"You need to be in bed," Tony growled, and surprised them both when he swung Lily up in his arms.

"Tony, what are you doing?"

Cradling her as if she weighed no more than a feather, he asked himself the same thing. They were alone together in his apartment in the middle of the night, and he wanted her so badly he physically ached.

The only problem was she was a guest in his home—only there because she needed his protection. But how could he release her when she felt so right in his arms?

"I'm carrying you to bed, if that's okay with you."

When she hesitated, he thought she was going to say no. Then she looped her arms around his neck and looked him right in the eye. "That depends," she said quietly.

Surprised, he arched a dark brow at her. "On what?"

"Whether you're taking me to my bed or yours."

Dear Reader,

The weather's hot, and so are all six of this month's Silhouette Intimate Moments books. We have a real focus on miniseries this time around, starting with the last in Ruth Langan's DEVIL'S COVE quartet, *Retribution*. Mix a hero looking to heal his battered soul, a heroine who gives him a reason to smile again and a whole lot of danger, and you've got a recipe for irresistible reading.

Linda Turner's back—after *way* too long—with the first of her new miniseries, TURNING POINTS. A beautiful photographer who caught the wrong person in her lens has no choice but to ask the cops—make that *one particular cop*—for help, and now both her life and her heart are in danger of being lost. FAMILY SECRETS: THE NEXT GENERATION continues with Marie Ferrarella's *Immovable Objects,* featuring a heroine who walks the line between legal, illegal—and love. *Dangerous Deception* from Kylie Brant continues THE TREMAINE TRADITION of mixing suspense and romance—not to mention sensuality—in doses no reader will want to resist. And don't miss our stand-alone titles, either. Cindy Dees introduces you to *A Gentleman and A Soldier* in a military reunion romance that will have your heart pounding and your fingers turning the pages as fast as they can. Finally, welcome Mary Buckham, whose debut novel, *The Makeover Mission,* takes a plain Jane and turns her into a princess—literally. Problem is, this princess is in danger, and now so is Jane.

Enjoy them all—and come back next month for the best in romantic excitement, only from Silhouette Intimate Moments.

Yours,

Leslie J. Wainger
Executive Editor

Please address questions and book requests to:
Silhouette Reader Service
U.S.: 3010 Walden Ave., P.O. Box 1325, Buffalo, NY 14269
Canadian: P.O. Box 609, Fort Erie, Ont. L2A 5X3

LINDA TURNER

Deadly Exposure

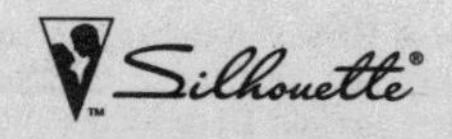

INTIMATE MOMENTS™

Published by Silhouette Books

America's Publisher of Contemporary Romance

ISBN 0-373-27374-6

DEADLY EXPOSURE

This edition published by arrangement with Harlequin Books S.A.

Visit Silhouette Books at www.eHarlequin.com

Printed in U.S.A.

Books by Linda Turner

Silhouette Intimate Moments

The Echo of Thunder #238
Crosscurrents #263
An Unsuspecting Heart #298
Flirting with Danger #316
Moonlight and Lace #354
The Love of Dugan Magee #448
**Gable's Lady* #523
**Cooper* #553
**Flynn* #572
**Kat* #590
Who's the Boss? #649
The Loner #673
Maddy Lawrence's Big Adventure #709
The Lady in Red #763
†*I'm Having Your Baby?!* #799
†*A Marriage-Minded Man?* #829
†*The Proposal* #847
†*Christmas Lone-Star Style* #895
***The Lady's Man* #931
***A Ranching Man* #992
***The Best Man* #1010
***Never Been Kissed* #1051
The Enemy's Daughter #1064
The Man Who Would Be King #1124
***Always a McBride* #1231
††*Deadly Exposure* #1304

*The Wild West
†The Lone Star Social Club
**Those Marrying McBrides!
††Turning Points

Silhouette Desire

A Glimpse of Heaven #220
Wild Texas Rose #653
Philly and the Playboy #701
The Seducer #802
Heaven Can't Wait #929

Silhouette Special Edition

Shadows in the Night #350

Silhouette Books

Fortune's Children
The Wolf and the Dove

Montana Mavericks:
Wed in Whitehorn
Nighthawk's Child

The Coltons
The Virgin Mistress

Silhouette Christmas Kisses 1996
"A Wild West Christmas"

A Fortune's Children Christmas 1998
"The Christmas Child"

Crowned Hearts 2002
"Royally Pregnant"

A Colton Family Christmas 2002
"Take No Prisoners"

Under Western Skies 2002
"Marriage on the Menu"

LINDA TURNER

began reading romances in high school and began writing them one night when she had nothing else to read. She's been writing ever since. Single, and living in Texas, she travels every chance she gets, scouting locales for her books.

Prologue

Hesitating in the doorway of the Liberty Hill High School cafeteria, Lily Fitzgerald seriously considered slipping outside and leaving before anyone saw her. She shouldn't have come. She'd long since lost touch with the few friends she'd made in school, and she didn't really care for reunions. All everyone ever talked about was how many children they had and how successful they were, and that left her with little to say. She'd never married, let alone had children, and she didn't measure success in dollars and cents. So what if she had a healthy back account? She couldn't remember the last time she'd been happy.

"Lily! You came! I didn't think you would."

Glancing up from her thoughts to find Natalie Bailey sitting by herself at the table closest to the door, Lily had to smile. She and Natalie had been in biology together their junior year and shared a frog in lab. She wouldn't have said they were close friends exactly, but they'd enjoyed working together, and today, she appreciated a friendly face in the crowd.

"I almost didn't," she admitted honestly, joining her at the table.

"Me, neither," Natalie replied. "Then I felt guilty for *not* wanting to come, which is ridiculous. I'm thirty-three years old, for heaven's sake! I shouldn't let guilt control my life."

"Don't beat yourself up over it," Lily advised. "We all do it."

Her tone was casual enough, but she didn't fool Natalie. Her blue eyes narrowing sharply, she said, "I thought that out of all of us, you'd be the one who did your own thing and found happiness. You were always so together."

Lily almost laughed out loud at the idea of her ever being *together*. For as long as she could remember, she'd never felt as if she'd had any control over anything, least of all her life. "It was a front," she said honestly. "I was just doing what my father and teachers wanted me to do, being who they wanted me to be. I figured if I played the game the way they wanted me to play, one day I'd be old enough to live my life the way I wanted."

"So has that day come?" Natalie asked, arching an eyebrow at her. "Are you doing what you've always wanted?"

She almost said yes because that was what was expected of her. All her life, she'd always done what was expected of her. But she wasn't a little girl anymore, and she was just so tired of telling people what they wanted to hear. "No," she said quietly, "I'm not."

"Neither are we," Rachel Martin said, blatantly eavesdropping from a nearby table with Abby Saunders and making no apology for it. Joining them, she frowned.

"So what's wrong with us? How come we're not married to a wonderful man and raising little angels like Susan Phillips? We're all as smart and pretty as she is. So why didn't we land butter side up in suburbia? Where did we go wrong?"

"I always let my father influence the decisions I made, and he never wanted what I wanted," Lily said grimly. "Making him happy seemed more important than making me happy."

"I didn't think I was pretty enough to get a good man," Abby said quietly. "Which is why I'm dating Dennis. No one else seems to be interested."

"What?" Rachel exclaimed, shocked. "Of course they're interested! You just have to have more confidence in yourself. At least you're not stupid like I am. All I ever wanted was a baby, and what did I do? Waste years on a man who had a vasectomy without telling me. How dumb is that?"

"Stop that!" Natalie scolded. "You're not stupid. He's the bad guy, not you. You just believed the man you loved. I did the same thing. I worked six years to put Derek through college and law school because he told me I'd get my chance to go to school when he graduated and opened his own firm. Of course, he also told me he loved me, and all the time, he was playing around on me with his paralegal. So much for love. Now he's living on a Caribbean island with his new wife, and I'm raising our eight-year-old daughter by myself. And there isn't a damn thing I can do about it."

"Yes, there is," Lily told her. "It's not too late for you to go to school yourself. Get your degree and laugh in the jerk's face."

"That's easy for you to say," she retorted. "When are you going to stop letting your father control your life?

And when is Abby going to have the confidence to go out and find herself a good man?''

''And what about me?'' Rachel chimed in. ''I want a baby and the clock is ticking. How am I going to get pregnant without a man?''

For the first time since she'd walked in the door, Lily smiled. ''You don't need a man, Rachel...just his sperm.''

''Oh, no!'' she said quickly. ''I'm not going there. If I'm going to have a baby, I'm going to do it the traditional way, with a man I love, a wedding ring, the whole nine yards.''

''And that's the problem,'' Natalie said quietly. ''We all wish our lives were different, but we're not willing to do what it takes to find happiness. Maybe that's the difference between us and them,'' she added, nodding toward the dance floor, where their happier classmates were dancing the night away. ''They went after what they wanted. We didn't.''

''Because we were afraid to take a chance and step outside our comfort zone,'' Abby said quietly.

Her expression grim, Rachel said, ''It's been fifteen years since we graduated from high school, and we're still afraid! How long are we going to live like this?''

Somber, they all just looked at each other. That was a question no one had an answer for.

Chapter 1

The newspaper ad had simply read, One-Bedroom Upstairs Apartment for Lease in Georgetown. But it was so much more than that, Lily thought with a grin as she grabbed a stack of boxes from the back seat of her SUV. It was hardwood floors and tall ceilings and narrow cobblestone streets. It was the smell of lasagna in the air from the Italian restaurant that occupied the space below her apartment, and the big hug that Angelo Giovanni, her new landlord, neighbor, and the owner of the restaurant, gave her when she signed the lease. It was the old-fashioned gas lights that lined the street, and quaint shops and restaurants and the used bookstore on the corner that looked as if it had been there since Lincoln occupied the White House.

But best of all, it was freedom! Freedom from the past, from her father, from a life that belonged to the woman she'd never wanted to be. An accountant…just thinking about the years she'd spent doing a job she'd hated made her cringe. All she'd ever wanted to be was a photographer, but her father wouldn't hear of it. From the time she was old enough to talk, he'd drilled it into her head that she had to get a *real* job, one that paid well and allowed her to have a home of her own and money in the bank. She could never have that with a career in the arts.

So she'd done as he'd advised to keep the peace and win his approval and gotten a job with the IRS in Washington, D.C., but she'd never given up her dream. She'd spent the last fifteen years after graduating high school secretly taking classes, studying, learning everything she could about photography, while she waited for the magical day when she would have the guts to do what *she* wanted, not what her father wanted. That day might have never come if she hadn't gone to her high-school reunion....

Making the decision to take a leave of absence from her job and follow her dream was one thing, sticking with it, another. Her father hadn't talked to her since she'd told him what she planned to do, and she didn't fool herself into thinking that he would forgive her any time soon. After all these years, she knew him well. As long as she continued to live her life in a way he disapproved of, he would keep his distance.

And then there was Neil, her...former...fiancé. He'd lectured her as if she were a child for disappointing him and her father, and in the process, he'd sounded so much like her father that it was frightening. She'd realized then that he was never going to support what she wanted to do with her life. How could he? He didn't have a single dream in his head and never had. He would do nothing but try to drag her down, back to her old life, and she couldn't allow that. So she'd ended their relationship.

She was on her own, completely alone, and she didn't regret it. She felt as if she'd just been released from prison. Lifting her face to the steady rain that fell from the gray sky above, she wondered if her father was some kind of warlock who'd summoned up the storm to rain on her parade. If he had, he'd wasted his time. Let it rain. She felt like Gene Kelly in *Singing in the Rain.* All she wanted to do was laugh out loud and jump in a puddle.

It was all working out, she thought happily as she danced across the rear parking lot behind the building. She had a new apartment, she'd bought a new 35mm camera and lenses and started taking advanced black-and-white photography classes at the local community college. With time, she hoped to buy an enlarger and set up a darkroom in the apartment's laundry room. She'd never developed her own pictures before. She couldn't wait.

Her eyes sparkling at the thought, she couldn't remember the last time she'd been so happy. And despite her father's silent treatment she'd done the right thing and left her new address and phone number on his answering machine. He hadn't called her back, but she refused to feel badly about it. She was finally living the life she'd always wanted, and he was just going to have to accept that.

Overhead, thunder rumbled, reminding her of the worsening weather. Shaking off thoughts of her father, she pulled open the back door to the stairwell and hurried inside. She was halfway up the stairs when she started to lose control of the boxes she carried.

''Oh, no!'' she exclaimed.

''You look like you could use some help.''

Struggling to catch the top box before it fell and her underwear ended up all over the stairs, Lily didn't see the man coming down the stairs until he was just a few steps above her. Surprised, she glanced up and had a quick impression of coal-black hair, green eyes and a chiseled jaw, then the boxes in her arms gave up their fight with gravity. With a muttered curse, she tried to juggle them, but it was too late. They went flying, and so did her sheets, towels and clothes, tumbling all over her and the man above her on the stairs.

"I'm so sorry!" she cried, hot color firing her cheeks as she hurried to snatch up her things. "I shouldn't have tried to carry everything at once. Here, let me get that."

"It's okay," he said with a chuckle. "It's my fault. I didn't mean to startle you. I thought you heard me." Pulling a washcloth from where it had landed on his shoulder, he held it out to her, his green eyes twinkling. "I believe this is yours."

Lily looked from the washcloth to his face and felt her breath catch in her throat. She wasn't the type of woman who generally lost her head over a handsome man, but in the dim light of the stairwell, shadows carved his face in chiseled angles, fascinating her. Where was her camera when she needed it? she thought, dazed.

She'd always been intrigued with light, with darkness and shadows and mood, and he had the kind of face the camera would love. His green eyes glistened with wicked humor and were surrounded by the kind of beautiful thick lashes a woman would kill for. With a will of their own, her eyes dropped to his mouth and the smile that lurked there, waiting for just the right moment to appear. Even as she watched, his smile broadened into a crooked grin, framed by dimples, and she couldn't look away. With nothing more than that grin, he stole her breath right out of her lungs.

"Hello?" he teased, waving his hand in front of her

face when she just looked at him. "Is it something I said?"

His words registered then, and with a soft gasp she glanced up to find his dancing eyes waiting for hers. Heat tinged her cheeks, and too late, she realized she was blushing like a teenager who'd never had a boy smile at her before.

Mortified, she wanted to sink right through the floor. She couldn't remember the name of the last man who had struck her dumb. She hadn't even done that with Neil the first time she'd met him, and she'd eventually fallen in love with him. What in the world was wrong with her?

Hurriedly turning away, she quickly snatched up the rest of her things. "Of course not," she retorted. "I was just distracted. You surprised me."

"Pleasantly, I hope."

When she glanced back over her shoulder at him and lifted a delicately arched eyebrow, he laughed. "You're good, lady. I've never had anyone shoot me down without saying a word. I like that." Grinning, he held out his hand to her. "I'm Anthony Giovanni, Angelo's nephew. I live in 201. You must be the new tenant in 202. Angelo said you'd be moving in today."

Somehow her hand ended up in his, and in the time it took to draw in a quick breath, the spicy scent of his aftershave licked at her senses. Irritated with herself, she gave his hand a perfunctory shake and quickly released it. "I'm Lily Fitzgerald. Angelo said you had the apartment across the hall from me." What he hadn't said was that Brad Pitt didn't hold a candle to his nephew. "If you'll excuse me, I need to get these things upstairs."

Looking past her, he frowned as he brought his gaze back to hers. "You have someone to help you, don't you? You can't get your furniture upstairs all by yourself."

"I hired a moving company," she informed him coolly. "They delivered the larger pieces this morning. I can handle the smaller things myself."

Thanks, but no thanks. She never said the words, but Tony got the message nonetheless. "So you don't need my help," he said. "Is that what you're telling me?"

"No—"

"Good." His grin wide, he took the box of personal items from her and laughed when she tried to snatch it back from him. "Oh, no, you don't. You just said you needed my help."

"I did not!"

"Sure you did. So where do you want this?"

Irritation knitting her forehead, she glared at him. "Are you always this persistent?"

"No. Sometimes I'm worse. It drives my family crazy." Grinning, he turned and started up the stairs.

If Lily hadn't been so frustrated, she would have laughed. What did it take to tell this man no? "I'm not a helpless female, you know," she called up the stairs after him. "I packed everything in my car without any help—I can certainly carry it up the stairs by myself!"

"I never said you couldn't," he retorted from the top of the stairs as he returned to the landing after setting the box just inside her front door. "But why would you want to when you can have someone help you? I'm not an ax murderer. If you don't believe me, ask around. All the little old ladies around here will tell you I'm a real sweetheart."

"I'm not a little old lady!"

"No, you're not," he chuckled as he started back down the stairs. "I noticed that right off." He had, in fact, noticed a heck of a lot more than that. She had a heart-shaped face, a pert nose and a stubborn chin. Top that with the curly blond hair she'd pinned on top of her head and a slender little body with curves in all the right places, and you had trouble with a capital *T*.

She was going to add some spark to the old place, he thought with a smile. Life could be on the verge of getting damn interesting.

"Just for the record," he said, "I like helping ladies—old, young and in-between. So let's get the rest of your stuff. Hold the door, okay?"

Not waiting for an answer, he made three quick trips to her car, then upstairs, and in a matter of moments he'd unloaded her car and stacked everything neatly in her living room. "All done," he announced with a grin. "I'd offer to help you unpack, but somehow I don't think you'd let me get anywhere near your underwear."

Biting her lip, Lily almost choked on a laugh. The man was incorrigible. "You thought right. Now that we've got that settled..."

"I'll take you to dinner to welcome you to the neighborhood. Don't say no. I know a great Italian restaurant."

He was speaking of his uncle's place, of course, and had the circumstances been different, Lily had to admit she might have been tempted. He was, after all, an incredibly good-looking man, not to mention charming, and the twinkle in his eye was hard to resist. She wasn't, however, looking for a man, a date, or anything that even resembled a relationship. For once in her life, she didn't have her father or a fiancé telling her what to do or how to do it, and she planned to keep it that way.

"I appreciate the offer, but I can't. I've just got too much to do."

There was no doubting her sincerity...or the stubborn set of her chin. Studying her, Tony had always liked a challenge, and he had to admit that one as pretty as Lily Fitzgerald definitely intrigued him. With time, he liked to think he had a better-than-even chance of changing her mind, but that was the catch. When did he have time? He worked long hours at the police station, had his son every chance he could, and was lucky if he got five hours of sleep a night.

His smile rueful, he said, "Maybe another time, then. If you need anything, just holler. If I'm not around, you can usually find Angelo downstairs in the restaurant."

"I'll do that," she said quietly. "Thank you."

Leaving her to her unpacking, he let himself out and tried to take comfort in the fact that even if he could find time to squeeze a woman into his busy schedule, he didn't really want one. The last one he'd let into his life had caused him nothing but grief.

His good humor faded at the thought of Janice. He'd fallen for her like a ton of bricks the moment he'd met her, and as soon as he'd been able to talk her into it, he'd rushed her down the aisle before she could change her mind. They should have grown old together. Instead, they'd only been married seven years when she started fooling around on him. The ink hadn't even been dry on their divorce papers when she walked down the aisle and married another man.

He wanted to hate her for that, but how could he? Because of her, he had a son, and she hadn't tried to take him away from him when they'd divorced. She had custody, but she was very generous with visitation. He had Quentin as much as she did. More, in fact. Janice was seldom home. Tony knew that she loved Quentin, but all her focus was on her career and making a name for herself at the high-powered law office where she worked.

She worked late nearly every night and sometimes had to go into the office on weekends.

He, on the other hand, could adjust his schedule when he needed to. As a D.C. police officer, he was able to work a shift that allowed him to be with Quentin in the afternoon and for dinner on the nights Janice worked late. So Quentin didn't have to spend any more time than necessary with Larry, his new stepfather, who didn't have a clue how to get along with a nine-year-old boy. By the time Tony took Quentin home, Janice was usually just getting home from work. According to Quentin, all he generally saw of his mother was when she tucked him into bed.

Janice had the weekend free for once, however, so he didn't have Quentin. Normally, Tony would have worked, but just yesterday, a co-worker had asked him to trade shifts with him, so he'd worked a double shift and had today off. Heading down the stairs, he could hear laughter and the clatter of dishes coming from his uncle's restaurant and knew without looking at his watch that the dinner crowd was already gathering. Miss Independence upstairs might not want his help moving into her new apartment but he knew his uncle would appreciate an extra pair of hands. The waitstaff was usually shorthanded, especially on a Saturday.

Stepping through the stairwell door into the restaurant kitchen, he moved to the dining room and wasn't surprised to find the place packed. Angelo's Italian Restaurant was famous not only for its food but for his uncle's hospitality. He catered to families, and over the years, his regular customers had become like family. They came to Angelo's to celebrate birthdays and anniversaries and graduations, and they came when they were down and needed a sympathetic ear.

There were no sad faces today, however. There was a line of customers waiting at the front door, every table was full, and waiters were hurrying to keep up with orders. And in the middle of the organized chaos was his uncle. Totally unruffled, he was in his element as he seated customers, directed waiters, and even bussed tables when everyone else was busy.

Spying Tony immediately, he grinned as he grabbed some menus from the stack by the front door. ''It's about time you got here. Carlos is getting married today, Thomas broke his arm, and Roger had car trouble and won't be in for another hour. How about taking over the private dining room for me? It's Mrs. Stanlowski's eighty-fourth birthday, and the whole family's there. You'll make sure they have a good time.''

He didn't have to ask him twice. Mrs. S. had owned the candy store down on the corner for as long as Tony could remember, and she'd always been as sweet as the chocolate she sold. ''Do we have a cake for her? What about champagne?''

''It's all taken care of,'' Angelo assured him. ''You just go see after Mrs. S.''

''This'll be the best birthday she ever had,'' Tony promised. But before he could head for the private dining room, a woman slipped through the crowd waiting near the front door for a table and he found himself face-to-face with his ex-wife. Surprised, he stopped in his tracks, his gaze instinctively moving past her in search of Quentin. There was no sign of him.

''What are you doing here?'' he asked sharply. ''Where's Quentin? Is something wrong?''

Tall and regal and always cool to the touch, Janice said, ''He's fine. Really,'' she insisted when he looked unconvinced. ''He's at a birthday party with some school friends. Are you busy? I need to talk to you.''

If another woman had said such a thing, Tony would have laughed and told her to look around. Of course he was busy when the restaurant was packed! But for as long as he'd known Janice, she'd had an irritating tendency to assume the world revolved around herself. That, obviously, hadn't changed.

He should have told her to take a hike—Mrs. S. was waiting, dammit, and Janice had a hell of a nerve walking in here expecting him to drop everything just because *she* wanted to talk to him! She could call him on his day off.

But even as he opened his mouth to tell her they'd have to talk another time, he shut his mouth with a snap. When they'd divorced, he'd promised himself he wouldn't fight with her the way most people did with their exes. She hadn't always made it easy for him to keep that promise. They'd been divorced two years, and in that time everything had to be done her way. He liked talking face-to-face, but if she had something to discuss with him about Quentin, she either e-mailed him or called him. Why the change? What the devil was she up to?

''What's this about, Janice?'' he asked, scowling. ''What's going on?''

When she hesitated, Angelo, who'd been watching their entire exchange from across the dining room, stepped forward and said quietly, ''Why don't you two talk in my office? It'll be quieter in there and you won't be interrupted.''

Tony almost said no. There was a knot in his gut that warned him that he wasn't going to like whatever she had to say, but she'd already headed for Angelo's office off the kitchen. Swearing under his breath, he followed.

''Okay,'' he growled, shutting the door behind him the second they were both inside. ''What is it?''

Her cool blue eyes narrowed at his curt tone, but she only said, ''I wanted you to know that I'm changing law firms. I got a new job.''

Whatever he'd been expecting, it wasn't that. Perplexed, he said, ''Okay. Congratulations. So what's that got to do with me?''

''It's in Florida. I start the second week in October.''

''Like I said...congratulations,'' he began, still not seeing what her change in employment had to do with him. Then it hit him. ''Oh, no, you're not! If you're trying to tell me you're taking Quentin with you, you can think again. It's not going to happen.''

Far from impressed with his roar of outrage, she warned, ''Don't try to fight me on this, Tony. I have custody. That gives me the right to take him with me wherever I go. This is a wonderful opportunity for me—''

His eyes narrowed angrily. ''It's always about you, isn't it? What about Quentin? Have you even thought about what this is going to do to him? You're taking him away from his father, his friends at school, everything familiar. How is that good for him, Janice? Explain that one to me, because right now, I don't see how this new job could be good for anyone but you.''

''He'll adjust,'' she said with a shrug. ''He has to, and so do you. I'm not passing up a chance to work in one of the most prestigious law firms in the country just because you and Quentin might not like it. You don't have any say in the matter, so get used to it. He's going with me and Larry to Miami and there's not a damn thing you can do about it.''

Chapter 2

She stormed out, leaving Tony swearing after her. Damn her! How dare she threaten to take his son away from him! She knew how close they were. They went fishing together, watched sports together, cooked dinner together just about every evening. Quentin was his pride and joy, the rock that grounded him. From the time he'd first held him when he was only a few minutes old, his son had taught him what life was all about. He couldn't lose him. Janice might not care about what this would do to him, but what about Quentin? He'd be devastated. Surely Janice had to know that. Why was she doing this?

"Tony? Are you all right? I saw Janice leave. She looked a little miffed. What's wrong?"

Glancing up from his tortured thoughts to find his uncle standing in the doorway, Tony laughed without humor. "What's wrong? Everything! Janice is moving to Florida and she's taking Quentin with her."

"What? She can't do that! Who's going to take care

of him after school and cook dinner for him every night when she's working? That robot husband of hers? He doesn't even like the boy.''

It was that, more than anything, that tore Tony apart. From the moment he'd first laid eyes on Larry Coffman, he'd known he was a man who didn't like children. Janice had claimed he was just reserved, but Tony saw right through him. He was autocratic, condescending and had no sense of humor. For a nine-year-old boy like Quentin, that could only spell misery.

''She refused to even listen to reason,'' he said bitterly. ''He's *her* son. She has sole custody and she can take him wherever she likes. And there's not a damn thing I can do about it.''

''Sure there is,'' Angelo said. ''You can fight for full custody.''

If he hadn't been so miserable, Tony would have laughed at the mere idea of taking on Janice in a courtroom. ''Are you serious? She's an attorney, Angelo! How can I take her to court? She works with a whole office of high-dollar attorneys who'd be only too willing to help her. I wouldn't stand a chance.''

''You don't know that,'' Angelo said with a frown. ''Just because you can't afford a big-league lawyer doesn't mean you can't find someone who's good. And if you're worried that the cards are stacked against you because the mothers always get the kids, times have changed. It's not like the old days. I know a lot of fathers who have custody of their children. You know Chris Barrili. He has his twin daughters—''

''Because his ex-wife is an alcoholic and set the house on fire when she was drunk,'' Tony said dryly. ''That's a different matter completely. Janice isn't a bad mother. She doesn't drink or use drugs, and she'd cut off her arm before she'd put Quentin in danger. She's just so damn indifferent. All she cares about is her career."

"You got that right," his uncle retorted. "I've never seen a mother who spends so little time with her son. You've been keeping a record of when you have him, haven't you?"

"Yes, but I only did that in case the IRS audited me for claiming him and I had to prove how often he was in my custody."

"I know, and you were smart to do that. But those records also prove how little Janice has the boy," he pointed out. "I think a judge would be interested in that."

Unconvinced, Tony said, "I don't know. She's a lawyer, Angelo, and a damn good one, at that. She's not going to roll over and give me Quentin just because I want him. There's nothing she loves more than a good fight. And she knows judges."

"So?"

"So if I was crazy enough to fight for custody, she'd pull a few strings and have the judge in her pocket before we even stepped in the courtroom. What's the point?"

"Your son," Angelo said quietly. "He's the point."

His words struck Tony in the heart. He was right, of course. Quentin *was* the point. And nothing was more important than his happiness and security. If Tony didn't find a way to stop her, Janice would take him a thousand miles away to Florida and leave him with a stepfather who didn't even like him while she spent all her time at the office making partner. Just thinking about how lonely and unhappy Quentin would be sickened him.

"Don't misunderstand me," he told his uncle gruffly. "It's not that I don't want him. You know I do. I've always wanted him, but when we divorced, Janice wouldn't even consider giving me full custody. When she promised to let me see him whenever I wanted if I didn't fight her on custody, I went along with it because I knew I would have Quentin most of the time, anyway. It never entered my head that she'd one day decide to move.''

''You should talk to your lawyer. He needs to know what's going on.''

''It won't do any good. She has the right to live where she wants.''

And that was what was so frustrating. Anguish twisting in his gut, he'd never felt so helpless in his life. ''I can't lose him, Angelo,'' he said huskily. ''I speak to him every day. We have dinner together nearly every night. How can I help him with his homework if he's in Florida? My phone bill will be through the roof. And when will I be able to afford to see him? You know what my salary is. With what I make, I'll be lucky if I can fly down there once a year!''

''Janice is the one taking him away,'' Angelo replied. ''She should be the one who has to pay to send him home.''

''Even if she does, I'll still only get to see him a couple of times a year.'' Despair filled him at the thought. Swearing softly, he said, ''I don't know what to do. If I sue for custody, Quentin will be put in the position of having to pick between me and Janice. Regardless of what I think about her, she is his mother and he loves her. He won't thank me for making him choose between the two of us.''

''But if you don't, you'll lose him.''

''Exactly,'' he replied grimly. ''And it scares the hell out of me. If I thought I had a chance of beating her in court, I'd go to court tomorrow if I could. But I can't see a judge granting me custody just because Janice is moving away.''

''Talk to your lawyer,'' his uncle suggested again. ''He'll tell you if you've got a fighting chance. Then do what you can live with.''

It was sound advice. Because whatever he decided to do, he wasn't the only one who would have to live with the consequences. Ten years from now, he didn't want Quentin blaming him for a miserable childhood.

Two days later, Angelo was waiting for him when he walked into the restaurant after a meeting with David Lye, his lawyer. ''Well?'' Angelo asked, arching a grizzled eyebrow. ''How did it go?''

''Just about the way I expected,'' he said with a grimace. ''The courts generally like a child to stay with the mother until they're at least twelve.''

''But he's still your son! How can Janice just drag Quentin off to Florida without your permission?''

''David felt that was a good question to put before the court. Janice has the right to live her own life, but that doesn't mean she can take Quentin out of state, away from me and the court, without even discussing it.''

''So he thinks you have a shot at winning custody?'' he said with a sigh of relief. ''Thank God!''

''Don't start celebrating yet,'' Tony cautioned. ''This isn't going to be easy. Custody battles are very expensive, and David warned me there's a good chance I could lose.''

''You won't lose,'' Angelo assured him. ''Just remember—you're doing the right thing for Quentin.''

''I know,'' he said gruffly. ''I don't care what it costs—I've got to stop her.''

"Don't worry about the money. I'll loan you whatever you need."

Surprised, Tony blinked. "I beg your pardon?"

"You heard me," Angelo growled. "I love that boy, too. I want to help you keep him. I've got the money. Why shouldn't I loan it to you?"

"Because you might need it," he replied. "You never know what's going to happen. You could get sick or have some kind of accident—"

"And I could win the lottery!"

Tony grinned. "First you have to play."

Not the least amused, Angelo scowled. "I want to help, dammit! What good is money if I can't use it to help someone I love?"

"If you want to help me, give me a job instead of a loan so I can work off the money," Tony told him. "David said I could make payments, just like I did for the divorce, but I still want to pay him off as quickly as possible. In order to do that, I've got to take a second job. If I wait tables here during the day and work my regular shift at the police department at night, I'll be able to get by and hopefully still pay David off within three or four months."

"But what about Quentin?" Angelo pointed out. "You're not going to be able to see him very much if you're working round the clock."

"It's only until I pay David off," he replied. "And I can adjust my schedule at the precinct so I can spend some quality time with him. I don't want to do the same thing to him that Janice is doing. And that may not be an issue, anyway. David's starting the paperwork immediately, but if he isn't able to stop Janice from taking him to Florida before the custody issue is settled, I won't be able to see Quentin, anyway."

"I don't think you have to worry about that. David sounds like he knows what he's doing."

"I'm counting on it," he said grimly. "I can't even think about losing Quentin."

"Good. Because it's not going to happen." Squeezing his shoulder, Angelo blinked back tears. "You're a good man. I wish Leo had lived to see you grown. He would have been so proud of you."

"He and Mom died too young," Tony said huskily. "They weren't even forty."

"Thankfully, they didn't suffer," his uncle said. "I don't think they even saw the truck that hit them until it was too late." With a sigh, he shook off the sad memory and smiled. "They were as crazy about you as you are about Quentin. I wish they were here to help you, but since they're not, I am. Even working two jobs, you're going to have a tough time paying your bills and paying David off early...which is why I'm going to reduce your rent."

"Oh, no, you don't! I can't let you do that."

"You can't stop me," Angelo retorted with a grin. "It's my building. I can lower the rent if I want to."

"But you need that income—"

Snorting, he said, "*Please!* The building's paid for and the restaurant's making money hand over fist. You could live here the rest of my life without paying a nickel rent and I'd never miss the money."

"I would never do that, and you know it."

Angelo chuckled. "Like I said, you're just like your father."

"I don't want your money," he said stubbornly.

"I won't touch my savings if you'll let me lower your rent. You'll be able to pay David off quicker, and I'll feel like I'm doing something to help you keep Quentin. Please, Tony, let me help.''

Put like that, Tony couldn't refuse him. ''Okay. If you insist.''

''I do.'' Pleased, he grinned again, his green eyes twinkling. ''Now, back to that job you were asking about. You're just the kind of waiter I've been looking for. If you don't show up for work, I know where you live. When can you start?''

For an answer, Tony smiled and reached for an apron hanging on a hook by the door. ''How about now?''

Later that evening, Lily walked into Angelo's restaurant with a smile as big as Texas lighting her face. Champagne. She wanted champagne! After the day she'd had, she deserved it. And a steak, she decided, already tasting it. One of Angelo's specialties was a grilled steak that smelled incredible, and she'd been promising herself that one day soon, she'd try it. Today was the day. She might even order dessert.

''Somebody must have had a good day. You're beaming.''

Her thoughts on dessert, Lily looked up to find Tony Giovanni standing before her dressed in black slacks and a white shirt, with a waiter's white apron tied around his waist. She hadn't seen him since he'd helped her move in two weeks ago, but she would have known that sexy grin of his on the dark side of the moon. Every time she stepped into the stairwell, she thought of him and, like it or not, found herself smiling.

For that reason alone, she shouldn't have been pleased to see him, but nothing could dampen her spirits today. Flashing her dimples at him, she said, ''I had an incredible day. The best! What about you? What are you doing here?''

''Waiting on you,'' he said simply.

''You work here?''

''Starting today,'' he said. He arched an eyebrow at her. ''I take it we're celebrating?''

''You bet we are, Mr. Giovanni. I need champagne. Lots of champagne.''

He grinned. ''That can be arranged. But call me Tony. All my dates do.''

Too happy to take exception to his flirting, she said, ''But we're not dating. Remember? I've just got too much to do.''

''Then we should take advantage of the moment. I'm here, you're here, and we're in that great Italian restaurant I told you about. So what if I'm working? Let's take what we can get.''

She should have said no. Her heart was already pounding, and the man was far too easy on the eyes. To make matters worse, he was far too good at flirting. A wise woman would have taken one look at that glint in his eye and requested another waiter, or, better yet, gone to a different restaurant. But what harm could a little flirting do? He was working and this was probably the closest they would ever come to a date. Why shouldn't she enjoy it?

''You know, you're absolutely right,'' she said with a smile. ''What's the fun of celebrating alone? It's a beautiful evening. Is there an available table on the patio? I'd love to eat under the stars.''

''Whatever the lady wants, the lady gets.'' Grabbing a menu from the stack on the counter near the front door, he led her out to the patio and a table for two. With a charming smile, he pulled her chair out for her. ''You know, you really do look fantastic. So what are we celebrating? Did you get a raise? A new car? Win the lottery? Whatever it is, you'd make a fortune if you could figure out a way to bottle it."

Bursting to share her good news, she confided, "I just had a meeting with the owner of the gallery around the corner."

"Susan Richards?" he said, surprised. "She comes in here all the time."

"I know. She said she'd known Angelo for twenty years. She's going to hang two of my photographs in her gallery."

Confused, Tony frowned. "I didn't know you were a photographer. I could have sworn Angelo said you were an accountant."

"I was," she admitted with a smile. "In my other life. Then I had a midlife crisis and decided that if I was ever going to do what I wanted to do instead of what my father thought was best for me, I'd better get started."

"It sounds like you made a wise move. Susan has a reputation for accepting nothing but the best. You must have really impressed her." Nodding at the portfolio she'd laid on the table, he asked, "Mind if I take a look?"

In the past, she'd never been shy about showing her photos to her friends and anyone else who cared to see them, but for reasons she couldn't explain, she hesitated to show them to Tony. *Idiot,* she chided herself. There was no reason to be nervous. His opinion was just that—an opinion. He was certainly entitled to it, but it didn't mean any more to her than anyone else's.

Still, she could feel a blush stealing into her cheeks as she said, "I don't have copies of the ones from the gallery with me—I left them with Susan—but I have some others from the same roll of film."

When she handed him the portfolio, Tony was amazed to see how shy she was. He wouldn't have thought she was a woman who ever lacked confidence about anything. Then he opened the portfolio and found himself amazed all over again.

Glancing up sharply, he said, "You did these? I thought you were a beginner."

A slow smile spread from her mouth to her eyes. "I guess you could say I'm a late bloomer. I've been studying photography for years, going to conventions, entering contests…that kind of thing. I loved it, but I never felt like I was quite ready to try my hand at it professionally. Then I went to my high-school reunion this summer and everything changed."

"You realized that life was passing you by?"

"Something like that," she replied with a rueful smile. "All I ever really wanted to be was a photographer. If I was ever going to be happy, I had to take a chance and turn professional. So I did."

"And today proved you've got what it takes."

"Well, I don't know if I'd go that far, but it certainly proved that I was right to believe in myself. Of course, I'm still learning, still taking classes, still picking the brains of professional contacts I've made over the years and trying to be the best I can be."

From what Tony could see, she was already damn good. Studying the black-and-white photos that had been taken in the park on a rainy afternoon, he couldn't get over the quality of the prints. He knew the street where she'd taken the pictures—it formed the southern boundary of Rock Creek Park—and over the years he'd jogged through that same area hundreds of times. He'd seen it every which way there was to see it and would have sworn he knew it backward and forward, but he'd never seen it the way Lily had captured it on film.

When she'd taken the picture, a thunderstorm had obviously just blown through. It was late afternoon, but the sky was dark and the streetlights had sprung on. The normally busy entrance to the park was deserted—joggers and vendors had vanished—and a hot-dog cart that had been hastily shut down had been left behind. Rain still dripped from the trees, but it was the steam that rose in a wispy mist from the warm sidewalk and pavement that drew the eye.

It was a lonely scene, haunting. Somehow, Lily had made the image grainy, which only added to the mood. With no effort whatsoever, Tony could almost smell the rain on the hot pavement and feel the humidity in the air.

"These are incredible," he said huskily, turning to the next picture, then the next. "Did Susan see these? I can't believe she didn't take them all."

She smiled at that. "She wanted to start slowly and give me time to finish the rest of the classes I'm taking. She also wanted to give me time to build up a portfolio of work. If everything goes well, she's talking about doing a show in the spring."

Not surprised, Tony grinned. "Aha. I knew it! Susan's pretty sharp at spotting talent, and you've got to know you've got it in spades."

"I hoped," she said with a modest shrug. "But I'm prejudiced. I was afraid I was just seeing what I wanted to see."

"You can stop worrying about that. You've got a great eye." Closing the portfolio, he laid it on the table, then straightened with a grin. "Now, about the celebration.

You know, if you put yourself in my hands, you won't regret it."

"Yeah, right," she chuckled, her blue eyes twinkling. "I bet you say that to all your dates."

Caught off guard, he burst out laughing. "That's quite an impression you have of me. I'll have you know I haven't been out on a date in six months!"

"Are you kidding?"

"Not at all. And the only woman I asked out in all that time turned me down flat," he confided. Mischief dancing in his eyes, he added, "I don't understand it. I was charming, helpful—I even helped her move into her new apartment. And what did she say when I asked her to dinner? She was too busy! Can you believe it? I was devastated."

She grinned. "Maybe she was busy."

"Maybe," he agreed. "Maybe she'll give me a second chance."

She shrugged. "Maybe she will. I guess you'll have to ask her again sometime and find out."

"You know, I think I'll do that. So…now that you've put yourself in my hands—"

"I beg your pardon?"

"For your celebration," he reminded her. "Just sit back and let me take care of everything. I promise you won't be disappointed."

Fighting a smile, Lily studied him through narrowed eyes. "Why do I have a feeling I'm going to have to watch you like a hawk?"

"Me?" he said innocently. "I'm harmless."

"Yeah, right," she said. "And I'm Lucille Ball. Okay, Harmless, I'm in your hands…for dinner. I know you'll make sure it's wonderful."

His gaze drifting to her mouth, Tony hardly heard her.

Damn, she was cute when she laughed. Her whole face seemed to light up. So why didn't she do it more often? She was celebrating tonight, and with good reason, but he had a feeling that most of the time she was far too serious.

He'd like to see her let down her hair and kick up her heels and enjoy life. He hadn't been kidding when he said he just might ask her out again—he hoped she hadn't been, either. He'd take her somewhere fun—

Suddenly realizing what he was doing, he swore silently. Dammit, he had been working too hard if he was seriously thinking about asking her out again. Hadn't he had enough trouble with women? Janice had caused him nothing but one heartache after another, and now she was threatening to take his son. He had a hell of a court fight ahead of him, a second job, and with every other thought, he worried about losing his son. The last thing he needed right now was to get involved with someone else, even on a casual basis.

Still, he was tempted. And that was all the reason he needed to walk away. ''I'll be right back with your champagne,'' he told her quietly, and hurried to the kitchen to put in her order, then collected a chilled bottle of champagne and a champagne glass from the bar.

When he returned with the wine, Lily almost asked him to stay. Celebrating by herself didn't seem like much fun. She could have called her father, but he would only spoil the moment for her by pointing out that in spite of the fact that she had somehow managed to land some of her pictures in a gallery, she had yet to sell anything. Tony, at least, seemed to appreciate what she had accomplished so far. Maybe she'd ask him to join her on his break.

But even as he delivered her champagne, the opportunity was lost. A large crowd swarmed through the door at that moment, drawing him away. Watching him as he seated the boisterous group and joked with them, she told herself it was for the best. Susan Richards may have given her her first break, but she still had a long way to go to establish herself as a photographer. All her energy needed to be focused on that, not a charming flirt like Anthony Giovanni.

Still on cloud nine, Lily hardly slept that night. She still couldn't believe her photographs were hanging in a gallery. Six years ago, when she'd met Jeffry Garrison, an agent at a photography convention, and he'd told her he could get her work in a gallery if she ever wanted to turn professional, she hadn't really believed him. But after she'd had the rolls of film she'd taken in the park developed and she'd seen how good the pictures were, she'd called Jeffry immediately. When he'd set up a meeting with Susan Richards, she still hadn't believed that he or anyone else would be able to get her work in a gallery so soon after she'd turned professional. Obviously, she'd been wrong.

Just thinking about how that single phone call to Jeffry could eventually change her life kept her awake for hours.

Finally drifting off to sleep around three, she should have slept in the following morning—it was Saturday, and she didn't have anything to do but clean her apartment and do laundry. Instead, she was up with the sun. It was a beautiful day and she couldn't make herself stay inside, doing housework. So she made a mad dash through the apartment, picking things up and vacuuming while she did several quick loads of laundry. By ten o'clock, she had everything done and was checking her camera bag to make sure she had plenty of film. A few moments later, she hit the streets.

There was nothing she loved more than Saturday morning in the park. The playground was always teaming with kids, joggers pounded down the trails, and inevitably, someone somewhere was playing Frisbee with their dog. She could spend hours there and never run out of subjects for her pictures.

But even as she turned the corner and headed for the park at a brisk walk, she found herself thinking about her meeting yesterday with Susan Richards. With a will of their own, her feet turned toward the gallery. She wouldn't stay long, she promised herself. She just had to see her pictures hanging on the wall one more time. Susan would probably laugh at her, but that was okay. She had to make sure she hadn't dreamed the whole thing. Maybe while she was there, she'd take a picture of her pictures hanging on the wall.

Grinning at the thought, she stepped into the gallery, only to stop short at the sight of Susan standing in front of her photographs, talking to a tall, thin older man who was impeccably dressed in a navy-blue suit. He had an umbrella, even though there was no sign of rain, and pointed at the subject of the photo—a jogger running through the park in the rain—as he talked enthusiastically with Susan.

They *were* talking about her work! In the time it took to draw in a quick breath, her heart was pounding with excitement. She told herself not to jump to conclusions. Just because the two of them were discussing the picture didn't mean the man wanted to buy it. He could just be one of those people who visited galleries like they were museums and had no intention of purchasing anything.

"Lily! Just the person I wanted to see." Spying her in

the doorway, Susan crossed to her with a wide smile and took her arm. ''Come,'' she said eagerly. ''There's someone I want you to meet. Lily, this Julian Edwards. Julian was just admiring your photographs,'' Susan told her, her blue eyes dancing with excitement behind the lenses of her glasses. ''He's an interior designer.''

For a moment, Lily was sure her heart stopped dead in her chest. A designer! How had Susan gotten a designer interested in her work so quickly? Her pictures had only been hanging in the gallery for twenty-four hours.

Her imagination going crazy and her fingers not quite steady, she smiled and held out her head. ''It's a pleasure to meet you, Mr. Edwards.''

''Oh, no, my dear, the pleasure is all mine,'' he assured her. ''I was just telling Susan how talented you are. I've been a decorator for thirty years and I've never seen anything quite like your pictures. It's amazing how much they look like paintings. The lighting's perfect. How long did you have to wait to catch it just that way? It must have been hours. And did you know the runner or did he just come by by chance? He looks so mysterious, shrouded in the drizzle the way he is.''

Lily grinned. ''He does, doesn't he? I couldn't believe it when he came running out of the trees just as I was about to snap the shutter. The picture would have been good without him, but there's just something about the way he appeared out of the mist that grabbed me. I'm so glad you like it. It's the best picture I've ever taken.''

''They're both excellent,'' he said, studying the second print, which was of a mother and small daughter laughing together as they ran for cover from a sudden unexpected shower. ''I have several clients who would be thrilled to have your work hanging in their offices. Especially *The Runner*,'' he added, naming the piece that Lily had yet to name. ''Technically, it's not a sports photo, but that's what makes it so effective. It would look incredible in the lobby of Harold Sergeant's corporate offices.''

Stunned, Lily nearly dropped her camera bag. ''Harold Sergeant?'' she gasped. ''The owner of Titan Sporting Goods?''

''The one and only,'' he replied, smiling. ''He commissioned me to decorate his offices three weeks ago.''

Her head reeling, Lily couldn't believe this was happening. ''I don't know what to say.''

''I can't make any promises yet—''

''Oh, I know,'' she said quickly. ''I'm just thrilled that you're even considering my work. I never expected a response this quickly.''

Smiling at her like a proud grandmother, Susan said, ''I told you you were good.''

The taste of panic sharp on his tongue, Sly Jackson darted through the first doorway he came to, only to curse when he saw the dozen or more people mingling in what he realized with a scowl was a gallery. There was nowhere to hide.

''Damn!'' Swearing under his breath, he whirled to face the broad windows that gave a clear view of the street outside, and even though it was far from hot in the gallery, he could feel the sweat popping out on his forehead. In the pocket of his khakis, the cocaine he'd bought only moments before seemed to flash like a neon sign, drawing all eyes.

Don't be an idiot, a voice in his head growled. *No one saw you make the deal, especially the idiot cop walking his beat down the street. All you have to do is act cool, blend in and kill some time. No one will suspect a thing.*

Normally, he could have pulled off cool without a

blink of an eye. He was a stockbroker and a damn good one—he could handle pressure. Or at least, he had until two weeks ago.

Stiffening, he told himself not to go there, but it was too late. Stark, violent images played in his head, haunting him, tormenting him. Swearing, he reached for the coke in his pocket and would have sniffed it up his nose if there'd been an opportunity. He needed a line, dammit! For the last two weeks, he'd acted like a scared little boy cowering in the closet, hiding out from the bogeyman, and he was sick of it. The drugs would give him back his edge.

But even as he considered finding the restroom, he knew the policeman he'd seen down the street was slowly making his way toward him. And he had coke in his pocket. He had to get the hell out of there!

A red Exit sign glowed in the back lefthand corner, but when he turned to run, the thunder of his blood loud in his ears, he never even saw it. He took two steps, only to freeze as his gaze fell on a picture on the wall.

What the hell! No! It couldn't be, he thought wildly. There had to be some mistake.

But as much as he tried to convince himself that his eyes were playing tricks on him, there was no denying what was hanging on the wall right in front of his nose. The black-and-white photo had been taken near the duck pond in the park on a drizzly afternoon two weeks ago. The old-fashioned streetlights glowed in the mist, and the photographer had captured on film forever the single jogger who came running out of the misty rain.

The play of rain and shadows on the runner's face partially concealed his features, but Sly would have known him in the black pit of hell. Because *he* was the jogger, and when the unseen photographer had snapped his picture, he'd been running away from the scene of a murder.

How had this happened? he wondered, enraged. When he'd picked up a hooker on the street, then taken her to a secluded place in the park, he'd made sure there was no one around. He'd wanted to have sex with her, but all she'd wanted to do was talk about how much she charged. Irritated that she demanded to be paid ahead of time, he'd grabbed her, forced her to do as he'd wanted, then taunted her by threatening not to pay her a dime. That's when she'd threatened to turn him in to the police.

Even now, two weeks later, the memory made him livid. No one threatened him. No one! He'd slapped her, and that's when she'd started to scream. The only way he'd been able to shut her up was to strangle her.

He'd run then, his only thought to pretend to be a jogger out for a run. Concentrating on keeping his pace unhurried, he hadn't seen anyone with a camera, and with good reason. That particular day had been foggy as hell. The photographer could have been twenty feet away and he wouldn't have seen who it was.

"Your first sale is a done deal, Lily, my dear," a cultured feminine voice said happily, carrying across the room to interrupt his silent raging. "Julian just told me that if Harold Sergeant didn't buy *The Runner*, then he would. That's how much he loves it. So congratulations are in order. You just made your first sale."

His head coming up sharply, his eyes searching, Sly immediately found the woman who had just spoken. Decked out in jeans and a green sweater, her white-blond hair twisted up on top of her head, she stood with another woman in front of the picture of the runner, beaming at *his* photo as if she'd just won the lottery.

His gaze shifting to her companion, it didn't take a

rocket scientist to figure out that the mysterious Lily at her side was, in all likelihood, the photographer who'd taken his picture. She, too, was studying the photo, and she was far too excited for someone who didn't have a vested interest in it.

Bitch, he thought bitterly. She was probably the only person in the world who'd seen him in the park that day, but maybe she hadn't heard about the murder on the news. The police had no leads, no one had seen him pick up the hooker on the street that day, and after the story of her murder hit the news, it quickly fell from the headlines. The media and the public showed little interest in a prostitute murdered by an unknown john in the park.

He planned to keep it that way, he thought grimly. The only one who could place him anywhere near the murder scene was the woman standing across the gallery from him, and she had yet to make the connection. He had to find a way to eliminate her before she did.

Chapter 3

Outside, the policeman walking his beat strolled past the gallery with only a cursory look and continued down the street. Trying to appear nonchalant, Sly watched him disappear from view and soundlessly released the breath he'd been holding. At least he'd avoided one problem. Now it was the bitch Lily's turn.

He liked to think of himself as a civilized man. He always kept a tight rein on the rage that burned in his gut like an eternal flame—until he was crossed. That damn prostitute had threatened him and lived to regret it. That should have been the end of it. He'd been sure he was safe. He should have been, dammit! But now the oh-so-pretty Lily threatened him by her mere existence, and she didn't even know it. Stalking her, killing her, was going to make up for all the grief she had unwittingly caused him. Now he just had to decide how he was going to do it. He preferred choking the life out of her, but he wasn't a man who limited himself. He'd do whatever he had to to make sure she was never a threat to him again.

A tight smile of anticipation curling his mouth, he would have liked nothing more than to eliminate her right there and then, but he could hardly do that in a gallery full of people. So he forced himself to be patient and blend in with the other people milling about, studying the art. Ducking his head and praying no one recognized him as the man in the photo, he gradually made his way closer to his own picture. All he needed was Lily's full name, and he could track down where she lived. Then, sometime next week, he'd slip into her place while she was sleeping and take care of her. It was that easy.

An uncomplicated plan was always the best, but when he was finally able to stroll close enough to the photograph to see the name of the photographer on a little plaque next to the blown-up image, there was only one name printed there. Lily. Infuriated, he swore under his breath. Bitch! Still, no matter. Not knowing her last name was only a minor setback.

Quietly slipping out of the gallery before anyone had a chance to notice the resemblance between him and *The Runner*, he quickly crossed the street and found a hiding space in the alley directly across from the gallery's front door. All he could do then was wait.

Fifteen minutes passed, then another ten, and with every tick of the clock, Sly felt his rage grow. Damn her, what the hell was she doing in there? Had she somehow recognized him and put two and two together? Was she even now calling the police to tell them that she suspected he was the murderer who'd been in the park that day?

His paranoia building like lava in a volcano that was about to burst, he started toward the entrance to the alley, his only thought to get away before the cops arrived. He'd only taken two steps, however, when the door to the gallery opened and the woman he was quickly coming to hate stepped outside. She had her camera bag slung over her shoulder and didn't even look his way as she turned to the right and started walking down the street. With a tread as soundless as a panther's, he slipped out of the alley and quietly followed her.

Walking on air, Lily couldn't remember the last time she'd been this happy. She had a sell! Grinning, she still couldn't believe it. When she'd decided to quit her job and really make a living from her photography, she'd thought it would be at least six months before she'd be able to generate any kind of income at all. Even then, she'd worried that she was being too optimistic. Never in her wildest dreams had she dared to imagine that her new career would take off so quickly. And this was just the beginning. Susan had told her that once Julian Edwards used a photographer or artist's work, he had a tendency to buy their pieces again and again.

Sending up a silent prayer of thanks, she wanted to laugh and dance and hug the entire world. Her father, however, had taught her to show more decorum. So she restrained herself and headed for the duck pond at the park instead. The sun might be high in the sky and the shadows short, but she didn't care that the lighting wasn't the best. It was Saturday and a beautiful late-summer day. She had her camera and all was right with the world.

When she reached the pond, it didn't take long for her to lose all concept of time. There were mothers there with their babies while the fathers tended the older kids and directed miniature sailboat races on the pond. Giving out her business card to parents who expressed an interest in getting copies of the pictures she'd taken of their children, she spent hours snapping shots of everything that moved.

The afternoon was gone before she realized it. Suddenly out of film, she glanced up with a frown, wondering how she could have possibly used all her film, only to gasp at the sight of the sun sinking low in the sky. "Oh, no!"

Glancing at her watch, she swore softly and hurriedly began gathering up her equipment. How could she have forgotten the time? Abby Saunders was in town for a convention and they were supposed to have dinner together at seven. She had to hurry or she was never going to make it.

Wondering if their high-school reunion had affected her old classmate the way it had her, she made one last check around the area to make sure she hadn't left anything, then strode quickly toward home.

A dozen yards behind her, Sly hurried to keep up. What the hell had gotten into her? he wondered with a scowl as he tried not to look as if he was running after her. One minute, she'd been taking so many shots, he'd been afraid she'd get another picture of him, and the next, she'd stuffed her camera in its case and rushed toward the park exit. What the devil was going on? Had she remembered something? His blood running cold at the thought, he followed at a quick pace, his expression grim. If she even thought about going to the police...

All his attention focused on keeping her in sight, he didn't notice that she'd reached her destination until he was within twenty yards of her and closing fast. Biting off an oath, he quickly stepped into a recessed doorway, but he needn't have worried. When he cautiously peeked around the corner a few seconds later, she was slipping a key into the lock of a door halfway down the block.

She'd hardly turned the key in the lock when she disappeared inside.

Swearing, Sly darted after her, but it was too late. The door swung shut behind her and locked. Irritated that he'd lost her so easily, he peered through the glass door and saw a narrow hallway and a flight of stairs that obviously led to apartments that were located above the Italian restaurant that appeared to occupy most of the lower floor of the small, old building. Outside, next to the private street-level entrance that gave access to the second floor, there were three mailboxes. None of them were labeled, but Sly wasn't concerned. If there were only three apartments, Miss Candid Camera wouldn't be hard to find. Now that he knew where she lived, all he had to do was bide his time, wait until the conditions were right, and she'd be history.

The minute she entered her apartment, Lily took time only to store her camera case in the closet in the apartment's small entry hall, then headed for the bathroom. She had only thirty minutes before she was supposed to meet Abby. She'd have to hurry, and the apartment didn't have a shower. Quickly putting the stopper in the old-fashioned claw-foot tub, she turned the water on full blast, poured in her favorite bath oil, then rushed to the bedroom and laid out some clean clothes.

She would have loved nothing more than a long soak, but there just wasn't time. Peeling out of the T-shirt and capris she'd worn to the park, she tossed them in the hamper, set a clean towel on the old vanity stool she kept in the bathroom and stepped into a tub of cold water.

"Aaagh!" Screeching, she hopped out like a scalded cat. "What the—"

Quickly turning on the hot water, she groaned when

nothing but cold water gushed out. No. When she'd rented the apartment, Angelo had warned her that the pilot on the hot-water heater was sensitive and sometimes blew out if the wind even thought about blowing. It couldn't have gone out today, she thought. She didn't have time for this.

But when she once again tested the water running out of the spout, it wasn't even close to being warm. Grabbing her terry-cloth robe from where it hung on the back of the bathroom door, she shrugged into it and strode into the kitchen to the phone.

"Angelo," she said thankfully when he answered the restaurant phone a few seconds later. "This is Lily. I know you must be busy getting ready for the dinner crowd, but I don't have any hot water."

"I told you the heater was finicky," he said apologetically. "I've had it repaired twice already, and it still keeps blowing out. I guess I'm going to have to bite the bullet and buy a new one. Hang on, and I'll be up in a minute to relight the pilot for you."

"I don't mind doing it—"

"Oh, no, no," he said hurriedly. "It's too dangerous—it's a gas heater. I'll do it."

Promising to be right up, Angelo hung up, then turned to find his head chef, Stephen Talerico, standing in front of him, looking not only disgusted but decidedly green around the edges. Frowning, he said, "Are you all right?"

"I'll make it," he retorted. "We've got a problem."

Angelo wasn't surprised. It had been one of those days when everything that could go wrong had gone wrong; and the look on the other man's face told him he wasn't going to like what he had to say. "Don't tell me," he growled. "Let me guess. We're out of mozzarella."

"No, but we're low," Stephen retorted. "That's not a problem—we can send someone to the grocery store if we have to. We can't, however, send someone to the store for a new oven."

"What?"

He nodded grimly. "It looks like the heating element went out in the big stove. We can make do with the smaller one, but we've got a full house already and we're not going to be able to work fast. The customers aren't going to be happy."

Angelo swore roundly. "How many steaks do we have in the cooler?"

Already guessing where he was going, Stephen said, "Enough to feed every customer in the place, and then some. If we run short, there are always more in the freezer."

"Good. Then we've got a new special for the evening. I'll inform the waitstaff and the customers, then call around and see if I can get a repairman in tonight." Cocking his head, he studied Stephen's weak eyes and pale face and didn't like what he saw. "You're sick, aren't you?"

The other man didn't deny it. "That doesn't begin to describe it."

"Then why are you here? You should have called in sick."

"And leave you with two rehearsal-dinner parties and one oven, all with no notice? I don't think so."

Angelo appreciated the thought, but he couldn't let him stay and they both knew it. "You know you can't handle food when you're sick. If the health inspector knew you were here, he'd have a stroke. Go on—get out of here. Take some chicken soup home with you and don't come back until you're feeling better."

"But what about the stove?"

"I'll call a repairman if I get a chance. If not, I'll handle it. I started this restaurant with only one stove—I can certainly get through the evening without a second oven. So don't worry. We'll be fine."

Stephen was a loyal employee—Angelo wasn't surprised when he hesitated. But he was obviously feeling miserable and had no business being anywhere but in bed. "Okay," he said gruffly. "You win. I'll go."

Washing his hands and tying on an apron, Angelo quickly stepped into the chef's place and went to work, his only thought to avert disaster. He sent one of the kitchen staff to post the new special near the front door and to inform the waiters of the change, then sent one of the busboys to the store for more mozzarella. Avoiding that disaster, he completely forgot about Lily and her lack of hot water until he retrieved some just-cooked spaghetti from a pot of boiling water.

"Damn!" Taking a quick glance at the clock on the wall above the door to the dining area, he swore again. He had steaks on the grill, waiters rushing in every few minutes with new orders, and forty people arriving shortly for the two rehearsal dinners. How was he going to find the time to go upstairs?

"Man, this place is a madhouse tonight," Tony said, pushing his way into the kitchen through the swinging door from the dining room. "There's a line out the front door of people waiting to get in. What's going on? You've got that frazzled look, the one you always get when the kitchen sink backs up and the health inspector is eating out front. What's wrong? Where's Stephen?"

"I sent him home," Angelo retorted as he hurriedly slapped steaks on the grill. "He was as green as a gourd.

Unfortunately, he couldn't have picked a worse time to get sick.''

''You're not kidding,'' Tony said, suddenly remembering. ''There are two rehearsal dinners tonight!''

''Oh, it gets worse,'' Angelo said with a grimace, and quickly told him about the blown heating element in one of the ovens and the shortage of mozzarella. ''I've sent a busboy to the store for cheese, but I can't get a repairman tonight. I tried calling, but no one was available, which is probably for the best. How could I cook for a full house with someone taking an oven apart right in the middle of the kitchen?''

''You're right—you can't. But man, you've got your work cut out for you, trying to pull this all off with only one oven.'' Flashing him a grin, he said, ''I guess this isn't a good time to ask for the night off, huh?''

When Angelo's eyes narrowed dangerously, Tony laughed. ''Chill, Unc. I'm just teasing. What's the status on the party rooms? Are they set up and ready to go? What about the menu? Is it already set or is everyone ordering individually?''

''It was set, but with the oven out, I'm going to have to change that,'' he retorted, disgusted. ''When the two parties get here, I'll need you to explain the situation and offer them steak at no extra charge.''

Not surprised that Angelo would make such a costly substitute, Tony had to shake his head in admiration. ''It's no wonder you've got customers who've been coming here for thirty years. They know they're going to get treated right.''

''Make sure you remember that when you inherit the place,'' he told him. ''Everyone has a bad day once in a while, but it doesn't have to cost you customers. Be honest with them, apologize, and make it up to them. You remember to do that, and they'll forgive you just about anything.''

''I'll remember,'' Tony said gruffly. ''In the meantime, I expect you to stick around at least for the next thirty years or so and take care of your customers yourself. I'll help, of course, but this is still your baby. So what do you want me to do first? Check the party rooms or help you here in the kitchen?''

''Actually,'' he said, ''the first thing I need you to do is go upstairs and check the hot-water heater in Lily's apartment. The damn pilot light seems to be out again.''

Surprised, Tony frowned. ''I thought you got that fixed.''

''So did I,'' he said grimly. ''Lily offered to relight it herself, but I'd rather she not take a chance.''

''Oh, I get it,'' Tony said with a grin. ''You want me to blow up instead.''

''Remind me,'' Angelo told him with a matching grin. ''Why am I leaving this place to you? You give me nothing but grief.''

''Yeah, right. I'm your favorite nephew and you know it.''

''You're my only nephew!''

''Why would you need another when you've got me?''

''The more you stand around jawing, the more reasons I can think of,'' Angelo said dryly, grinning. ''Get out of here!''

He didn't have to tell him twice. Chuckling, Tony hurried over to the kitchen door that gave access to the apartment stairwell. ''I'll be back in a few minutes.''

Restlessly pacing her living room, Lily glanced at the clock on the mantel and frowned. She'd already called Abby and told her she was going to be late. Thankfully,

Abby was running late herself so her tardiness wasn't a problem, but she still hadn't expected to be *this* late. What was keeping Angelo? If he didn't hurry, she'd have to give up on a bath—it would just take too long to heat the water. She hated to call him again and pester him, especially when she could light the damn thing herself.

Marching into the kitchen, she was just searching through a drawer for matches to light the pilot light herself when there was a knock at the front door. "Finally!" The matches forgotten, she hurried into the living room and pulled the door open with a smile. "I was afraid you'd forgotten about me—"

Tony grinned crookedly. "How could I forget a woman who doesn't want to go out with me? You broke my heart."

All too aware that she was standing before him in nothing but her terry-cloth bathrobe, Lily felt heat climbing into her cheeks and there was nothing she could do but suffer through it. "I never said I didn't want to go out with you," she reminded him as she stepped back to allow him access into the living room. "I said—"

"Maybe," he finished for her. "So…is today my lucky day?" he said eagerly, teasing her. "It is, isn't it? You just pretended the pilot on your hot-water heater was out so Angelo would send me up here and you could surprise me. Sweetheart, that's so thoughtful of you." Grinning broadly, he opened his arms wide. "Give us a hug."

Laughing, she sidestepped him. "I don't think so. The pilot on the hot-water heater really is out. Sorry to disappoint you, but I was expecting Angelo. Where is he?"

"Running the kitchen," he replied. "The chef got sick, and two different wedding parties are expected any minute for their rehearsal dinners."

"Sounds like you've got a busy night ahead of you. And you wanted to go out," she chided teasingly. "When were you going to have time? Between two and three in the morning?"

"If necessary. Is that a yes?"

"No," she said quickly, laughing. "I told you—"

"I know, I know. You're busy. Damn, I hate it when that happens. Just for the record, I'm not giving up," he warned her with dancing eyes. "Some things are just meant to be. You'll see that eventually. In the meantime, I guess I'd better check out your hot-water heater before Angelo calls out the National Guard."

As she led the way to the kitchen pantry and the water heater, Lily couldn't stop smiling. So he wasn't giving up, was he? She had no intention of telling him, but secretly she was glad. Later, she knew she would worry about how easily he was slipping past her guard, but for now she was having too much fun with him to care.

It took Tony all of ten seconds to discover that the pilot light on the hot-water heater had, indeed, blown out. Quickly relighting it, he rose to his feet and grinned. "Okay, you're all set. Give it a few minutes, and you'll have all the hot water you need."

"Thanks for your help. I would have lit it myself, but I think Angelo was afraid I'd blow the place up."

He chuckled. "Don't take it personally. He's old-fashioned. There are certain things a man's supposed to do, and lighting pilot lights is one of them. Not because he doesn't think you're capable of doing it," he added quickly. "He just doesn't believe a woman should have to put herself in danger when there's a man around."

Arching an eyebrow, she met his gaze head-on. "And how do you feel about that?"

He didn't even have to think about it. "Pretty much

the same way,'' he said honestly. ''That doesn't mean I'm a chauvinist. I'm all for women doing anything they want, especially when it comes to education and working. But I'll admit it—I'm protective of women and children and the sick and the elderly. I'm Angelo's nephew. It's in the blood.''

''I think that's nice,'' she said with a soft smile. Wishing he could stay longer but knowing he couldn't, she walked with him back to the living room. ''I guess you're going to work all evening.''

''It's going to be crazy,'' he agreed. ''On top of everything else, the heating element in one of the ovens went out. Hey, what's this?'' he said, suddenly noticing several black-and-white contact sheets lying on the coffee table.

''Homework,'' she replied ruefully. ''Out of ten rolls of film, I have to pick out one shot that I think is the best of the lot and enlarge it into an eight-by-ten for a class competition.''

''And which one are you going to choose?''

Grimacing, she shrugged. ''At this point, I've narrowed it down to about fifty.''

''It looks like you've got your work cut out for you,'' he said. ''But look at the bright side. You've eliminated a hundred and ninety...if there's twenty-four on a roll. That's a damn good start.''

''Good point,'' she laughed. ''Things can always be worse—just ask Angelo.''

That should have been his cue to leave and return to work. By now, the dining room would be overflowing and Angelo would be wondering what the hell was taking him so long. But the more he got to know her, the more he wanted to know about her. Surely Angelo could get by without him for a few more minutes. She was dressed in a bathrobe, for heaven's sake. Granted, there wasn't anything the least bit revealing about it, but she'd twisted her hair up with some kind of clip, and loose curls brushed the delicate lines of her neck. He tried not to notice, but he wasn't made of stone.

That night he'd waited on her downstairs, she'd captivated him without even trying. He'd have sworn then that she couldn't get any prettier. He'd been wrong. She wasn't wearing makeup and she didn't need it. There was a natural blush to her cheeks, and her lips had a rosy color that he found impossible to ignore. With a will of their own, his eyes returned again and again to the enticing curves of her mouth. Were her lips as soft as they looked? he wondered, only to swallow a groan at the thought. What would she do if he tried to kiss her?

Half tempted to reach for her and find out, he took a quick step back before he gave in to temptation. "Speaking of Angelo," he said huskily, "I should be going. I'm sure he needs my help."

"With two private parties and a restaurant full of people, I'm sure he does," she agreed.

But he didn't move toward the door, and when she didn't, either, he felt inordinately pleased. "You know, I hate to repeat myself, but I think we need to talk about that date you promised me again."

A slow smile curled the corners of her mouth. "Maybe."

Heat spilled into Tony's stomach. "Don't start that," he groaned, half laughing, only to frown when his cell phone rang, destroying the moment. Cursing silently, he jerked it from the holder attached to his belt. He didn't have to look at the caller ID to know who it was. "I'll be right there," he growled.

"You said that fifteen minutes ago," Angelo retorted.

"What's taking so long? I'm getting swamped down here!"

"I know. I was just hanging around a few minutes to make sure that the pilot stayed lit."

If his uncle noticed that his voice was husky or that he didn't explain what he'd been doing for the last fifteen minutes, he made no comment. Instead, he said, "Tootsie's coming in for dinner. She was hoping you might have a recent picture of Quentin. She hasn't see him in ages."

Tony winced and swallowed a silent groan. He loved his aunt Tootsie dearly, but she wasn't shy about asking him questions about his love life, and he wasn't in the mood to be grilled. "School pictures haven't been taken yet, but I've got a few recent snapshots. She can have one of those."

"Good," he said, satisfied. "She'll be here in ten minutes. You can wait on her. You always were her favorite nephew. She doesn't know you like I do."

Fighting a grin, Tony said dryly, "I always did think she was one of the smartest relatives I've got."

"Yeah, right," Angelo snorted.

Tony chuckled. "You're smart, too. There's no need to be jealous."

"Jealous, my eye," he said. "I'm just as smart as Tootsie, and on top of that, I've done everything in life I wanted to do. She's my sister, for heaven's sake! I love her."

"I never doubted it for a moment," Tony replied. "Family is family. Nothing else matters."

"You're damn right. And don't you forget it."

Amused, Tony grinned. "Now that we've got that settled, I'm going to check the pilot light one more time before I leave. I'll be down before Aunt Tootsie arrives."

When he hung up, he turned to find Lily watching him with dancing eyes. The need to kiss her hit him in the gut again, this time stronger than before. But Angelo needed him…and Aunt Tootsie would be here soon. If he kept her waiting, she'd want to know the reason. Once she found out there was a woman involved, he'd never hear the end of it.

Swallowing a silent groan, he quickly returned to the kitchen to check the pilot light, then shot Lily a smile that was little more than a grimace. "I guess I'd better be going. Angelo's getting antsy. If you have any more problems, all you have to do is call."

Giving in to impulse, he gave her a quick kiss on the cheek, wished her a gruff good-night and quickly let himself out. Her heart pounding, Lily pressed a hand to her cheek and almost called him back. For the past week, she'd worked hard to convince herself that he was just teasing about wanting to date her, that the attraction between them was nothing more than a game they both enjoyed. But there had been nothing teasing about the kiss he'd given her…or the heat in his eyes.

Somewhere on the edge of her consciousness, an alarm bell clanged, warning her to beware, but all through her quick bath, all she could think about was Tony. By the time she finally dragged herself out of the tub and dressed, she had ten minutes to get across town to meet Abby at her hotel. All thoughts of Tony flying out of her head, she grabbed her keys and rushed outside to her car.

"Abby! I'm so sorry I'm late. It's just been one of those days—"

"Hey, don't worry about it," her friend said with a smile as Lily quickly strode across the lobby of the hotel where she was staying. "I just got here myself. Look at you. You look fantastic. I guess I don't have to ask if you regret quitting your job.''

''Actually, I just took a leave of absence...just in case.'' Her smile rueful, she added, ''I am, after all, my father's daughter. I'm almost positive, though, that I won't be going back.''

''Things are going that well for you? Oh, Lily, that's wonderful. What about your father? Has he forgiven you yet?''

Her smile fading as they made their way to a corner table in the hotel restaurant, she shook her head grimly. ''He's the stubbornnest man I know. When I called to tell him that two of my pictures were already hanging in a gallery, he didn't say anything—he just changed the subject.''

''I don't understand why he can't see how talented you are,'' Abby said with a puzzled frown. ''Even in high school it was obvious how gifted you were. The school annual won all sorts of awards that year, mainly because of your photographs. He doesn't have to like what you're doing, but he could at least admit that you're good at it.''

''That's not his way,'' Lily replied flatly. ''It never has been. If he doesn't like what you're doing, he doesn't care how good you are at it, he's not going to praise you.''

''It must have been difficult growing up without your mother,'' Abby told her quietly. ''Your father was always so stern. I don't think I've ever seen him smile.''

''It's not something he does often,'' she admitted. ''He's been unhappy ever since my mother died. I don't think he realized just how much he loved her until she was gone.'' Sadness pulled at her, but she determinedly shook that off as the waiter arrived to take their order. When he hurried off to the kitchen, she turned to Abby and forced a bright smile. ''So tell me what's been going on in your life since the reunion. Are you still dating Dennis?''

Abby winced at the question and would have preferred not to discuss her personal life at all. After all, she knew what everyone thought about Dennis. It had been painfully obvious at the reunion that he talked too much and thought he knew everything, and she couldn't blame her friends for not wanting to be around him. After all, there had been times when *she* didn't want to be around him, either.

''I keep telling myself it will work if I just give it enough time,'' she said huskily. ''But how much is enough?''

''I used to think I would be happy if I just kept working at a job I hated,'' Lily confided. ''I was a damn good accountant. And it wasn't all bad. I was friends with the people I worked with, I had seniority, great benefits, everything anyone could want. I put in ten years, Abby. Ten years! And it never got any better. Not once did I ever look forward to going to work.''

''Oh, Lily, I'm so sorry. I had no idea you hated your job so much. You were always so good in math.''

''All I ever wanted to do was be a photographer,'' she said simply. ''That didn't seem to matter to my father. Not,'' she added, ''that I can blame him for the fact that I stayed with my job all these years. That was my fault. I knew quitting would cause a rift between us, and I didn't want that. He's the only family I have left. I hate being at odds with him.''

''But you did it, anyway,'' Abby said as the waiter delivered their food to the table. ''How did you work up the nerve?''

''I realized I just couldn't do it anymore. Not for my

father, not for anyone. This is *my* life, not his. I had to do what was right for me. If my father has a problem with that, he'll have to learn to live with it.'' She met Abby's gaze head-on. ''You have to follow your heart, Abby. You'll never be happy if you don't.''

''I know,'' she sniffed, blinking back the tears that suddenly welled in her eyes. ''It's just so hard. What if what's out there is worse than what I already have?''

''It won't be,'' Lily assured her. ''You're looking for something better, not worse, and you won't stop looking until you find it.''

''But I'm not like you. I never had much self-confidence.''

''I didn't either when it came to standing up to my father,'' Lily confessed. ''But I just felt the years slipping through my fingers and I had to do something. Life's too short to be miserable.''

''But what about Neil? Didn't he want to be part of your new life? You were engaged.''

''He couldn't accept what I wanted to do any more than my father could,'' she replied. ''As far as he was concerned, I had a good job with a secure retirement. He didn't care that I hated it. If I hadn't broken our engagement, he would have. He was furious with me for not taking his advice.''

''Dennis gets mad at me for the same thing,'' she confided huskily. ''I hate it. Do you think all men are like that?''

Lily started to say yes, but then she heard Tony's voice as clear as day in her head. *I'm all for women doing anything they want, especially when it comes to education and working.* He hadn't been just telling her what she wanted to hear—he was sincere. Even though she didn't know him nearly as well as she would have liked, every instinct she possessed told her he would be supportive of the woman he loved. What would that be like? she wondered. To have someone in her life who wouldn't treat her like a child or want to control her…

"Lily? Hello? What'd I say? I lost you."

Caught up in her thoughts, Lily blinked. "What?"

"You've met someone, haven't you?" Abby said, smiling at her curiously. "Just a minute ago, you had this look on your face—"

"No! Really," she insisted when her friend looked skeptical. "I was just thinking that it would be nice to meet someone who didn't want to control me."

From the glint in her friend's eye, it was obvious that Abby clearly didn't believe her, but she didn't push the issue. "If you say so. Enough about men. It's time to talk about something important…like dessert. When we finish with the main course, what are you having next? Cheesecake or the double-chocolate hot-fudge cake?"

Lily didn't even have to think about the answer to that one. Grinning, she quickly supplied, "Hot-fudge cake."

"Table number four's getting restless," Tony told his uncle as he hurried into the kitchen to retrieve the almond torte one of the wedding parties had ordered for dessert. "Their drink orders should have been taken ten minutes ago. Where's Maria?"

"Sick," Angelo retorted as he slapped more steaks on the grill. "I just sent her home. I think she's got what Stephen has. It seems to be making the rounds."

If he hadn't spent most of his adult life helping his uncle in the restaurant whenever he needed him, Tony might have panicked. But he'd learned from the best and it took a heck of a lot more than a flu virus decimating the waitstaff to make him panic. "No problem—I'll get

George and Cindy to take over her tables. How're things going in here?"

"Crazy," he replied. "Tomorrow I may not be able to move, but you won't hear me complaining. We haven't had a night like this in ten years. You were right about the band."

"Aha! So you admit it," he teased. "It's about time."

For the last six months, he'd been trying to convince Angelo to have live music on Friday and Saturday nights, but his uncle had been afraid that his older customers wouldn't like the change. He'd finally convinced him to at least give the band a try for a couple of weekends, and the payoff had been almost immediate. The reason the two wedding parties had decided to have their rehearsal dinners at Angelo's was because he'd promised them live music. Advertising, and, of course, reputation had brought in the rest of the crowd.

"Okay, okay, so I should have done it sooner," Angelo said with a wry grin. "Maybe I'll listen to you more often."

"Maybe you should," Tony said. "Aunt Tootsie said I'm one of your biggest assets."

"I know," he groaned. "She came back here before she left and told me the same thing. She also said the pretty brunette at table three has been flirting with you all night, but you didn't even notice. That doesn't sound like you at all. What's wrong? You're not sick, too, are you? I can't afford to lose you and Stephen all in one night."

"I'm fine," Tony replied. "I'm just busy. And I did notice the brunette. She just wasn't my type."

Even to his own ears, that sounded outrageous. Tony readily admitted that he liked women. He enjoyed them, enjoyed talking and laughing with them. He hadn't been kidding when he'd told Lily that he hadn't dated anyone in six months, but he still enjoyed flirting.

So why'd you ignore the brunette? an irritating voice in his head demanded. *She was gorgeous, and you didn't even give her the time of day. What were you thinking? Or maybe I should say who were you thinking about? Could it be the blonde in her bathrobe who needed you to light her hot-water heater? What's going on there?*

Nothing, he growled to himself as he made the excuse that he had to check on the wedding party in the main party room, then strode out of the kitchen. Nothing at all was going on. If he couldn't get the image of Lily in her bathrobe out of his head, that was perfectly natural. She was a beautiful woman, sexy as hell, and he liked teasing her as much as she seemed to like teasing him. There was nothing more to it than that.

Chapter 4

Standing in the shadows of the alley across the street from Angelo's Italian Restaurant, Sly Jackson felt rage ignite inside him like a wild fire fanned by a hot breeze. The bitch was gone—she must have slipped out the back—and he still didn't have a clue which apartment was hers. Cursing under his breath, he told himself it didn't matter. The building wasn't that big, and he'd search every apartment in it if he had to in order to find hers. Then he'd sit and wait. She had to come home eventually. When she did, he'd make her wish she'd never picked up a camera, let alone taken his picture.

But first he had to find a way inside the damn building.

His cold, steely eyes narrowed on the glass door at the front of the building that gave access to the stairwell and stairs that led upstairs. He'd tested it earlier and, not surprisingly, found it locked. There wasn't a doubt in his mind that he could pick the lock, but there was, for the moment, a slight problem. The sidewalk tables at the restaurant next door were crowded with diners and people lingered near the entrance, waiting to get in. With so many witnesses on the street, he couldn't move without someone seeing him.

Cursing again, he wanted to lie low until the streets emptied, but he couldn't, dammit. Everyone else in the building would be home by then, and the odds of him finding the bitch, Lily, without anyone hearing him would be slim to none. No, he decided, if he was going to break in, he had to do it now and take advantage of the fact that everyone was gone. Then, when Miss Candid Camera finally came home, he'd be waiting for her. In the darkness of the alley, he allowed himself a tight, cold smile of anticipation. He was going to enjoy this.

In the meantime, however, he still had to find a way into the building. His gaze shifted from the entrance to the apartment stairwell to the diners just fifty feet away. Grimly, he had no choice but to accept that he had to find another way in. And he couldn't do that by staying where he was.

A muscle ticking in his jaw, he straightened his shoulders, smoothed his hair and dragged in a bracing breath. A split second later, he stepped out of the dark shadows of the alley, crossed the street and turned away from the restaurant as he headed for the corner. Fighting the urge to hurry, he kept his pace slow and easy as if he was out for a stroll in the moonlight. Anyone seeing him would think he didn't have a care in the world, but on the inside, he was wound tighter than a time bomb on the verge of exploding.

The second he turned the corner, darkness immediately enveloped him, and he released a silent sigh of relief. The cross street was empty and full of shadows, but there were no watchful eyes here to note his progress as he soundlessly strode down the block to the back alley that ran behind the restaurant.

In the quiet of the night, the muted music from the live band inside Angelo's throbbed like a heartbeat. Pleased, Sly smiled coldly in the darkness as he approached the rear entrance to the apartment stairwell. There was nothing like a good band to drown out the sound of someone breaking in. He couldn't have planned this better if he'd tried.

Unlike the street-side entrance to the stairwell, which was glass, the rear one was steel. Undaunted, Sly reached into his pocket and pulled out a small tool kit he took with him everywhere. In the darkness, his fingers immediately found a penlight that was no bigger than a fountain pen, then a lock pick. Taking a quick look around to make sure he was truly alone, he silently went to work. And all the while, the band played on.

In the restaurant kitchen, Angelo was in the process of pulling another pan of lasagna from the one working oven when he suddenly stopped in his tracks and cocked his head, listening. Across the room, Tony glanced up from where he was dishing up cheesecake for table twelve and studied him in amusement. "What are you doing?"

"Listening," he said with a frown. "I thought I heard something."

"It's probably rats," Tony replied. "It's time to get up on the roof again and check the covers on the vent pipes. I'll do it tomorrow, after my shift ends."

Still listening to the noise in the stairwell, Angelo frowned. "I had those covers fixed two months ago. They shouldn't be loose again so soon."

"Maybe that storm last weekend loosened them. The winds were pretty strong."

Unconvinced, Angelo shrugged. "Maybe. I don't think so."

Tony had to admit that his uncle usually had good instincts. He certainly wasn't in the habit of imagining things. If he thought he'd heard something, then he probably had. "You want me to check it out? I can put out some traps in the stairwell—"

Angelo hesitated, then shook his head. "We're too busy. I'll do it later, when I close up."

"You're sure? Okay," he said. "Then I guess I'd better get this cheesecake to table twelve." Hefting a tray laden with desserts, he pushed open the swinging door that separated the kitchen from the dining area. "We've still got a full house," he warned his uncle. "It's going to be a long night."

With a soft click, the lock opened. His heart pounding louder than the restaurant band, Sly quietly stepped into the stairwell and shut the door carefully behind him. The light overhead made him clearly visible to anyone who might suddenly appear, but he wasn't deterred.

Ten seconds later, he reached the upstairs landing without incident, only to stop in his tracks with a muttered curse. This was just great, he thought grimly. Three apartments opened off the upstairs hallway, but it might as well have been ten. There wasn't a name anywhere to indicate which apartment belonged to which tenant.

Furious, he didn't even consider backing out now—not when he'd come this far. He had to choose an apartment, and he had to be pretty damn quick about it. Because every second he stood in the hallway, he was risking discovery.

Lightning quick, he chose the apartment closest to the stairs and immediately picked the lock. Amused, he almost laughed aloud at the ease in which he did it. Damn, he was good! One of these days, he'd have to go back to Brooklyn and thank old man Thompson for teaching him everything he knew about locks when he'd worked for him that summer he was sixteen. Over the years, he'd lost track of how many times that little skill had come in handy.

In the quiet stillness of the upstairs hallway, he slipped into the apartment like a dark shadow, not making a sound. No lights had been left on, and the second he shut the door behind him, darkness swallowed him whole. His nerves now as steady as an executioner's, he leaned back against the door and waited for his eyes to adjust.

It didn't take long, and almost immediately he noticed that the living-room windows, which faced the busy street, were uncovered. If he turned on a light, he would be clearly visible to anyone who happened to live in the upstairs apartments across the street. He'd have to search the place in the dark.

Quietly stepping away from the door, he proceeded to examine the living room in the dark, but from what he could see, the furnishings were generic and could have belonged to anyone. The apartment wasn't very large, and within a matter of moments he found the bedroom. It, too, faced the street, and the blinds were wide open. In the darkness, he could make out the outline of the bed and dresser, and little else. Muttering a curse, he moved to the closet and pulled open the door.

Not surprisingly, the inside of the closet was as dark as pitch and he couldn't see a damn thing. Scowling, he pulled his penlight from his pocket, then pulled the closet door half-shut behind him so that the small beam of the flashlight couldn't be seen by anyone through the windows. Only then did he turn on the light.

"Son of a bitch!"

His eyes riveted on the police uniforms hanging right in front of his nose, he swore and jerked back like a scalded cat. A cop, dammit! How the hell was he supposed to know there was a cop living in the building?

He had to get away. Panicking, he started to slam the closet door shut, only to remember just in time that the noise might carry down to the restaurant below. Muttering another oath, he managed to shut it quietly, but he was shaking with rage as he quickly made his way to the apartment's front door.

He had to regroup, rethink his strategy. As much as he wanted to find that bitch and eliminate her before she could destroy him, he couldn't do it when there was a damn cop in the building. Sly liked to think he was gutsy enough to take a chance when someone else might cut and run, but he wasn't a complete fool. He wanted nothing to do with a cop.

Downstairs, the music continued to play—obviously it would be a while before the restaurant closed for the evening. Sly didn't care. His only thought was to get away, he rushed out of the apartment, and in his haste to leave, never noticed that he didn't quite pull the door completely shut.

By the time the last customer left, the band cleared out and the kitchen and dining area were clean, it was going on midnight, and Tony was beat. He'd sent Angelo upstairs an hour ago and closed up for him. With Stephen out sick and all the other problems that had cropped up, there hadn't been time to draw a deep breath, let alone take a break, all evening long. By eleven, it was clear

Angelo was worn-out—otherwise, he never would have allowed Tony to talk him into leaving the cleanup to him. That just wasn't his way. For as long as Tony could remember, his uncle had always been the first one in in the morning and the last one to leave.

Time was catching up with him, Tony thought as he headed upstairs. And he hated that. Angelo was like a father to him. After his parents had died in a car accident when he was sixteen, Angelo was the one who'd stepped forward and taken him in. He'd always been there for him whenever he needed him, and he didn't like to think of his uncle getting older and slowing down. If the time ever came when he couldn't cook for people and make them comfortable the way he loved, Tony intended to make sure he was able to spend time at the restaurant whenever he wanted, even if he had to wheel him in in a wheelchair. After everything Angelo had done for him, it was the least he could do.

Lost in his thoughts as he locked up, then climbed the stairs to his apartment, he didn't notice anything was amiss until he started to insert the key to his front door in the lock. The second he touched it, the door silently swung open.

"What the—"

Frowning, he studied the open door through narrowed eyes. Hadn't he locked the apartment earlier? He would have sworn he had. In fact, he couldn't ever remember *not* locking his front door. He just wasn't that careless.

An image stirred in his head, one of Lily answering her door in her bathrobe. In spite of that, she couldn't have looked more proper—or showed less skin—and she'd still somehow managed to distract the hell out of him. Was that what had happened? he wondered with a scowl. After he'd left her apartment and stopped by his to pick up the pictures of Quentin for Aunt Tootsie, had he just walked out without even checking to make sure he'd shut the door? Because of Lily?

Or did someone break in while he was downstairs working?

No, he thought, immediately rejecting the idea. The neighborhood was safe—he couldn't remember the last time Angelo or any of his neighbors had had a problem with crime. Still, he couldn't completely reject the idea, not when his door was standing wide open and he didn't know how it had gotten that way.

Every nerve ending in his body on alert, he quietly pushed open the door until it came to rest against the wall. Good, he thought in grim satisfaction. There was no one hiding behind it. Hopefully, there wouldn't be anyone in the rest of the apartment, either.

Quietly stepping across to the kitchen, he repeated the same procedure he'd used in the living room, then did the same in the bedroom and bathroom. Only when he was satisfied that there was no one in the apartment did he finally relax. Then he began to thoroughly search the place to make sure no one had been there.

Fifteen minutes later, he didn't have any more answers than he had when he'd first noticed his door was open. As far as he could determine, nothing was missing and there was no sign that anyone had been there. Obviously he *had* left the door open, though he had no memory of doing so.

Shaking his head, too tired to wonder anymore how he could have done such a thing, he checked the door a second time to make sure that it really was locked this time, then flipped off the lights. Exhausted, he stumbled into his bedroom and was asleep before his head even hit the pillow.

* * *

Sly didn't sleep much that night. Nothing had turned out the way he'd expected, he fumed, pacing the confines of his apartment like a death-row inmate counting the days. He shouldn't have had so much trouble finding the bitch's apartment. How difficult could it be? There were only three apartments in the whole damn building! So what had he done? Stumbled into a cop's! Son of a bitch! Talk about bad luck. It didn't get any worse than that.

It wasn't over, though, he told himself grimly. Miss Candid Camera might have been able to evade him tonight, but her turn was coming. Oh, yeah, he'd get her. He had to—she was the only one who'd seen him running in the park that day, the only one who could place him at the scene of the murder. He wasn't, however, going to risk getting caught trying to find her apartment again. Not when there was a damn pig in the building who could show up at any moment.

No, there was a better way to take care of her, he decided. The lady was a photographer, and from what he'd seen of her work in the gallery, she didn't work in a studio. She had to get out in the world, and when she did, he would be waiting for her, watching. Granted, there would be more people around, but she'd be much more accessible on the street. If he was lucky, she'd go back to the park, to the spot where she'd taken that damning picture of him, and then he'd have her…because he knew the park like the back of his hand. He'd been jogging there for years, and he knew all its secrets. There were areas not far from the fountain where he could drag her and no one would ever hear her scream.

Packing her bag with backup batteries, film and her camera, Lily couldn't wait to hit the streets. It was a beautiful morning, crisp and sunny, and fall was definitely in the air. The days were already growing shorter, and the first cold front of the season was only weeks away. Soon the leaves would be changing and summer would just be a memory. Mothers would still take their children to the park, but instead of playing in the fountain, toddlers would chase the falling leaves, and the bigger kids would play football with their friends. With her mind's eye, she could already see the pictures.

Grinning at the thought—Lord, she loved what she was doing!—she grabbed her purse and the camera bag and rushed out of the apartment. With her bag over her shoulder and a skip in her step, she turned right and headed for the park and never saw the man who quickly stepped out of the building across the street and began to follow her.

Keeping a safe distance, Sly dodged other pedestrians and tried not to look as if he was tailing her, but the bitch didn't make it easy for him. She moved along at a fast clip, and in order to keep up with her, there were times when he had to practically run—especially when the light changed at the next corner and a stream of moving cars abruptly cut him off from her. Swearing, he prowled back and forth on the curb, not caring that he was jostling people as he watched Lily draw farther and farther away from him.

"Dammit to hell!" he muttered. He was losing her, and thanks to the lights and traffic, there was nothing he could do about it. Every time he even thought about stepping off the curb, the cars racing past blasted him with their horns.

Watching her disappear around the next corner, he swore again. Like last time, he checked the traffic, but this time, he saw a break. Ignoring the Don't Walk sign, he stepped off the curb and darted across the street. All around him, drivers laid on their horns, but he only made a rude gesture and never even bothered to look at them. His eyes trained on the corner where Lily had turned, he started to run.

Nearly ten minutes later, he spied her entering the gates of the park. She was less than fifty yards ahead of him, and there weren't nearly as many people in the park as there had been on the street. If Lily had glanced over her shoulder, she would have seen a man walking his dog, an old lady pushing a baby in a stroller and him.

Would she recognize him? he wondered. He looked nothing like he had that day in the park when she'd taken his picture. Instead of a jogging suit, he wore a polo shirt, khakis and loafers, and dark sunglasses hid his eyes. It wasn't much of a disguise, but he'd been using a self-tanner, so he looked considerably darker than he had when she'd seen him last.

Still, he wasn't taking any chances. The damn picture was hanging in a gallery, for God's sake. She must have looked at it—and his face—a dozen times or more...which was why he wasn't getting too close to her. If she recognized him, all his plans would be shot to hell.

So he kept his distance, falling farther behind as he casually followed her down the trail. As she walked farther into the park, however, he started to sweat. Where the hell was she going? Had she somehow sensed he was following her? Was she leading him into some kind of trap? It could happen, he reasoned. He didn't know for certain that she hadn't figured out that he was the one who'd killed that girl in the park that day. She must have seen it on the news by now. What if she'd put two and two together? She didn't know his name, but she had a picture of him. What if she'd gone to the police with it and her suspicions. For all he knew, a damn posse could be waiting for him around the next curve in the path.

Fear a bitter taste on his tongue, he almost bolted into the trees. But before he could take a single step, Lily stopped to set up her tripod for her camera. It was only then that he noticed that the path she'd taken was a shortcut that led to an area of the park set aside for dog lovers. The street served as a boundary on one side, but the open field for the dogs was set well back from the street.

Setting up her camera about twenty feet from the curb, she immediately changed to a more powerful lens, then went to work taking pictures of several of the dogs and their owners who were playing Frisbee. If she knew he was fifty feet behind her and watching her every move, she gave no sign of it.

The tension draining out of him, Sly almost laughed aloud. He didn't know why he was so worried about the bitch—killing her was going to be so easy. She was right by the road, for God's sake. He could take her out in full view of everyone in the park and the passing traffic, and the cops would never be able to trace it to him. But first, he had to leave to make a few arrangements. Luckily, he didn't have to worry about her disappearing on him while he was gone. If her previous trips to the park were any indication, there was enough activity in that area of the park for her to be busy for hours.

Hurrying back to his apartment, he couldn't stop smiling as he planned her murder in his mind. The story would, no doubt, make the front page. After all, a hit-and-run in the park was big news. In fact, he couldn't remember it ever happening before. People would be outraged. And Lily, poor thing, would never know what hit her. Her killer, of course, would never be found, but hey, those were the breaks. The police couldn't find a man who didn't exist.

His eyes glinting with cold, wicked humor, he stood in front of the mirror and adjusted the wig he'd chosen for the occasion. No doubt about it, he thought gleefully, red was definitely his color. Any witnesses who happened to catch sight of him would be so busy looking at the hair, they wouldn't even be able to tell the police what he looked like.

Removing the wig, he stuffed it, along with several other props, inside the oversize T-shirt he wore, then he hurried back outside. Turning away from the park, he turned down the next side street and began to check the neighborhood for a car. He found it four blocks away, parked in an alley. It couldn't have been more perfect if he'd wished it into existence.

It was a fifteen-year-old Volkswagen, beat up and far from pretty, with faded red paint and a rear bumper that was hanging onto the vehicle by a thread. It wasn't the kind of car that was even worth stealing, but as far as Sly was concerned, it had one redeeming quality that made it invaluable…it looked like something a down-on-his-luck pizza-delivery-boy would be driving.

Glancing around cautiously, Sly studied the building the car was parked behind, but there was no sign of life in the building or the alley. Not wasting another second, he slid behind the driver's seat, quickly hot-wired the car, then donned his red wig and a paper hat from a local pizza parlor. Next he pulled out a 3-D magnetized sign that he'd stolen off the roof of a pizza-delivery car just last night and slapped it on the roof of *his* new car.

Checking his image in the rearview mirror, he grinned, his eyes glinting with sinister pleasure. Damn, he looked good! His mother wouldn't have recognized him—not that she'd ever given a damn about him. But that was something he could get drunk over later. For now, he had a murder to commit, he thought in satisfaction as he put the transmission in Drive. A split second later, he headed for the park.

Lily had never had a dog—when she was a child, her father had refused to even consider the idea—and once she moved to D.C. and had a place of her own, she never seemed to have time to devote to a pet. But watching through the viewfinder of her camera as the black-and-white terrier mix caught the Frisbee his owner threw to him again and again, Lily couldn't help but be envious. They looked as if they were having so much fun.

On the street bordering the park, cars zipped by less than twenty feet away from where she'd set up her tripod, but Lily never looked up. Caught up in the action taking place across the field where the terrier and other dogs played with their owners, she snapped picture after picture and only stopped to change film.

When a horn blared two blocks down, she didn't even look up…until other drivers joined in, voicing their displeasure. Startled, Lily straightened from her camera and looked down the block, only to gasp in horror as a small car with a pizza sign on its roof careened down the street, wildly changing lanes and scraping against other vehicles. Tires screeched as drivers slammed on their brakes, trying to avoid an accident, but the driver of the pizza-delivery car never even checked its speed.

"My God, he's a madman!" she cried, and instinctively turned to grab her camera. All around her, people screamed and began to run away from the street, and Lily caught it all on film in a series of lightning-quick shots that she knew in an instant were the best pictures she'd ever taken. She didn't, however, have time to think about that. She took the last picture on the roll, the film automatically began to rewind, and quickly, she reached for her camera bag without once taking her eyes from the drama unfolding before her.

The idiot driver was in the outside lane and would pass right by her, she realized suddenly, startled. Instinctively, she took a step back, her heart in her throat. In the time it took to blink, he was closer. She caught a flash of red hair, but before she could get a good look at his face, the car swerved again. Suddenly, it was racing right toward her.

Her search for film forgotten, she watched in horror as he drew closer and closer. "Turn," she muttered. "Turn!"

He could have—all it would have taken was a simple turn of the wheel—but he didn't. Instead, he accelerated and the car jumped forward as if it were shot from a gun.

Horrified, Lily froze. *Move!* a frantic voice screamed in her head, but her feet felt like they were encased in blocks of concrete. She couldn't move, couldn't think of anything except she was about to die and she wasn't ready. On the edge of her consciousness, she heard a woman scream and only then realized it was herself.

"No!" Another scream ripping from her throat, she almost waited too long. She could feel the heat from the engine when she screamed again and jumped behind a tree.

A heartbeat later, the car brushed against the tree so hard, it groaned. The driver, however, never slowed down. Bouncing off the tree, tires squealing, he jerked the car back onto the road and raced away. Taking the next corner on two wheels, he disappeared without ever looking back.

Chapter 5

Lily hit the ground, hard, face first. Her forehead hit the ground, and her knee came into sharp contact with an exposed tree root. Grunting in pain, she knew she would have bruises tomorrow, but there wasn't time to worry about that now. Scrambling to her feet, she squinted after the car that was just disappearing around the corner.

"Focus!" she told herself fiercely. But all she could see were the numbers six and three. Swearing, she impatiently wiped her eyes with the back of her arm, but she might as well have saved herself the trouble. The car was gone, and she'd been so busy trying to get the license number that she couldn't even say what the make or model was.

A sob rose in her throat. "No!"

The young man who she'd been taking pictures of with his dog suddenly appeared at her side, a worried frown knitting his eyebrows. "Are you all right, ma'am? I thought that jackass had killed you. Here, let met help you. You look like you're going to pass out."

"I'm okay," she said faintly, swaying. "I'm just feeling kind of nauseated."

"You are looking a little pale. What can I do? Do you need some water? Ice? My mother always wants a cold cloth on her head when she's not feeling well."

Feeling as if she was going to toss her cookies any second, Lily shook her head. "No…thank you, but I don't need anything. Except to lie down."

"Here?"

She nodded miserably. "Right here, right now, or I'm going to be sick."

With a soft groan, she sank to her knees, and he was instantly beside her, whipping off his cap so that she could lay her head on it. "I think I should call an ambulance," he said worriedly, studying her. "You're limping. And you've got a nasty scrape on your forehead. It looks like you took a pretty good hit."

Suddenly too weak to even open her eyes, Lily gingerly felt the wound on her forehead. "I don't remember much about what happened after I jumped behind the tree. I must have fallen."

Beside her, she heard a dog whine. Surprised, she stirred, forcing her eyes open just a crack. At the sign of the terrier she'd taken rolls of pictures of, she smiled faintly. "I hope you don't mind that I took pictures of you and your dog. You just looked like you were having so much fun."

"Hey, no problem," he assured her. "Jack's a ham—he loves performing for people. I was just about to show you our best trick when I heard the horns blaring. That's when I saw that jackass heading straight for you."

She swallowed thickly. ‘‘I thought he was going to kill me.’’

‘‘You aren’t the only one. It did look like he was deliberately trying to run you down. I’ll call the police for you, if you like. Somebody needs to turn the idiot in. He could have seriously hurt you.’’

She winced at the idea of all the questioning she would be put through for nothing. ‘‘But I didn’t even get a license-plate number. What can the police do?’’

In the distance, the whine of a siren signaled that someone had already called 911. Still flat on her back on the ground, Lily saw a police car pull up at the curb and closed her eyes with a groan. ‘‘I can’t believe this is happening.’’

‘‘Do we need an ambulance?’’ the officer began as he exited the cruiser, only to swear. ‘‘Son of a bitch! Lily? Is that you? Are you all right? What happened?’’

Lately, Lily had heard that same voice in her dreams too many times not to recognize it. Her eyes flew open in surprise, and she looked up to find Tony leaning over her, shock clearly visible in his eyes as he frowned down at her in concern. It wasn’t his unexpected appearance, however, that stunned her. It was the policeman’s uniform he was wearing.

Confused, she rubbed at the knot on her forehead. ‘‘I must have hit my head harder than I thought—my eyes aren’t working right. You’re not a cop.’’

His expression somber, he allowed himself a small smile. ‘‘Actually, I am. I just work at my uncle’s part-time. Are you all right? I got a call there was a hit-and-run.’’

‘‘He didn’t hit me,’’ she said huskily. ‘‘I jumped out of the way.’’

‘‘It was close,’’ the young man at her side said frankly.

Introducing himself, Patrick Barnes added, "I was playing with my dog across the park and saw the whole thing. If she'd waited another second to jump, she probably would have been dead. He was aiming right at her."

"I'm okay," Lily insisted. Still ashen, she struggled to sit up. "I just hit my head."

"Whoa, whoa," Tony said, squatting beside her to lay a gentle hand on her shoulder. "Just sit there a minute while I take your statement. You're still pretty pale."

"I'm fine."

"I just want to make sure you're okay," he assured her. He noticed another patrol car pulling up behind his vehicle and told Patrick, "That's my partner, Stan Kitchen. He's going to take your statement while I finish up with Miss Fitzgerald."

"No problem," he said, rising to his feet. "I just need to get my dog some water first. She's been running pretty hard."

"Thank you so much for your help," Lily said. "I don't know what would have happened if you hadn't been here."

"You would have done fine," he said with a smile, patting her hand. "I'm glad I could help. I hope you're okay."

Tony motioned for Stan to take the man's statement, then turned back to Lily. "Are you sure you're all right? I can call for an ambulance."

"No, please. I hate for you to go to all that fuss. I'm just a little shaken up."

Even as she spoke, Lily could feel herself start to shake in delayed reaction, and there didn't seem to be a damn thing she could do about it. Then tears welled in her eyes, horrifying her. "I'm sorry," she choked out, wiping at a stray tear that slipped over her lashes. "I'm not usually such a crybaby. I just—"

"Never had anyone almost kill you before," he said gently when she struggled to find words. "Trust me, it's understandable. The first time someone sent a bullet flying over my head, I went home and threw up. Wait here. I'll be right back."

Stepping over to his car, he retrieved a blanket from the trunk, then returned to where she still sat on the ground. Going down on one knee beside her, he quickly draped the blanket around her shoulders. "Is that better?" he asked, smiling into her eyes.

More tears welled. "No!" she said. "Don't be nice to me—it just makes me want to cry."

Pulling the blanket closer around her, he chuckled softly. "I like being nice to you. If you'd just go out with me, you'd see that."

"Don't start," she warned, but a smile tugged at the corner of her mouth. Thankful for the comfort of his teasing, she glanced over at the traffic that streamed around his patrol car and that of the other officer and felt her heart stop. "I hadn't realized how close I still was to the road," she said, sobering. "Would you mind if we moved over there?"

When she nodded to a bench under a tree thirty feet away, he understood perfectly. Without a word, he stood and offered her a hand. "Let me help you."

His fingers closed gently around hers, warming her all the way to her heart, and just that quickly, she found herself overcome with emotion. Even as she tried to blink the tears away, they spilled over her lashes.

"I'm sorry," she choked as he carefully helped her to her feet. "I guess I'm more shook up than I thought."

"You wouldn't be human if you weren't," he told her,

and with no more warning than that, pulled her gently into his arms.

How had he known she needed to be held? She hadn't known it herself. Comfort wasn't something she'd received much from the men in her life, and she'd never felt the loss until now. Giving in to the need, she buried her head against his chest. "I'm sorry," she sniffed. "This isn't going to get you in trouble, is it?"

"Of course not," he said roughly, tightening his arms around her. "You just had a nasty scare, and we're dating. Why shouldn't I hold you?"

"Because we're not dating, and you know it."

"That's just a technicality," he said with a chuckle. "And a matter of time."

"Tony—"

"Have I told you that I love it when you say my name like that…when you bristle up and try not to laugh? Go ahead, do it again."

She laughed, she couldn't help it, and pulled back to find him grinning down at her. "That's better," he told her as he helped her over to the bench. "You're doing great, by the way. If this had happened to my aunt Tootsie, you would have heard her all the way up on Capitol Hill. Of course," he added wryly, "we're Italian. When we're scared or hurt or mad, everybody's going to know it."

Her hand somehow finding its way into his, Lily smiled wistfully. "That sounds wonderful. You don't know what it's like to grow up in a house where there's no noise. My father was always so self-contained and proper. Sometimes when I was a kid, I just wanted to scream just to see what it felt like. Of course, I didn't. Father would have been horrified."

"Is your father still alive?" he said quietly. "I'm sure

he'd be raising his voice if he knew you'd almost been flattened by a hit-and-run driver.''

''He would be worried,'' she agreed, ''and upset with me for moving to Georgetown. He's not happy with the changes I've made in my life recently, so there's no point in calling him. He's not speaking to me.''

As a father, Tony couldn't imagine not speaking to his son just because he'd chosen to lead his own life. What kind of man was her dad? Didn't he realize what he was losing?

Frowning, he wanted to ask her a dozen questions, but this wasn't the time. ''He's the one who's losing out,'' he said quietly. ''Now...tell me what happened. You were standing by the tree?''

She nodded. ''I'd set up my camera and tripod there and was taking pictures across the park. I was focusing on that when I heard cars start honking their horns down the street. That's when I turned and saw a pizza-delivery car racing in and out of traffic.''

Glancing up from the quick notes he was jotting down, he frowned. ''Did you happen to see what company the driver worked for? Or the license-plate number? Or the driver? Was it a man? Were you able to get any kind of description of him?''

She named a national chain, then said, ''I'm sorry—I didn't even think to get the license-plate number until it was too late.''

''What kind of car was it?''

''Maybe a Volkswagen...I think. I'm not sure, but it wasn't in very good shape. It had faded red paint and looked older, but I'm not good at models.''

''You're doing great,'' he assured her, jotting down notes. ''What about the driver?''

Grimacing, she shook her head. ''It seems like I caught

a flash of red hair, but I was so horrified when he turned the car right at me that I couldn't take my eyes off it long enough to get a good look at him. I'm sorry."

"Don't be," he said. "You were scared." His words suddenly registering, he looked up at her sharply. "What do you mean...*he turned the car right at you?* Are you saying he was deliberately trying to run you down?"

She nodded grimly. "That's the way it seemed to me. He obviously had control of the car when he was weaving in and out of traffic. Then, all of a sudden, he was aiming right for me, and he didn't turn away until I jumped out of the way and he found himself heading right for the tree. If that's not deliberate, I don't know what is."

Tony had to agree with her. Frowning, he studied her through narrowed eyes. "Do you have any enemies? An ex-husband? A boyfriend you ditched who wants to get back at you?"

"I did break up with my fiancé," she admitted, "but I can't see Neil doing something like this. He's just not the type."

"I'll need to talk to him," he told her. "Whose idea was it to break up? Was there a fight? How long ago was this?"

"Earlier in the summer," she replied. "And no, there wasn't a fight. Actually, I think he was relieved."

Surprised, he lifted a skeptical eyebrow. "Your fiancé was relieved you broke your engagement?"

"Like I said, I changed a lot this summer," she replied. "My father wasn't the only one who had a difficult time dealing with that. Neil couldn't accept the fact that I wanted to be a photographer. He wanted me to be the accountant he fell in love with. I was never going to be that again, so I broke things off."

Personally, Tony thought the man was a fool for not

accepting her for who she was. Did he have a clue what kind of woman he let slip through his fingers? "I still need his name and address," he told her.

She gave it to him, then said, "While you're checking Neil out, you might as well check out my former boss. Not that she would ever do anything like this," she quickly amended, "but she's the only other person besides Neil and my father who's irritated with me. She thinks I'm crazy to walk away from a government job to be a photographer."

"Obviously, she hasn't seen your photographs," he retorted with a quick grin. "And thinking you're crazy and wanting to kill you are two different things. How are you feeling?"

He switched the subject so quickly that he caught her in the act of rubbing the knot on her forehead. Grimacing, she smiled ruefully. "Okay, it hurts," she admitted. "And so does my knee. I have no one to blame but myself. When I saw what was happening, I should have immediately jumped behind the tree, but like an idiot, all I could think of was getting some pictures—" Suddenly realizing what she'd said, she gasped. "Oh, my God! My camera! I completely forgot."

Forgetting her injured knee, she whirled, only to cry out as pain shot up and down her leg. "Aaagh!"

Lightning quick, Tony scooped her up as she started to fall and quickly set her on the nearby bench. "Sit," he growled. "I'll get your camera."

If she'd given him one word of argument, Tony told himself he was going to dump her in his patrol car and take her to the hospital himself. Something in his expression must have warned her not to push him—she didn't move. Relieved, he turned to look for her camera and found it not far from the curb. He took one look at it and swore. It was in pieces the manufacturer never intended it to be.

He didn't want to show it to her, not after all that she'd been through, but he didn't have any choice. Striding back to her, he sat down on the seat next to her and held it out. "I'm sorry, Lily."

She didn't, as he'd feared, take one look at the ruins of her camera and burst into tears. The tears were there, but she blinked them back and sniffed, "I was afraid of that. And the film's ruined, too. Damn. I was hoping I at least got a picture of the driver."

Amazed, Tony had to laugh. "You're something else. You know that?"

"Why do you say that?"

"Isn't it obvious? You broke off your engagement with your fiancé, left a government job, and irritated your family and friends by changing careers. But what do you say when some idiot nearly kills you? *Damn, I was hoping I at least got a picture!*"

"Cameras can be insured...and replaced," she pointed out. "You only get one chance to take a Pulitzer Prize–winning photo."

"And that's what you're aiming for?"

She shrugged, smiling. "Maybe."

Not surprised that she'd set herself such a goal, Tony had a feeling that if anyone could pull off a Pulitzer, Lily could. The lady had guts, and he liked that. He liked *her,* dammit, more than he should. But he didn't have time to worry about that right now, not when whoever had nearly killed her was still on the streets.

"I need to call this in," he told her. "Just sit there and take it easy, then you've got to see a doctor."

"Oh, no, I'm sure I'm fine."

Tony had no intention of arguing with her. Stepping

over to his partner, who had finished questioning the dog owner, he checked with him to compare notes and wasn't surprised that the other witness hadn't gotten the license-plate number of the pizza-delivery car, either. Like Lily, he'd been too caught up in watching the destruction caused by the out-of-control car to notice the driver or license-plate number.

"I'll start canvassing the crowd," Stan said, eyeing the people who stood around the sidewalk, watching them work. "With so many witnesses around, hopefully someone saw something."

The odds on that were slim since no one else had come forward, but it was the only hope they had. Leaving Stan to the crowd, Tony stepped over to his car to call in a report. When he returned to Lily, his expression was grim. "The car was reported stolen fifteen minutes ago. It'll probably show up eventually, but we'll be lucky if we ever find the driver. He'll ditch the car in a remote area and just walk away from it."

"But there must be a way to catch him. He can't just get away with it. I really think he was trying to kill me."

"I know, and he may have been," he said regretfully. "But hit-and-runs are almost impossible to solve when it's just a random act of violence. And that's obviously what this was—you, yourself, said you can't think of anyone who would want you dead. So some crackhead stole a car and went for a joyride. When he comes down from his high, he'll wipe down the car so there won't be any fingerprints, then walk away when no one's looking. And the only thing we know for sure about him is that he has red hair. Of course, he could dye that as soon as he gets home—or his hair could already be dyed."

Her shoulders slumping in defeat, Lily felt like crying.

"So what are you saying? That I should just forget this ever happened?"

"No, of course not. But don't tie yourself in knots worrying about catching the jerk. A lot of things have to come together for that to happen, and you don't have control over any of them. All you can do is take care of yourself and get on with your life. Now that we have that settled, you need to see a doctor."

"No, I don't."

"Oh, really? Then maybe you should take another look at your knee. I bet it's swelling. And that knot on your head isn't too pretty, either. You could have a concussion, and that's nothing to fool around with. When I was a kid, one of the neighbors fell and cracked his head when he tripped over his cat. He died, Lily. You're going to the doctor."

"That's not necessary," she argued. "I'm fine. Really."

Hesitating, he studied her pale face with eyes that missed little. "I'd feel better if a doctor checked you out. But I'll make you a deal. You can let me call an ambulance for you or I'll drive you to the hospital myself. It's your call. Take your choice."

"That's not a deal. Anyway, you're working."

"Actually, my shift ended ten minutes ago," he said with a grin. "All I have to do is file my report, and I'm free."

After the day she'd had, the last thing she wanted to do was spend two or three hours in a hospital emergency room, but he was right. Even though there didn't appear to be anything seriously wrong with her, she had a pretty good bump on her forehead. She probably did need to have a doctor check it out. Giving in, she sighed, "Okay,

I'll go. But no ambulance! If you really don't mind taking me, I'd appreciate the ride."

"No problem," he said easily. "I'll be ready in just a moment."

The emergency room was packed due to a ten-car pileup on I-95, and the place was a zoo. Mothers held crying children, a woman, worried about her seriously injured husband, sobbed in the corner, and nearly every chair in the waiting room was occupied by someone with a bloody head or a hurt neck or an arm that didn't quite hang right.

Surveying the scene as she and Tony stepped through the hospital's electronic doors, Lily decided she wasn't that badly hurt, after all. "You know, I don't need to do this today. I'll just wait and go to my doctor on Monday."

"Oh, no, you don't," Tony said, quickly sidestepping to block her path when she would have walked out. "We have a deal. You agreed to see a doctor today. We're here. You might as well stay."

"But this could take hours!"

"So? At least I'll be able to sleep tonight knowing you're not lying in your apartment with a concussion. C'mon, be a good girl and do the right thing."

That was the wrong thing to say to a woman who had been fighting her entire life for her independence. Narrowing her eyes at him, she said silkily, "I think jumping out of the way of that car must have affected my hearing. What did you say?"

Undaunted, he grinned, his green eyes dancing wickedly. "Oh, did I mumble? I'm sorry. Angelo's always getting on to me for not speaking up. I said I've always admired women with spunk and courage, and you've got both. How's that?"

Her lips twitching, she nodded in approval. "Better. Is it true?"

"What? That I've always admired women with spunk and courage or that you've got both? Okay," he laughed when she gave him that look he was coming to recognize from her. "I'm just pulling your chain. Of course it's true," he said. "It took a hell of a lot of courage for you to try to take pictures of a maniac determined to flatten you with his car. Not that it was your smartest moment," he added. "He could have killed you."

Honesty forced her to agree. "I wasn't thinking. If I'd seen someone else do the same thing, I would have been horrified." Glancing around at the nearly full waiting room, she grimaced. "We're going to be here most of day. You know that, don't you?"

Smiling, he said, "I've got nothing but time. Now that we've got that cleared up, I'll see if I can find us a seat while you check in with triage."

Resigned, she headed for triage, where she presented her ID and insurance paperwork. As the nurse took down the information about her injuries, Lily had to admit that Tony was right to insist that she stay until she saw a doctor. Her head was throbbing, and over the course of the last half hour, her knee had stiffened up considerably.

"Okay," the nurse said, finishing the report. "Find a seat, and the doctor will be with you shortly."

When she found Tony and eased into the chair beside him, she repeated what the nurse had said, then warned, "You know what shortly means, don't you? Hours! You don't have to stay. I'll be fine. I'll take a cab home."

She might as well have saved her breath. Stretching his legs out, he crossed his feet at the ankle and said,

"Did I ever tell you about the time my cousin and I were at my grandmother's house in Virginia and I fell out of the hayloft into the pigsty?"

Horrified, Lily couldn't help but laugh. "You're making this up, aren't you? To make me laugh, right?"

Mischief dancing in his eyes, he neither confirmed nor denied it. "Maybe. Maybe not."

She should have laughed and tossed back a teasing remark, but suddenly, she felt like crying. Her smile slipped, and abruptly, her eyes were once again swimming in tears.

"Hey, what's this?" he said in concern, leaning close to catch the tears that spilled over her lashes. "Is your head worse? Do I need to get a nurse?"

"No, no," she choked out, catching his hand when he would have risen to his feet, then pulling him back down beside her. "I'm fine. Really," she said when he lifted his free hand to trace the tear that trailed down her cheek. "You're just being so wonderful to me, and all I want to do is cry."

"So cry," he said with a small smile. "I can handle it."

Lily didn't doubt that he could. He seemed to be able to handle just about anything that was thrown at him, and that amazed her. She'd never known a man like him. Both her father and Neil had little patience with tears, so she'd learned long ago to control her emotions. But Tony not only didn't have a problem with tears, he encouraged her to give in to them if she needed to.

And that only made her want to cry again. He was so accepting of who she was. And he didn't seem to have a clue of how special that made him. Her own father couldn't accept who she was. Where had Tony been all her life?

Emotions filling her heart, she wanted to turn to him, to tell him everything she was feeling, but it was all too new. Then a nurse stepped into the waiting room and called her name. "Lily Fitzgerald?"

Caught up in the emotions hitting her from all angles, Lily hardly heard her. Then Tony squeezed her hand and gently pulled her to her feet. "Time to see the doctor. Are you all right? I'll be happy to go with you if you like."

"What? Oh! I'm sorry—I guess I was drifting. I'm fine," she assured him. "I shouldn't be long."

An hour and a half later, the emergency-room doctor released her to go home. Exhausted, she walked stiffly into the waiting room and greeted Tony with a tired smile. "Well, I don't have a concussion," she said wryly. "That's the good news. But I do have a twisted knee and a sprained wrist. The doctor said tomorrow I'm going to feel like I got hit by a Mack truck. I already do."

"It could have been worse," he said sympathetically as he stood. "If you'd really been hit by a truck, you wouldn't be standing here discussing it. C'mon. Let's go home."

Lily had never heard sweeter-sounding words. "You won't hear me complaining. The doctor gave me a shot for the pain. If I don't get horizontal soon, I'm going to end up flat on my face."

"Oh, no, you don't." Not waiting to hear more, Tony ushered her outside. "The car's right here."

His patrol car, was, in fact, parked in a tow-away zone just steps away from where the ambulances pulled up before the emergency-room doors. When Lily just arched an eyebrow at him, he had the grace to blush. "Okay, so it's one of the perks of the trade. I should have moved it while you were in with the doctor, but I was afraid you'd come out while I was gone and think I'd left.

"Okay," he said when she continued to just look at him with amusement. "I didn't want you to have to walk any farther than you had to. Happy? I was just thinking about you."

Her smile weary, she would have hugged him if she'd had the strength. "That was very thoughtful of you. Did I thank you for all your help? I don't know what I would have done if you hadn't showed up this afternoon."

"You don't have to thank me," he said gruffly. "I was happy to help. Here, let me help you into the car."

She looked so fragile that Tony would have liked nothing more than to scoop her up and settle her in the front seat as if she were a china doll. As tired as she was, however, he wasn't sure she'd allow that. So he opened the door for her instead and carefully helped her ease down into the passenger seat. Seconds later, they were headed for Georgetown.

"Are you sure you're going to be okay?" Tony asked with a frown as he walked her to her door. "I don't like the thought of you being alone. I can stay until you fall asleep…just in case you need something."

Lily felt her heart catch at the thought of him being somewhere nearby when she fell asleep. Don't go there, she warned herself, but it was too late for that. Something had changed between them today, something she couldn't even put a name to, and she didn't want her time with him to end. Not yet.

She tried to tell herself her defenses were down because of everything she'd been through and the pain pills the emergency-room doctor had given her, but she knew it was more than that. It was Tony himself. For weeks now he'd flirted with her and teased her, and she'd never seen the real Tony Giovanni...until today. He was sweet and protective and caring and nothing like Neil or her father. How was she supposed to deal with such a man? All she wanted to do was step into his arms.

Why, she wondered with a silent groan, had the fates put him in her path now? The timing couldn't have been worse. She had classes to complete, a new career to establish. All of her energy needed to be focused on that—not a man. Especially a man like Tony. How was she supposed to resist him when he was so wonderful? "If you need anything, just call me," he said, handing her a card with his home-phone and cell numbers on it. "I'll be home the rest of the night. Okay?"

"Okay," she said softly. "I don't know how to thank you—"

"No thanks are necessary," he cut in, stopping her. Taking her keys from her, he opened her door for her, then handed the keys back to her. "Go to bed, Lily." And with that, he kissed her on the cheek and gently pushed her inside her apartment. A second later, he quietly wished her good-night and shut the door.

Later, Lily couldn't have said how long she stood there, staring at the closed door as if she'd never seen it before. This was the second time he'd kissed her on the cheek. And this time, just as the last, she couldn't help wondering what it would have been like if he'd kissed her square on the lips as she wanted him to.

The next day she wasn't fit to kill, just as the emergency-room doctor had warned. The knot on her forehead was a throbbing purple egg, her knee was so stiff that she cringed just at the thought of moving it, and every muscle in her body ached. It was nearly ten o'clock in the morning when she woke up, and even then she couldn't bring herself to get out of bed when she was feeling so awful. Switching on the television in her bedroom, she lay in bed the rest of the morning and just vegged.

By two o'clock in the afternoon, the walls of her apartment were closing in on her with a vengeance. She had to get out. Changing into a blue-jeaned skirt and her favorite red T-shirt, she slipped into flats and grabbed the keys to her apartment.

The second she stepped into the stairwell, the mouthwatering scents of Angelo's cooking drifted up the stairs to her and she realized that she was starving. Carefully making her way downstairs, she favored her knee with every step she took.

"What are you doing downstairs?" Angelo said by way of a greeting when she slowly walked into the restaurant. "Tony said the doctor said you were supposed to rest all day."

"I know," she said with a grimace. "But I was going crazy just lying in bed. And I haven't eaten all day. Spaghetti and meatballs sound good."

"You could have called. I would have brought a plate up to you."

Not surprised, she smiled. "Now I know why Tony's the way he is. It must be a genetic thing."

"You're hurt," he said simply. "Of course he would come to your aid. That's why he's such a good cop. He really cares about people. But enough about Tony. You need to rest your knee." Pulling out a chair at a nearby table, he motioned for her to sit, then frowned. "I'm sorry. I should have asked if you'd rather sit somewhere else. The patio's available—"

"No," she said quickly, horrified at the idea. "I don't think I'm ready to go near the street yet."

Pulling a chair out for her at the table by the window, he squeezed her shoulder, understanding perfectly. "The memory will fade with time. You just rest. I'll get your food."

When he disappeared into the kitchen, Lily glanced around the restaurant and wasn't surprised to find it nearly empty. It was well past the lunch hour, and the dinner crowd wouldn't pick up until around five. Content to have the place to herself, she propped her injured leg up on the chair across the table from her and sighed in contentment. Maybe she'd just stay here for the rest of the afternoon. She couldn't say why, maybe it was the wonderful scents spilling from the kitchen, but the restaurant felt much more like home than her apartment did.

Maybe she needed to get a cat so she wouldn't be so alone, she thought with a frown.

"Here you go," Angelo said cheerfully, suddenly appearing at her elbow with a tray that was laden with fresh bread sticks, salad and a steaming plate of spaghetti and meatballs. "Dinner's on me," he added as he set the food in front of her. "And that includes dessert."

"Oh, Angelo, no! This is too much. I can't possibly eat all this—"

"Of course not," he agreed, winking at her. "But you can take the leftovers upstairs with you and heat them up in the microwave later. You shouldn't have to cook when you're not feeling well."

"That's very sweet of you," she said. "I don't know what I'd do without you and Tony. You've both been wonderful."

Color warming his cheeks, he grinned. "We look out

for people we like. So…what about your camera? Tony said it was destroyed.''

''Flattened,'' she said with a grimace. ''It could have been worse, though. I could have been the one who was flattened.''

Angelo nodded grimly. ''True. Your angels were watching out for you. A camera can be replaced. You can't.''

''I don't think I'll be taking pictures in the park for a while. Just the thought of going back there…'' Images flashed before her mind's eye, and with a shudder she quickly pushed them away and forced a smile. ''I've been thinking that I might set up a darkroom in the laundry room of the apartment and spend more of my time working there for a while. There are some things I'd like to try.''

''What do you need?'' Angelo said promptly. ''A sink? Tables? I know nothing about photography but I'll help you if I can.''

Touched, she cocked her head at him and studied him with amusement. ''If you do this for me, you have to let me do something for you in return. I'd love to take some pictures for the restaurant, maybe do a photographic montage of you and your steady customers. What do you say? We could use that wall over there.''

When she nodded toward the wall opposite the kitchen, Angelo grinned in delight. ''Are you serious?''

''Of course. It'll be fun. So…do we have a deal?''

''Are you kidding?'' he said, holding out his hand. ''When can you start?''

''Just as soon as I can buy a new camera. How about tomorrow?''

''Sounds good to me,'' he said.

Lily placed her hand in his and shook. They had a deal.

Chapter 6

The front door to the restaurant opened then, and Angelo turned to greet the young boy who came charging in like a lightning bolt. "Hey, there's my boy!" he said with a smile. "How was school? How'd you do on your English test?"

A broad grin flashed across his face. "I aced it! My teacher couldn't believe it!"

"All right! I knew you could do it!" Pleased, Angelo held up his hand and gave him a high five. "How about your own personal pizza to celebrate? But first come and meet Ms. Fitzgerald. She's my new renter."

Turning to Lily, Angelo smiled proudly. "Lily, this is my great-nephew, Quentin. And he really is a great nephew."

Quentin stepped forward and offered his hand. "It's nice to meet you, Ms. Fitzgerald. My dad told me about you. He said you're a photographer."

Surprised, Lily took his hand. Tony had a son? He'd

never mentioned it. Why? "I didn't know Tony had any children," she told Quentin with a smile. "But I would have known you anywhere. You're the spitting image of your dad." When he wrinkled his nose, she liked him immediately. "I bet a lot of people tell you that."

"All the time," he confessed. "Especially Aunt Tootsie. Dad's her favorite. She sneaks me candy when no one's looking."

"You're lucky," she replied. "My dad wasn't anybody's favorite. Of course, he didn't have much family, so there wasn't anyone to spoil me."

"Bummer. What about your grandparents? Did they spoil you? Or wouldn't your dad let them?"

"They all died before I was born. But don't feel too sorry for me. My father really believed in education, so during the summers, I went to special camps all over the country. I even went to space camp at NASA one summer."

"Wow! Did you get to meet any astronauts?"

"Actually, I did. It was great."

"I'm going to ask Dad if I can go to space camp," he told his uncle eagerly. "Do you think he'll let me?"

Angelo smiled. "That's something you'll have to discuss with him, hot rod. Maybe you should bring your math grade up before you ask him, though."

"I'm trying, but I don't understand what we're doing right now. Mrs. Green said I need a tutor, but Dad said he'd try to help me. Is he home yet?"

"Not yet. He had to testify at a trial, and you know how that goes. It always takes longer than anyone expects."

Quentin's face fell. "Do you think he'll be back before it's time for me to go home? Mom'll help me if I ask her, but she really stinks at math. Whenever she can't figure out a problem, she asks Larry to help her." He wrinkled his nose in distaste. "He makes me feel stupid. I don't want him to help me."

Taking in the bits and pieces of information Quentin casually dropped, it was clear to Lily that Tony and his wife were divorced and that the boy didn't care for Larry, who was probably the new man in his mother's life. Lily sympathized with him. She couldn't imagine what she would have done if her father had married someone she couldn't stand after her mother died.

"I've got a degree in accounting," she impulsively told Quentin. "I can help you with your homework if you like...if your dad and uncle don't mind."

"You won't get any argument out of me," Angelo said with a quick grin. "You need a recipe for scallopini, I'm your man. But math—especially that stuff they're doing in school today—is a complete mystery to me. Sometimes I can get the right answer, but I haven't got a clue how I came up with it."

Lily understood that perfectly. Her father used to say the same thing when she was in school. "He has to prove how he got the answer, doesn't he?"

Angelo nodded. "That's the whole problem. If I can't prove it, how can he?"

"What about Tony? Maybe he'd rather help Quentin himself. I don't want to interfere—"

"Are you kidding? Most of the time he has trouble balancing his checkbook. Geometry and algebra are like a foreign language to him. Trust me," he assured her, "if you can help Quentin, he'll be thrilled."

Lily would have preferred to have the okay from Tony himself, but since he wasn't available, Angelo's reassurances were the next best thing. Glancing over at Quentin, she smiled. "Well, it looks like the two of us are going to be working together. If you like."

"Yeah! I mean, yes, ma'am," he quickly corrected himself, giving her an engaging grin that set his blue eyes twinkling. "I can use all the help I can get."

"Then pull up a chair and let's get started," she said.

She didn't have to tell him twice. Angelo quickly cleared the table for them, and within seconds Quentin had pulled his chair close to hers and spread his homework out in front of her. Amused, Lily couldn't help but like him. He was a cute kid and not a bit shy.

"Okay," she said, "what seems to be the problem?"

With a grimace of dislike, he pointed to the very first problem his teacher had assigned for homework. "The answers to the even problems are in the back of the book, but that doesn't help much. In order to solve the problem, I have to get *x* on one side of the equal sign and everything else on the other. I get that. But how do you get rid of the fraction in front of *x*?"

"Aha. I see what you mean. If I remember correctly, I had a problem with this, too, when I was your age. Let me show you how it's done."

On a piece of scratch paper, she quickly wrote out the problem, then inverted the fractions. "See...once you invert it, and multiply it times the original fraction, they cancel each other out. But whatever you do to one side of the equation—"

"You have to do to the other," he finished for her. "Mrs. Green says that to us all the time."

Biting back a smile, Lily said, "That's because she wants you to remember it. Math is all about rules. Remember the rules, and you should be able to solve whatever problem is thrown at you. Let's try another one."

When he quickly wrote down the next problem, then

hesitated, Lily didn't rush him. She watched a frown tug his eyebrows together, then he started talking to himself. Waiting patiently, she didn't interfere, giving him time to work it out himself. Then, just when she thought he wasn't going to be able to solve the problem without her help, he mumbled, "Oh, yeah. Dummy. How could you forget that?"

Lily watched his expression change from frustration to comprehension to exhilaration. "I got it!" he told her, shocked. "I can't believe it! This is easy!"

"It's all a matter of just knowing the rules and applying them," she said encouragingly. "See? The next problem is very similar to the one you just did. Just work it the same way."

"Okay!" Thrilled, he started to work the next problem, only to look up in alarm when she shifted in her seat. "You're not going back to your apartment yet, are you? Just in case I need more help?"

"Are you kidding? Of course I'm not going anywhere. I want to see your face when you finish. Trust me, you'll have this done in nothing flat."

Fifteen minutes later, he finished the last problem. "Yeah!" he crowed, punching the air above his head with a fist. "I never did my homework this fast before. Sometimes it seems like it takes hours and hours, and I still don't know what I'm doing. Thanks, Ms. Fitzgerald."

"Lily," she replied, smiling. "You can call me Lily. I'm glad I could help. It was fun."

"Can you teach my dad to do this so he can help me next time? This was so cool."

He was so excited, Lily had to laugh. "You're so funny. Of course I can teach your dad, if you like. But I think it would be easier if you just dropped by my place whenever you have a problem Tony can't help you with."

"You wouldn't mind?"

"No, of course not. I should warn you, though, that I might not always be home," she added. "I'm a photographer, so I'm out a lot in the afternoons, taking pictures."

"You make money taking pictures?"

Amused by his wide-eyed expression, she laughed. "Sometimes. I'm still getting started, but it's starting to pick up. I have a couple of pictures in a gallery, and as soon as I get a new camera, I'm going to start doing some work for Angelo." She nodded toward the wall across from their table. "That entire wall is going to be filled with pictures of customers. Before too much longer, you'll be up there yourself."

"Really? And my dad, too? Cool!"

She had to agree. "It is going to be pretty cool. I'm looking forward to it. I've never done anything like this before."

"Maybe I'll ask for a camera for Christmas," he said eagerly, suddenly taken with the idea. "I wanted a PlayStation, but a camera would be better. Then I could do the same thing on my bedroom wall that you're doing here. Wow, that'd be great! Could you teach me how? Then it wouldn't matter where I had to live, I would still feel like I was at home."

Puzzled by that statement, Lily almost asked him what he meant, but his mood had changed, and there was a pain in his eyes that she recognized from her own childhood. "Of course I could teach you how," she said quietly. "I'm going to set up a darkroom in my laundry room, so if you use black-and-white film, I can also show you how to develop it. Now, *that's* fun."

"Really? You mean it? You're not just saying that? That'd be *so* cool! My friends at school aren't going to believe it. I've got to go call them."

He started to run to the kitchen, only to remember his manners. Before Lily could even suspect his intentions, he threw himself into her arms for a giant hug. "Thank you, Lily!"

"You're welcome," she said huskily, hugging him back.

"This is going to be so much fun. I've got to go tell Uncle Angelo and call my friends. Maybe he can convince my dad to buy me a camera."

He was off like a shot, hopping and skipping and jumping as he disappeared through the swinging door into the restaurant kitchen. Grinning, Lily followed at a slower pace, gingerly favoring her knee. "Thanks for the meal, Angelo," she told him, holding up the leftovers he'd put in a container for her. "It was delicious, as usual."

"It was my pleasure," he told her. "If you need anything, just call."

Carefully making her way back upstairs, Lily let herself into her apartment and was immediately enveloped in silence. Normally, that wouldn't have bothered her—she'd lived alone for years—but as the afternoon shadows grew long and evening approached, the loneliness of her existence weighed on her in a way it hadn't in years. Did Tony know how lucky he was? she wondered. Granted, his son didn't live with him, but he was in his life. After meeting Quentin and helping him with his homework, Lily knew that he had to bring Tony a great deal of joy. He was a fantastic kid.

And then there was Angelo. He not only worked with Tony and lived right across the hall from him, he was like a father to him. They might be uncle and nephew, but they shared an incredibly close relationship.

You have a father, too, a voice in her head pointed out. *Call him. Maybe he's feeling lonely, too, and will talk to you this time.*

She was tempted, but she hesitated. She loved her father, and there wasn't a doubt in her mind that he loved her. His pride wouldn't let him call her, but that didn't mean she couldn't make the first move and be the one to call. If she acted as if no harsh words had been spoken between them, she knew he would, too.

Until the subject of her career came up again.

She told herself he couldn't help it. He was one of those men who naturally took charge of situations and people without even thinking about it. She knew that and accepted who her father was. That didn't mean, however, that she could continue to accept his interference in *her* life. For no other reason than that, she couldn't call him. It was a matter of principle. When he was ready to accept her and her choices in life, *he* would call her.

She didn't fool herself into thinking it would be any time soon.

The dinner crowd was already starting to fill the restaurant dining room when Tony strode into the kitchen, pulling at his tie and looking more than a little irritated. "I'm sorry I'm late," he told his son, who was sitting on a tall stool at the end of the work island, eating a slice of pizza. "The trial ran long, and I didn't get to testify until nearly five. Then, of course, I got caught in traffic. Has your mom called? I'll help you with your homework as soon as you finish eating."

Unperturbed, Quentin took another bite of his pizza. "It's okay, Dad. I already finished my homework and talked to Mom. She said she didn't have a problem with me staying late as long as I was home by nine."

"Good. Then I'm going to run upstairs and change—" Suddenly realizing what Quentin had said, he stopped halfway to the door, frowning. "What you mean...you already finished your homework? What about your math?"

"Done," he said with a flash of dimples. "And I got every single problem right. Mrs. Green's going to be shocked."

"Mrs. Green's not the only one," Tony retorted. Studying him through narrowed eyes, he couldn't miss the fact that Quentin was feeling damn good about something. In fact, he couldn't remember the last time he'd seen him look so happy.

"Okay, what's up?" he asked suspiciously. "I know Uncle Angelo didn't help you with your homework—"

"Hey!" Angelo said indignantly from the grill. "I could if I had to."

"And I could be Columbo," Tony told him with a grin, "but I'm not and you didn't. So what's going on, son? Just the other day, you told me you needed a tutor and now you're doing your homework on your own and being pretty darn cocky about it? I'm sorry, but things don't usually turn around that quickly. Spill your guts. Who helped you with your homework?"

Quentin exchanged a grin with Angelo, then said, "She's the coolest lady, Dad! And she lives right here in the building. You know her...Ms. Lily Fitzgerald."

For a moment, the name didn't register. When it did, Tony blinked. "Do you mean *Lily?* Lily, the new tenant in 202, upstairs? *She* helped you with your math?"

His blue eyes twinkling, Quentin grinned. "Yep."

"I see," Tony said, his lips twitching. "And just how

did this meeting with Lily come about? I didn't even know you knew her."

"I didn't until this afternoon," he replied. "But she was having lunch in the dining room when I came home from school and Uncle Angelo introduced me to her."

"And then you asked her to help you with your math?"

"No! C'mon, Dad, I know better than that."

Grinning at his son's indignant tone, Tony reached over and ruffled his hair. "I'm just kidding. I know you wouldn't just come out and ask a total stranger for help unless you were desperate."

"I was desperate," he confessed. "But she offered to help me when I told Uncle Angelo that I hoped you got home in time to help me with my homework because Mom really stinks at math and I didn't want to ask Larry. That's when she said she had a degree in accounting and would be happy to help me. She's cool, Dad! Did you know she's a photographer? She's going to take some pictures of us and the customers for Uncle Angelo. And she said anytime I needed help with my math, I could knock on her door…as long as it was okay with you."

"Well," he said, surprised, "it sounds like a lot happened this afternoon."

"So, can I ask her for help when I need it? Please, Dad? She's better than Mrs. Green. And when she showed me what I was doing wrong, I finished my homework in fifteen minutes flat. It was awesome."

Amazed, Tony couldn't remember the last time he'd seen his son so excited about homework. In fact, he'd shown little enthusiasm for anything since his mother had told him she was moving to Florida and taking him with her. What in the world had Lily said to him that had fired him up so much?

"I'll talk to her," he promised. "I'm sure she was serious when she made the offer, but I just need to make sure we don't take advantage of her. You did thank her for her help, didn't you?"

"Dad! I have manners."

"I beg your pardon. I lost my head," Tony said, biting back a smile. "Of course you have manners. That's because your parents made sure you knew how to behave. Good manners—"

"Will take you a long way in this world," Quentin said with him, grinning cheekily. "I know, Dad."

"Monster child," Tony said affectionately. "Just wait until you have kids. I'm going to remind you of this conversation one day and laugh my head off." Smiling at the thought, he grabbed Quentin before he suspected his intentions and threw him over his shoulder. "Now that we've got that settled, it's time to go upstairs, monster. Where's your backpack?"

"By the door," he laughed, hanging upside down over Tony's back. "Wait, Dad!" he cried, still laughing as Tony strode across the kitchen. "I have to tell Uncle Angelo good-night."

"Oh. You're right. I forgot *my* manners." Striding over to his uncle, Tony turned around, presenting his back…and his son. "Say good-night, Quentin."

"Good night, Quentin." Quentin giggled, grinning upside down at his uncle.

Laughing, Angelo said, "I'll see you tomorrow. Sleep tight, monster."

His grin the replica of his son's, Tony said, "I'll be back in a few minutes," and headed out the rear door of the kitchen with a giggling Quentin still hanging over his shoulder.

* * *

By the time Tony finished his own dinner and loaded Quentin and his backpack into his car to take him home, it was nearly nine o'clock. Beside him in the front seat, Quentin stared out at the darkened night and chatted absently about school. Tony couldn't help but notice, however, that as they drew closer and closer to Janice's house, his son grew quieter and quieter.

When Quentin leaned his head back against the headrest and closed his eyes, Tony thought he'd fallen asleep. Then he said, "Dad? Can I ask you something?"

Whenever Quentin spoke in that quiet, pensive tone, Tony's protective instincts jumped into overdrive. Bracing for God knew what, he said easily, "Of course. I've always told you that you can ask me anything you like. Is something wrong?"

"No…not wrong, exactly," he said, grimacing. "I was just wondering… I know Mom has custody and everything…"

When he hesitated, Tony knew where the conversation was headed and wanted to kick Janice for putting their son in such an untenable situation. If she would just do what he did and put Quentin and his needs first, all three of them would be a hell of a lot happier. But she wasn't about to change—nothing mattered but what *she* wanted. The sooner he and Quentin accepted that, the less unhappy they would be.

"Yes, she does have custody," he replied. "We talked about this. Because you were so young when we divorced, the judge felt it would be better if you lived with her."

"But she's going to make me move to Florida with Larry. Do I have to?"

Tony had never wanted to say no so badly in his life. But he'd never made his son a promise he wasn't sure he could keep, and he wasn't about to start now. He hated the idea of him moving to Florida, of him being there all alone except for a mother whose main priority was her career and a stepfather who made no secret of the fact that he didn't like him. He wanted to grab his son and hug him and tell him there was no way in hell he was letting Janice or anyone else take him away, but he couldn't. Because ultimately, it would be left to a judge to decide where Quentin would live.

Sickened by the thought that some stranger would have that kind of power over his son, he said huskily, "I can't promise that you won't have to go, but I want you to know that I'm doing everything I can to see that you're happy. Okay? So try not to worry."

He was asking the impossible—how could Quentin *not* worry about moving to another state with a stepfather like Larry? The man didn't understand kids and made no effort to. As far as Tony was concerned, he was a self-centered, pompous bore who didn't love anyone but himself. He would never understand what Janice saw in him...or how she could leave a son that she claimed to love in the care of such a jackass.

One day soon, he was going to ask her that, he promised himself as he arrived at her house to find the outside lights on and Janice waiting by the front window. The second he pulled into the driveway, she stepped outside and watched with a carefully blank expression as Tony walked Quentin up the front walk.

There'd been a time when Tony had thought she was the most beautiful woman in the world, but that was before she betrayed him with another man, before she became so ambitious that all she cared about was money and success and how she could have more of both. If he hadn't had a child with her, they would have had nothing in common, and that twisted in Tony's gut like a knife. How had it come to this?

"Sorry we're late," he said by way of a greeting. "It's been one of those days."

"Don't worry about it," she replied. "Actually, I got home late, myself, so this works out for both of us. Have you got a minute? I need to talk to you."

Tony stiffened. The last time she'd told him she needed to talk to him, she'd informed him that she was taking their son with her to Florida and there wasn't a damn thing he could do about it. All his senses on alert, he said, "All right." Turning to Quentin, he gave him a quick hug. "Go in and go to bed, son. And remember what I said, okay?"

Worry knitting his forehead, Quentin looked back and forth between his parents, then nodded stiffly. "Okay, Dad. Good night." Giving him a fierce hug, he turned to give his mother one just as fierce, then darted into the house.

With his leaving, silence fell between them like a rock. His arms crossed over his chest, Tony arched an eyebrow at her. "Well?"

"I was wondering if you could take care of Quentin after school for the next few weeks. I've got a lot of work I need to finish up at the office before I make the move to Florida, and Larry is flying to Miami tomorrow morning to find us a place to live. Tina can take care of him after school, but she leaves at five. I won't come in until at least eight, and he shouldn't be here alone."

"Of course he can stay with me," he said without hesitation. That should have been a no-brainer for her—if the choice was his son staying with him or a maid, the choice was obvious. "I don't know if I'll be able to rearrange my shift so that I'm home every afternoon for a two-week stretch, but if I'm not, he can always stay with Angelo at the restaurant until I get home.''

''Good,'' she said, pleased. ''I want to thank you for being so reasonable about this move, Tony. I know you're not happy about it, but it's the best thing for me and Larry, and Quentin will adjust. I'll fly him home whenever you want to see him.''

Tony almost told her she could take her offer and stuff it, but he bit the words back just in time. No, he didn't want to antagonize her, he reminded himself. His attorney had warned him to guard his tongue around her—the last thing they wanted at this point was to give her advance warning she was about to be hit with a custody fight and a restraining order prohibiting her from taking Quentin out of the state. She'd find out soon enough, and when she did, Tony knew there'd be hell to pay. He had to admit he was looking forward to it. Quentin was his son, too, and it was about time she realized that he had as much say in his upbringing as she did, including decisions about where he lived. ''I find it interesting that you think it will be best for you and Larry but not for Quentin,'' he said coolly. ''Doesn't that bother you at all?''

''Like I said,'' she replied with a shrug, ''he'll adjust. He'll have to. He's a child, Tony. He doesn't get a vote. This is my life and my decision to make. I don't know what you're worried about, anyway,'' she added with a frown. ''It's not like he's one of those kids with social problems. He makes friends wherever he goes. He'll do fine.''

She was so cavalier and unconcerned that Tony wanted to shake her. This wasn't some kid down the street they were talking about, this was their *son,* dammit. How could she care so little about his happiness?

Irritated, he growled, ''I guess he'll have to, won't he?

At least I get to spend as much time as possible with him before you take him away from me. I guess I should thank God for that, if nothing else.''

''It won't be that bad, Tony,'' she said stiffly. ''Just give it a chance.''

''That's easy for you to say,'' he retorted. ''You're not the one losing him.'' She didn't argue with that, and that only angered him more. The discussion over as far as he was concerned, he said, ''Good night, Janice. I'll be happy to keep Quentin as long as you need me to.''

Returning to his car, he drove away without a backward glance, and for the first time since she'd told him she was taking his son away from him, he had no doubts whatsoever about fighting her for custody of their son. He didn't doubt that she loved Quentin, but not as much as she loved her career. She would never put his needs before her own, let alone his happiness, and for no other reason than that, Tony knew Quentin belonged with him.

Reaching for another one of the boxes that she'd piled in a corner when she'd moved, Lily told herself she should go to bed. She was tired, her knee was hurting, and she had no one to blame but herself. She should have followed doctor's orders and rested.

''Okay,'' she muttered, breaking the silence that surrounded her on all sides. ''So I unpacked a few boxes. So sue me. I couldn't stand lying around anymore. I'll be fine after a good night's sleep.''

But as she unpacked some of her photography books, she had to admit that she'd overdone it. The books were heavy and she ached in every bone in her body.

Exhausted, she put the books in the built-in bookcase in the short hallway that led to her bedroom, then headed for the bathroom for a hot bath. Maybe a nice long soak would help ease her stiff muscles, which were still feeling the effects from being almost run down yesterday.

Ten minutes later, the bathroom was filled with steam as she shed her clothes and carefully eased down into the hot water that nearly filled the old-fashioned claw-foot tub to the rim. Drawing in the scent of her favorite bath oil, she sighed with pleasure as the water closed over her shoulders. Maybe she'd just stay here the rest of the night.

Later, Lily couldn't say how long she lay there, letting the tension drain out of her. Somewhere in the distance, she thought she heard a phone ring, but she couldn't be sure if it was her phone or the neighbor's. It didn't matter—if it was hers, the machine would get it. Closing her eyes again, she soaked until the water grew cold.

When she stepped out of the bathroom twenty minutes later, the phone rang, and this time there was no question that it was hers. Surprised, she frowned. Who could be calling her at this time of night? Her friends never called after nine, and her father...well, he wasn't calling, period, so it wasn't him. Unless there was some kind of emergency.

Her heart jumping into her throat at the thought, she quickly stepped into the bedroom and picked up the phone on the nightstand. "Hello?"

Her only answer was silence, then a quick dial tone.

"Okay," she said ruefully, hanging up. Obviously, someone had the wrong number and no manners. At least there was no emergency, thank God. Her father wasn't dead or hurt or lying in a hospital bed having an attack of his conscience. He just wasn't talking to her.

Resigned to the fact that nothing had changed, she turned out the light and crawled into bed...just as the phone rang again. "Not again," she muttered. Searching in the dark for the phone, she finally found it and snatched it up. ''Hello?''

For a moment, she thought the caller was going to hang up again. Silence echoed in her ear. Irritated—she had no patience for phone games—she was just about to hang up, when a hoarse voice rasped, ''Lily? Is that you?''

Startled, she answered without thinking. ''Yes?''

''Do you know who this is?''

''No, I'm sorry I don't.''

''This is the man who's going to kill you,'' he growled. ''You lucked out in the park yesterday. You won't next time. Understand? Your days are numbered, lady. Make a will. You're going to need one.''

The line went dead, but Lily hardly noticed. *You lucked out in the park yesterday.* The words echoed in her head over and over again, horrifying her. No! she thought, fumbling for the bedside light with fingers that were suddenly shaking like a leaf. She must have misunderstood. That was the only explanation. No one tried to kill her. It was just an accident.

But even as she tried to convince herself that the phone call was someone's idea of a sick joke, images from yesterday flashed before her eyes, and all too easily she saw the moment when the driver of the pizza-delivery car had abruptly turned the vehicle right at her. He hadn't changed direction until she had jumped out of the way and he was in danger of hitting a tree.

Stricken, she felt the blood drain from her face. For the last twenty-four hours, she'd told herself over and over again that even though it seemed as if the driver had intentionally tried to run her down, she was just being paranoid. She didn't have any enemies. Why would anyone try to kill her? Her mind was just playing tricks on her.

Or so she'd wanted to believe.

Someone really had tried to kill her in the park yesterday, she thought, shaken.

And he knew where she lived.

Chapter 7

Fear hit her right in the stomach, terrorizing her. Her heart slamming against her ribs, she jumped out of bed and started to turn on the light, only to freeze. No! For all she knew, he could have been calling from a cell phone right outside her front door. If he broke in, her only advantage would be the dark. She knew the layout of the apartment—he didn't.

Swallowing a sob, she quickly stepped over to the closet and blindly grabbed a pair of jeans and a shirt and pulled them on. She wouldn't be caught in her nightgown if he broke in. Shoes! she thought frantically. She needed her tennis shoes so she could run. Dropping to her knees, she felt around for her shoes and hurriedly pulled them on. Her fingers were trembling, but somehow she managed to tie the laces.

A weapon, she thought, jumping to her feet. She needed something to defend herself with. But what? She didn't own a gun. Her friends had always told her she should get a pistol—a woman living alone needed something to protect herself with—but she'd never, ever thought that she'd be in this position. Not that it mattered. She hated guns and hadn't wanted even a pellet gun in the house. She couldn't regret that now.

"Think, Lily!" she told herself quietly, fiercely. But she had nothing…except a kitchen knife and an iron skillet. They would have to do. Hurriedly, she silently made her way down the dark hall to the kitchen.

Panic pulling at her, she sighed quietly in relief when her fingers closed around the handle of her grandmother's iron skillet. It might not offer much protection against a gun, she thought grimly, but it could do a lot of damage if she was able to surprise an intruder and bean him with it. If she wasn't able to knock him out, she could at least give him a serious headache. Then she'd have to run like hell because if he caught her, he would, no doubt, make her wish she'd never been born.

Quaking at the thought, she clutched the skillet to her chest, hugging it. In the tense darkness of her apartment, all she could hear was the wild beating of her heart.

Call the police, the voice in her head urged. *What's wrong with you? Someone just threatened to kill you!*

Shaken, so scared she couldn't think straight, she pressed her hand to her mouth, muffling a sob. *Idiot!* she chided herself. What was wrong with her? Of course she should call the police. But she'd left the phone in the bedroom. Whirling, she'd only taken two steps when there was a sudden hard knock at her front door. Horrified, she froze.

No! she wanted to scream. This couldn't be happening. This was just a sick dream, and any second now she was going to wake up. But in the silence of the apartment, a second, harder knock sounded like a gunshot. Her heart jumping into her throat, Lily stood with her feet rooted to the floor, unable to move. Oh, God, he *was* here! He hadn't just been playing a sick joke. He really was going to kill her!

Her blood turning to ice, she looked wildly around the darkened apartment for a place to hide, but she couldn't think. The closets were too obvious. The fire escape! There had to be one—

"Hey, Lily? Are you home?"

Through the fear that clouded her brain, it was several long moments before she recognized the voice of her visitor. "Tony?" she called in disbelief. "Is that you? Thank God!" Shaking in relief, she fumbled with the lock. "Hold on. Please…don't leave!"

"I'm not going anywhere," he said ruefully through the door. "I wanted to thank you for helping Quentin with—"

Lily finally threw the latch and snatched open the door. At the sight of Tony standing there with that familiar crooked grin on his face, tears spilled into her eyes. "Thank God!" she sobbed.

Tony only had time to notice that her face was totally devoid of color, her eyes wide with fright, and she wore a strange mismatch of black dress slacks and an old denim shirt that was faded and splattered with paint, before she threw herself into his arms. Stunned, he caught her, his arms instinctively closing around her to hold her close. For a split second, all he could think was how good she felt against him. Then his head cleared and he realized she was shaking like a leaf and clutching a cast-iron skillet to her chest.

"What is this?" he asked with a frown as he pulled the skillet from between them. "What's going on? I'd like to think you're glad to see me, but women don't usually throw themselves at me with an iron skillet. Are you okay? You're white as a sheet."

Her face still buried against his chest, she choked, "I know you think I've lost my mind, but just give me a second, okay?"

"No problem," he said. "Take all the time you need."

When one minute stretched into two, then three, and she made no move to step back, Tony settled his arms firmly around her and decided she needed more than holding to calm the unnamed fear that he'd seen in her eyes. "This is kind of nice," he said, hoping humor would not only distract her, but himself. Lord, she felt good in his arms. "You know, if I'd known knocking on your door would get this kind of reaction, I would have done it weeks ago. Think of the time we wasted. Do you have any other quirks I should know about? This could be fascinating. What happens if I call you? Will you go out with me then? Because I really, really, *really* want to go out with you."

He felt her shoulders shake and was afraid he'd gone too far. Then he realized she was trying not to laugh. "Stop," she choked out, chuckling as she punched him in the shoulder.

He grinned. "Is that a yes?"

"Can't you see this isn't funny?"

"Obviously, you haven't looked at that getup you're wearing," he teased, glancing down pointedly. "Do you normally paint in your best pants?"

"Paint? What are you talking about?" Confused, she stepped back to look down at herself, "I dressed in the dark and pulled on the first thing I grabbed from my closet."

"And was there a reason you didn't turn the light on? There are blinds on the windows—"

"I was afraid," she said huskily, her smile abruptly falling away. "Someone's trying to kill me."

Whatever he had been expecting her to say, it wasn't that. "Is that what this is all about? You're still worried about what happened yesterday? Oh, honey, I'm sorry. It's okay—"

"No—"

"I know it looked like the jackass tried to deliberately run you down, but we can't be sure that the car didn't have some kind of steering problem," he pointed out reasonably. "So try not to think about it. You were just in the wrong place at the wrong time, but it's over, thankfully. The jerk's gone. You're safe."

"He called me."

Confused, he frowned. "Who called you?"

"The man who tried to kill me," she said hoarsely. "He said that I lucked out at the park yesterday, but next time I won't be so lucky. Tony, he's going to kill me!"

Tears flooded her eyes, horrifying Tony. "Hey, it's okay. Don't cry," he said roughly, pulling her back into his arms. "There's got to be a logical explanation for this. C'mon, honey," he urged, coaxing her over to the couch. "Sit down and let's talk about this. Tell me again what the guy said. Are you sure he didn't have the wrong number?"

"No! He knew my name and everything that happened in the park yesterday." Suddenly chilled, she hugged herself and told him the entire conversation, word for word. "There was no mistake," she said flatly. "He knew who I was and he's determined to kill me."

"And you don't have a clue why? I need you to rack your brains, Lily. A man doesn't threaten to kill a woman he doesn't know just for the hell of it. He's got some kind of vendetta against you. Why? Who is he?"

"I don't know!"

"Think about his voice, sweetheart," he said, taking her hand in a warm, reassuring grasp. "Did you recognize anything about it? An accent or certain inflection that sounded familiar? Is there a possibility that he was trying to disguise it? Remember, there's a damn good possibility that this is probably somebody you know."

Closing her eyes, she frowned, concentrating on her tormentor's threats as his words played over and over again in her head. Finally, regretfully, she shook her head. "I'm sorry. I don't know this man—I'm sure of it."

"Then why do you think he wants to kill you?"

She would have given just about anything to know the answer to that. "I don't know why," she said. "I just know what he told me. Maybe he's crazy. Maybe he saw me in the park and wanted the place to himself. There's no telling what's going through his mind. I just know that he sounded dead serious."

"Do you have caller ID? How did he get your number? It is restricted, isn't it?" When she hesitated, he swore softly. "Dammit, Lily, you're a woman who lives alone. You should always have a restricted number. It's just safer."

"I've never had a problem before. And I wanted my old friends to be able to find me now that I've moved. Obviously, that was a mistake."

"Don't beat yourself up. Unless you work in the business, you just don't realize how much crime there is out there. Especially for a woman alone. Any nutcase who heard about your accident yesterday could have asked around and found someone who knew your name. All he had to do then was call information and he had not only your phone number but your address. So you can't assume that the man who almost ran you over in the park and the caller are one and the same. He could just be some sicko looking for a cheap thrill.''

''But doesn't he know he just set himself up to get caught?'' she asked. ''My phone records will lead the police right to him.''

''Not necessarily,'' he argued. ''We'll check it out, of course, but in all likelihood, the call was made from a pay phone somewhere and he left no fingerprints.''

''But why would he take such a risk by calling me?''

''To torment you,'' he said simply. ''There are a lot of twisted people out there, sweetheart. They get their kicks in weird ways. The bastard who called you knew the risk was minimal. In all likelihood, he stopped at a pay phone in the middle of nowhere, made a quick call and scared you to death without coming anywhere near you.''

''But his prints will be on the phone. All you have to do is trace it.''

''Trust me, he didn't leave any prints behind,'' he retorted. ''He wiped the phone clean, then probably went home. He'll get a good night's sleep tonight, while you'll lie awake, afraid to even shut your eyes, let alone sleep. And trust me, he knows that. The son of a bitch is reveling in it.''

Lily felt sick to her stomach. ''I want to file a report, Tony. Immediately,'' she insisted. ''He sounded so angry. If he could have gotten his hands around my throat, I know he would have killed me. I really think he wants me dead.''

She shuddered, hugging herself, and it was all Tony could do not to take her back into his arms again. Did she have any idea what she did to him when she looked up at him with those big blue eyes? He wanted to carry her off somewhere where no one could hurt her, then spend the rest of the night making love to her. And that was exactly why he wasn't touching her again. She was far too vulnerable, and lately, he'd been thinking about her a hell of a lot more than he should have.

Like tonight, he thought, disgusted with himself. He could have called her and thanked her for helping Quentin, but he'd wanted to see her again, so what had he done? Knocked on her door with the first excuse he could think of.

You've got it bad, Giovanni, that irritating little voice in his head drawled in amusement. *And she won't even go out with you! How the mighty have fallen.*

If he'd had any sense, he would have gotten out of there while he still could. But she was truly scared, and he just couldn't bring himself to leave her. "Of course I'll file a report," he assured her. "And if it'll make you feel better, I'll check the apartment for you and make sure all your locks are in good shape. If they're not, I'll talk to Angelo and he'll have new locks installed tomorrow. Then you call the phone company tomorrow and have your number changed and restricted. I'll run a check on the old number and see if we come up with anything interesting. Okay?"

"Okay." For the first time since he walked through the door, she let down her guard enough to relax. Giving him a rueful smile, she nodded at the skillet, which he'd tossed to the other end of the couch. "I guess you're wondering what I was doing with that."

He shrugged. "It's pretty obvious you were going to brain someone with it. Thankfully, it wasn't me."

"Thank you," she said quietly. "I don't know what I would have done without you. After I got that phone call, all I could think was that some maniac was going to kill me tonight and I had nothing to protect myself with. That's when I grabbed the skillet.''

''Thank God I said something before you opened the door, or I'd be on my way to the hospital right now with a head injury. You'd have used that thing, wouldn't you?''

She didn't hesitate. ''In a heartbeat.''

Grinning, he growled, ''Good. There's no point in having a weapon if you're not prepared to use it.'' Rising to his feet, he held out his hand to pull her up beside him. ''C'mon. I'll call in a report, then we'll check the place out.''

It didn't take him long to discover that her apartment wasn't nearly as secure as he would have liked. Several of the window latches were so loose, a child could have popped them free, and the front door to the apartment didn't have a dead bolt. Still, the place was relatively safe. It was on the second floor, and the windows faced the street. Anyone wanting to gain entrance through the windows would have to be an idiot. They'd have to use a ladder and would be in full view of anyone who chanced to be passing by. And even though the front door didn't have a dead bolt, the front and back doors at street level that gave access to the stairwell did have dead bolts and were kept locked at all times. A fire escape at the rear of the building was locked unless it was pushed open from the inside. If the bastard tormenting Lily really did come after her, he was in for a rude awakening if he thought he could just walk upstairs as if he owned the place.

''I'll talk to Angelo in the morning, and he'll get someone in here to make the place more secure,'' he told her as she walked with him to the front door. ''In the meantime, you can either jam a chair under the doorknob or move the couch in front of the door if it will make you feel safer. And here's my number.'' Quickly jotting down his phone number on a piece of paper, he handed it to her and said, ''I don't care what time it is, call me immediately if you get another phone call or you're scared for any reason. I can be here in thirty seconds.''

Her smile tremulous, she clutched the card like a lifeline. ''I don't know how to thank you. This makes me feel a lot better.''

''Don't worry,'' he assured her as he opened the door. ''I'm going to get this guy if I can. And if the caller really is the same man who tried to run you down, then he's the one who should be putting his affairs in order. His days are numbered.''

Lily had never seen him so grim before...or so determined. Reassured, she wished him a quiet good-night, then closed the door behind him and quickly locked it. She told herself she was fine—there was no reason to be afraid now that Tony was aware of the situation. Still, her heart was pounding as she turned off the lights and crawled back into bed.

Later, she couldn't have said how long she lay there, staring at the ceiling and waiting for sleep to come. Time dragged in the night. She heard every sound outside, including the low growl of a motorcycle blocks away. Resigned to the inevitable, she sighed in disgust and threw back the covers. She might as well get up and spend the rest of the night working on her homework. At least she'd be doing something productive, because she sure as hell wasn't going to get any sleeping done.

Before she could even turn on the bedside lamp, however, the phone rang, shattering the quiet of the night. Startled, she bolted upright in bed, her heart racing. ''Don't answer it!'' she said aloud, trying to calm herself.

"He'll only scare you again, and that's what he wants. He enjoys it. Don't play his game."

She almost didn't, but she was already afraid, and the ringing phone was only making it worse. With a muttered curse, she jerked up the phone. "Hello?"

"Lily? Are you all right? When you didn't answer the phone, I was afraid something was wrong."

"Oh, Tony, I'm sorry!" she said, wilting in relief. "I was afraid you were *him.*"

He cursed in the darkness. "No, I'm the one who should be apologizing. I should have told you I was going to call before you went back to bed. I just wanted to make sure you weren't lying there in the dark, scared to death."

Laughing shakily, she sank back onto the bed and positioned her pillow under her head. "I don't know that I would go that far, but I blocked the front door with the couch and put your number on speed dial. I'm not expecting to sleep tonight, but I'm not as jumpy as I was. Or at least I wasn't until the phone rang," she added wryly.

"Sorry," he chuckled. "You know what they say about good intentions. Well, I guess I should go and let you try to get some sleep. You had a rough day and it's late."

"No!" She spoke too quickly and sounded more than a little desperate, but she didn't care. He was her link to sanity in the darkness, the one person tonight who could make her feel incredibly safe. She tried to tell herself it was because he was a policeman—it was his job to make people feel safe. But it was more than that, and she knew it. It was Tony, himself. When she'd opened the door to him and thrown herself into his arms, she'd felt as if nothing in the world could hurt her as long as he held her close.

Later, she knew she was going to have to think about that, but for now he was on the other end of the line and the only person between her and the demons of the night. And all she wanted to think about was him. "Don't go," she said huskily. "I wouldn't sleep, anyway. I was hoping we could talk."

"Sure," he said easily. "So what would you like to talk about? Me, right? It's okay. I know I've bowled you over with my charm. I have a habit of doing that. It's a genetic thing—all the Giovanni men have it. Ask Angelo. He can be a real charmer when he sets his mind to it."

"I'm sure he can," she said dryly, enjoying his teasing. "Of course, he doesn't flaunt it like you do."

"Are you kidding? I guess you haven't seen him when the Rose Club has its monthly dinner at the restaurant. I'm telling you, it's embarrassing. He falls all over himself flirting with the little old ladies, and they love it. I just don't understand it."

"Stop!" she laughed. "Angelo's not like that. And neither are you. I've seen you working in the restaurant. You don't flirt with the customers…though the old ladies do seem to be especially fond of you," she teased.

"Hey! What can I say? What's not to love?"

Lily chuckled. "Has anyone ever told you you're outrageous?"

"On a regular basis," he replied promptly. "What about you? Do you have your outrageous moments?"

"Only when I left a government job to chase a dream," she said ruefully.

"There must be other times in your life when you did something outrageous. What about when you were in school? You must have done something that would have raised your father's eyebrows if he'd known about it. All teenagers do."

She wouldn't have ever described herself as outrageous, but then she remembered a night when she was in high school that she'd nearly forgotten about. "Actually, now that you mention it, I did help TP a boy's house one night when I was a junior in high school."

"You didn't! Why, Ms. Fitzgerald, I'm shocked!"

"I was, too," she said. "I'd never done anything like that in my life. I felt so guilty about it that I talked my friends into helping me clean it all up before anybody saw the mess. My father would have had a stroke if he'd found out."

"My dad would have laughed, then made me confess the next day and clean it up."

"And are you the same kind of father your dad was? Do you laugh at things Quentin does, then make him do the right thing?"

"Do you even have to ask?" he said in amusement. "That kid knows exactly what to do to make me laugh. Not that I let him slide on the serious stuff," he quickly amended. "Just because Janice and I are divorced doesn't mean I play Disneyland dad. He knows what the rules are, and most of the time he doesn't push his luck. He's a good kid."

"He's lucky to have a father who knows how to laugh," she said quietly. "I didn't."

"What about your mother?"

"She died when I was six. Sometimes it seems like yesterday."

"I know what you mean," he replied in a voice that was as husky as hers. "My parents were killed in a car accident when I was sixteen. I don't know what I would have done if it hadn't been for Angelo and Aunt Tootsie. They were both there for me."

"Tootsie? That's Angelo's sister, right?"

"Yeah. She's something else. You should see her and Angelo dance. Even now, people clear the floor for them when they dance together. Aunt Tootsie always used to say it was in the blood. Then she tried to teach me."

"Why do I have a feeling that that was a disaster?" she asked.

"She gave me lessons at her house, and she's got all this dainty furniture that I kept bumping into. By the time the dance lesson was over, I'd broken a footstool and a side table and Aunt Tootsie's little toe."

"Oh, no!"

"It's a good thing I'm her favorite or she would have disowned me for sure."

Lily smiled in the darkness as he told her about his childhood, his wild Italian family, and even perps that had led him a merry chase before he'd managed to arrest them. And in the process, he made her laugh until she cried. And as one story led to another, she forgot all about her fear and the threatening phone call earlier in the evening. The hands of the clock on her bedside table passed an hour, then another, and she never noticed...until it was nearly three-thirty in the morning.

"Oh, my goodness! Tony, do you realize what time it is? I shouldn't have kept you this long. You have to work tomorrow."

Far from concerned, he only laughed. "I don't go in until noon. Anyway, I wouldn't care if I had to go in at dawn. I enjoyed talking to you."

"It was very sweet of you to keep me company through the night," she said softly. "Thank you."

"My pleasure," he said huskily. "Do you think you can go to sleep now?"

"Mmm-hmm," she said drowsily. "I can't seem to keep my eyes open. Did I say thank-you?"

"Yes, you did. Good night, Lily."

Smiling, already sinking into sleep, she murmured, "Good night." She'd hardly hung up before she was dreaming of him.

Sometime during the night, the first cool front of the season blew into town, and Lily woke to find the sky robin's-egg blue and the air crisp and cool. She'd always loved fall—it was her favorite time of year—and as she watched leaves blowing in the wind, there was nothing she would have liked more than to grab her camera bag and head for the park. But after what had happened the last time she'd set up camp there, she had no desire to stray that far from home.

Not that she was going to take many pictures without a camera, she reminded herself with a grimace. Since hers was beyond repair, she had to buy another one, and she didn't fool herself into thinking it would come cheap. Resigned, she hurriedly dressed, pulling on black slacks and a green tailored shirt, then secured her hair off her neck with a clip.

Surveying herself in the mirror, she grinned. Not bad. The bump on her forehead was concealed with makeup, and in spite of the terrifying phone call she'd received last night, she felt surprisingly relaxed and rested. And she had Tony to thank for that. Long after she'd hung up and gone to sleep, he'd been with her in her dreams.

Smiling at the thought, she grabbed her purse and stepped outside. A cool wind kissed her on the cheek, and she could smell the scent of burning wood on the morning air. Somewhere nearby, someone was enjoying the first fire of the season in their fireplace. Just that easily, she was transported back to the mountains of Colorado...and home. Fall came early in Liberty Hill. Friends and neighbors she'd grown up with had, no doubt, already started burning leaves and making apple cider and chopping wood so their woodpiles would be well stocked by the first snowfall. Just thinking about it made her homesick.

"Don't go there," she said aloud. "You can't live in the same town as your father, let alone the same state, and you know it. You took the job in D.C. to get as far away from him and his control as possible, so be happy. You're where you want to be."

Watching the leaves fall and people hurry down the street at a brisk walk, she saw dozens of pictures she wanted to snap. Once again, she was reminded that she had no camera. Normally, she would have walked to the camera shop two blocks away, but she hadn't forgotten the threats made against her last night. She wasn't going to live in fear, but neither was she going to take any unnecessary chances. So she walked around the corner to where she'd parked her car and drove the short distance to the camera shop.

Fifteen minutes later when she walked out of the store, she'd bought a Nikon that was just like the one that had been destroyed, then she'd given in to temptation and splurged on the enlarger she'd been promising herself. The enlarger would be delivered to her apartment later, but she took the Nikon with her. One day in the not too distance future, she hoped she'd be able to afford a Hasselblad, but she still intended to keep her Nikon. It was the first real camera she'd ever owned, and she loved it. She could take a dozen rolls of film, change lenses from telephoto to wide angle and back again without even having to think about it. Eager to get started, she hurried back to her car, loaded one of the rolls of film she'd bought with the camera and headed back home.

It only took a few minutes to collect her camera bag and tripod, and then she hit the streets. She didn't, however, go far. She had a mural to do for Angelo, and she decided that the place to start was outside. The restaurant just wasn't the building and its customers—it was the neighborhood, too, the families that lived in the area, the street itself. So setting up across the street from the restaurant, she began snapping pictures.

Not surprisingly, she drew more than her fair share of interested looks. A young mother, pushing a stroller with a baby that was bundled up against the cool air, nodded and smiled at her, and halfway down the block, Mrs. Parnelli, the owner of the neighborhood market, stopped in the middle of sweeping the sidewalk in front of her store to watch her. Amused, Lily waved and kept snapping pictures.

She wanted photos from different times of the day, different angles of light, different weather conditions, and that could take months. Pleased with what she'd taken for now, she was in the middle of repacking her camera bag, when a voice suddenly said from behind her, "You've got quite a setup there."

Surprised, she turned to find a man watching her with curious eyes. Tall and lean, with sharp, hawklike features and dark brown hair that he wore slicked back like a sophisticated banker, he was dressed in a black suit that Lily knew cost a small fortune. "It makes the job easier," she said with a half smile.

"Do you mind if I ask you a few questions?" he said easily. "My girlfriend wants to get into photography and I thought I might buy a camera for her for her birthday. Are you a professional? What do you recommend?"

"Oh, well, that depends on how much you want to

spend," she said with a smile. "And yes, I'm a professional. I'm still taking classes, though."

"No kidding? My girlfriend's been thinking about signing up for some classes. Where are you taking them? Are you happy with what you're taking?"

"Oh, yes!" she replied. "I'm taking three classes at Georgetown, and they're excellent."

"I'll have to tell my girlfriend. What kind of camera did you say I should buy?"

"It just depends on what kind of bells and whistles you want it to have. Personally, if money wasn't an issue, I'd get a Hasselblad. But there's nothing wrong with a Nikon or Cannon, either. You need to talk to someone at a camera shop. They can advise you better than I can."

"Okay, I'll do that," he said easily. "Thanks. You've been very helpful."

With a nod and smile, he strolled on down the street and had just reached the corner when a patrol car pulled up beside her. "Well, if it isn't Ms. Fitzgerald," Tony drawled with a wide grin. "You're looking awfully pretty for someone who didn't sleep much last night. I take it there were no more phone calls in the middle of the night?"

Delighted to see him, Lily couldn't conceal it. Her blue eyes smiling into his, she stepped over to the car as if drawn by a magnet. "No calls," she confirmed. "I slept like a baby…thanks to you."

"It was my pleasure," he said, his green eyes twinkling with mischief. "For a first date, I thought it went pretty well."

Not surprised by the turn of the conversation, she laughed. "That was not a date, Tony. We were in two different apartments."

"Well, that's easily rectified," he retorted with a grin. "Let's go out to dinner tonight."

"Okay."

For the first time since Lily had met him, she caught him off guard. Stunned, he blinked. "Are you kidding?"

She shook her head. "Not at all. I think it's about time, don't you?"

It was past time, as far as Tony was concerned. But he had to admit that there was a part of him that was tempted to tell her that all this time he'd just been joking with her. She was changing their relationship, and in some ways that scared the hell out of him. He had so much on his plate already—how could he find time for a woman in his life? And then there was Janice. Not only had she broken his heart and betrayed him, she was now trying to take his son. He'd sworn he'd never give another woman a chance to hurt him again. He could flirt and tease, but that was as far as it would go.

But there was something about Lily. He hadn't been kidding when he'd told her he really, really liked her. He'd been thinking about her all morning, so much that he'd found himself heading for Angelo's without even stopping to think about it. And that stunned him. He couldn't remember the name of the last woman who'd interfered with his work. But then again, he'd never met anyone quite like Lily. How could he not go out with her?

Grinning, he said, "I was beginning to think this day would never come. There is one thing you need to know, though. I have Quentin tonight."

"That's okay. He's a great kid. Bring him along."

Reassured—what could happen with his son along as chaperon?—Tony said, "It looks like we have a date. What time should we pick you up?"

"What time do you get off work? Is six-thirty too early?"

"We'll meet you in the hallway," he replied just as his police radio crackled to life. Listening, he grimaced. "Duty calls. I'll see you later this evening."

Switching on the light bar on the roof of his car, he waved and drove off. Staring after him, her heart pounding, Lily couldn't stop smiling. What had she done? And why didn't she regret it?

Chapter 8

"We're just going to dinner—it isn't a real date. We're just going to dinner—it isn't a real date."

Lily repeated the mantra over and over again, but her heart wasn't buying it. Her cheeks were pink with excitement, her eyes sparkled, and she felt as if she'd just won the lottery. She was humming, for heaven's sake. And to make matters worse, she changed clothes *three* times before she was satisfied with the jeans and red cover girl–style sweater she finally chose. Then she redid her makeup when there was nothing wrong with it. She had to be losing her mind.

Every time she looked in the mirror, she reminded herself that her photography was the only thing that was important to her right now. She wouldn't try to please another man and be who he wanted her to be. But that thought flew right out of her head when she stepped out into the main hallway at six-thirty and found Tony and

Quentin waiting for her. She took one look at the two of them and felt her heart skip a beat in her breast.

They were, she had to admit, something else. They had the same smile, the same hair, the same square-cut face. Even their eyes were the same, though Tony's were green and Quentin's blue. The twinkle that was so darn charming, however, was identical. Lily took one look at the two of them standing side by side, dressed exactly alike in jeans and blue-and-white striped polo shirts, and wanted to hug them both. She was, she decided, in big, big trouble!

"How do you like our shirts, Lily?" Quentin asked eagerly. "Dad and I are dressed alike."

"I noticed," she chuckled. "You both look fantastic."

"I told Dad you would. You know what's cool."

"Well, I don't know about that," she said. "I try. So how's math going? Was your teacher impressed with your homework?"

"She couldn't believe it. I got an A!"

"All right!" she said, holding up her hand for a high five.

"I think that deserves something special," Tony said. "How about dinner at Mr. Moon's? What'da'ya think?"

Eyes that were already sparkling widened. "Really, Dad? You mean it?"

"If it's okay with Lily. She may not like pizza."

"Are you kidding?" she countered. "I love it. Especially Mr. Moon's."

Surprised, Tony lifted a dark eyebrow at her. "So you've been there?"

She grinned. "Of course. And I'll have you know that I'm pretty good at some of the games, too. I should warn you that I plan on beating the socks off of both you."

"Oh, really?" Tony said, amused. Looking down at

his son, he said, "Did you hear that, Quentin? Sounds like a challenge to me."

"Me, too," he said, his eyes dancing as his gaze bounced back and forth between Tony and Lily. "I think the winner should get a prize."

"My feelings exactly," he said. Glancing back at Lily, he said, "I should warn you that I hold the record for the most cumulative points scored at Mr. Moon's. If you don't believe me, ask Mr. Moon. He'll tell you."

Not believing him for a minute, she only chuckled. "Yeah, right. And I've got some swampland in Florida you might be interested in."

The challenge made and accepted, they grinned at each other like two kids having a throwdown and enjoying every second of it. Delighted, Lily laughed. "C'mon, Mr. Hotshot. Let's see what you can do. And you, too, Junior Hotshot. The winner gets to pick his—or her—prize."

"Yeah!" Quentin cried. "I want a hot-fudge sundae with extra nuts!"

"You haven't won yet," she said.

So excited he could hardly sit still, Quentin chattered all the way to Mr. Moon's Fabulous Pizza Parlor and Game Room. They ate first, then it was time to put up or shut up. Tony gave Quentin ten dollars for tokens, and the games began.

"All right! I'm top scorer," Quentin crowed, punching the air with his fist. "I can already taste my sundae. Did I say I wanted two cherries on top?"

"I wouldn't be so cocky if I were you, short stuff," Tony told his son with a broad grin. "We've still got four more games to play, and the last time we played ringtoss, I smoked you."

Clearing her throat delicately, Lily reminded them of her presence. "Did I happen to mention that ringtoss just happens to be one of my personal favorite games? You guys are toast.''

His green eyes twinkling with mischief, Tony stepped back and courteously motioned for her to precede him. ''By all means, please go first. We'll just stand back here out of your way and watch a master at work, if that's okay with you.''

''Of course,'' she said graciously, fighting a smile. ''An audience is always so flattering.''

She winked and turned to the bottles that were closely set on a table in front of them. Small signs with different points printed on them were randomly attached to different bottles, with the highest points awarded to the bottle at the back of the table. Studying them, Lily tossed one of the plastic rings she'd bought with three tickets. With a soft clink, it settled over the neck of one of the bottles with the second-highest points.

''Yes!''

''All right, Lily!'' Quentin said. ''How'd you do that?''

''Here...I'll show you. Stand right here.'' Positioning Quentin in front of her, she handed him one of the rings, showed him how to hold it the way she had, then demonstrated how to flick his wrist just right. ''Okay, now try it.''

The first ring he tossed sailed right over the table to the floor on the other side. ''Not with so much force next time. Easy...easy. That's it...''

He tried again, and this time, the ring rattled around the high-point bottle and settled neatly into place. ''I did it! Look, Dad, I did it!'' A broad smile splitting his face, he turned to throw himself against Tony for a fierce hug, then launched himself at Lily for another hug that was just as tight.

Laughing, Lily caught him close, then grunted and pretended to stagger under his weight, making Quentin giggle. Watching them together, Tony found himself impressed all over again with how natural and relaxed she was with his son. She didn't talk down to him or try to mother him—she just treated him with humor and respect and liking, and he responded in kind. She was definitely a woman who should have children of her own, he thought, grinning as she challenged Quentin to a ring-tossing contest. She would make a great mother.

Whoa, a voice in his head cried in alarm. *Don't even think about going there. You've been there and done that, and the last thing you need right now is a woman who wants to hear the patter of little feet. You've got a son—the only thing you're concerned with right now is keeping him. If Lily wants children, she's going to have to get someone else to play daddy.*

He didn't always agree with that irritating little voice in his head that invariably tried to make him do the right thing, but sometimes, he had to admit, his common sense really did know what it was talking about. And this was one of those times.

That didn't mean, however, that he couldn't be more attracted to the lady than he'd ever been to any other woman in his life, he ruefully acknowledged. He just had to keep reminding himself why he couldn't do anything about it.

She didn't make it easy for him. They used up the rest of their tokens, and he couldn't take his eyes off her. He'd always thought the prettiest women in the world were those who didn't seem to know just how gorgeous they were. Lily was one of those women, and he found that incredibly appealing. She didn't check her makeup constantly or mess with her hair, and when she laughed, it was from the heart. He could have spent hours just watching her smile.

"Did you hear that, Dad? Lily says I'm the winner because my ringtoss points put me over the top. I can have a sundae, can't I? Mom only lets me have dessert on weekends."

"I don't think an occasional dessert's going to hurt you," he replied. "After all, what's life without an occasional sundae with a cherry on top?"

"My sentiments exactly," Lily said with a grin. "Only make that two cherries. You earned it."

Quentin let out a whoop and ran to get his dessert, leaving Tony alone with Lily for the first time that evening. Taking advantage of it, he said, "You've been really great with Quentin. It's nice to see him enjoying himself so much."

Her gaze trained on Quentin as he made his own sundae at the dessert bar, she grinned as he piled cherries on top of a mound of whipped cream. "It doesn't take much to amuse him. I like that in a kid. You've done a good job with him."

"I don't know if I can take any credit for that," he said wryly. "He's just…Quentin."

The object of their discussion came bouncing over to them then and was pleased as punch with himself and his sundae. "This is the best! I've never done anything this cool before. Can we do this again sometime, Dad, and bring Mac? He's really good at ringtoss, but there's no way he's as good as Lily. He's going to be shocked when I beat him."

"Mac's his best friend," Tony explained to Lily, then turned back to his son. "Don't count your chickens before they hatch," he warned. "In the meantime, it's a school night. I hate to break this up, but I need to get you back to your mom's.''

''Oh, Dad, do we have to? It's still early!''

''I need to be calling it a night, too,'' Lily said easily. ''I've got an early class in the morning. But don't worry,'' she told Quentin when he looked disappointed. ''We'll do it again sometime.''

Glancing from his father to Lily, he reluctantly accepted the inevitable. ''Okay,'' he sighed as dug into his sundae and ate it in record time. ''But next time we come back, I want to buy twice as many tokens. There were tons of games we didn't even try.''

''Maybe we can come on a Saturday and stay all afternoon,'' Lily said with a smile as the three of them fell into step and headed for the car. ''Or we could take my camera and go to the zoo. I'd like to get some pictures of the pandas.''

His eyes as wide as saucers, Quentin stopped in his tracks. ''Oh, wow, could I take some pictures, too? And help you develop them? You did get your darkroom stuff, didn't you?''

''It was delivered this afternoon,'' she said with a smile.

''Dad, she's got her own darkroom! Can I have a camera? And a darkroom? It sounds like fun!''

Laughing, Tony ruffled his hair. ''Not so fast, hotshot. I can swing a camera, but a darkroom is something else. You may not even like photography.''

''That's right,'' Lily agreed. ''You can take pictures for years without having a darkroom. I did.''

Curious, Quentin asked her dozens of questions on the way home about the process of developing black-and-white film, then asked her everything there was to know about printing pictures. And Lily could have kissed him for it. Because the closer and closer they drew to home, the more she was aware of Tony's eyes on her. He didn't say much as he drove down the dark, narrow streets of Georgetown, only occasionally adding a comment to something Quentin said, but there was something about the heated looks he kept sending her that set her heart thumping like a teenager's on her first date. Horrified, she kept talking about photography and prayed she didn't sound like some kind of nitwit.

When Tony pulled into his parking space behind the building and cut the engine, Lily was a nervous wreck. Even with Quentin there as a chaperon, she was far too aware of Tony as he came around to open the car door for her, then fell into step beside her as he and Quentin escorted her upstairs to her apartment.

"We really had a great time," Tony said as the three of them reached the upstairs landing and came to a stop in front of her door. "Maybe next time we'll go to the zoo, like you suggested."

"Yeah," Quentin said eagerly. "That would be cool!"

Since she had been the one to bring up the zoo in the first place, she could hardly say no. Not that she wanted to, she quietly admitted to herself. Whenever his eyes met hers, something happened to her heart. Even now, with Quentin standing right beside them as a pint-size chaperon, she couldn't stop herself from wishing he could kiss her. Her heart pounded just at the thought.

"Lily? Hello?" Waving his hand in front of her face, Tony grinned down at his son. "I think we lost her. Women do this sometimes, you know. They just blink and they're gone."

"I'm not gone," she said dryly, returning to her surroundings with the same blink he'd just been talking about. "I was thinking."

His eyes dancing, he arched a dark masculine eyebrow at her. "About what? Or is that something you don't care to share with us?"

She could feel revealing color steal into her cheeks, and there was nothing she could do about it. "Of course not," she said with a toss of her head. "I just remembered that I was supposed to e-mail some pictures to an old high-school friend. With everything that's been happening, I completely forgot about it."

He didn't believe her—she only had to meet his gaze head-on to know that he had a fairly good idea what thoughts had been teasing her senses. Her cheeks burning, she said, "Anyway, I guess I'd better go in. I had a great time."

"We did, too," he said huskily. "Thanks for dinner."

Kiss him! Kiss him! Kiss Him! If nothing else, on the cheek.

She wanted to, but she didn't dare. "Good night, guys," she said softly, and slipped into her apartment before she changed her mind.

Staring at the closed door, a half smile curling one corner of his mouth, Tony swallowed a groan. If Quentin hadn't been there, if she'd given him the least bit of encouragement—hell, if she'd just stood there a second longer…

"Dad? What's wrong? Why do you look so weird?"

Suddenly realizing he was standing there staring at Lily's door like a love-struck idiot, he said ruefully, "This is what a man who's losing his mind looks like. Would you do something for me, son?"

"Sure, Dad."

"Run downstairs and see if Uncle Angelo needs anything from the grocery store. Since I'm going to be out, anyway, taking you home, I might as well save him a trip. While you're doing that, I'll see if Lily needs anything.''

It was a good story, one that Quentin might have accepted without question when he was a little younger. He wasn't a baby anymore, however, nor nearly as innocent as Tony had hoped. Cocking his head, Quentin grinned up at him and said, ''You're going to kiss her, aren't you?''

''I'm going to see if she needs anything, smartypants,'' he retorted, giving him a stern look that was totally ruined by the slight smile that curled the edges of his mouth. ''That's all you need to know. Go check with Uncle Angelo to see if he needs anything. I'll be down in just a second.''

To his credit, Quentin didn't argue with him further. But Tony didn't miss the little smile that played around his mouth as he ducked his head and hurried down the stairs. Grinning, Tony knocked on the door of Lily's apartment.

At his second knock, he heard her start to turn the dead bolt, only to hesitate. ''Who is it?''

Smart girl, he thought with a smile. ''It's me,'' he called softly through the door.

With a click of the lock, she opened the door to give him a puzzled smile. ''What's wrong? Where's Quentin?''

''Downstairs, checking with Angelo to see if he needs anything from the store, since I'm going to be out. Do you need anything?''

Surprised, she said, ''No, but thanks for the offer.'' When he just stood there, she frowned, confused. ''Why do I have the feeling I missed something? What's going on?''

''Actually, I think we both missed something,'' he said

ruefully. And with no more warning than that, he stepped forward and pulled her into his arms. ''Quentin wanted a sundae if he won the contest at Mr. Moon's,'' he said huskily. ''I wanted this.'' And lowering his mouth to hers, he kissed her right there in the hall.

Her head swimming and her heart threatening to beat right out of her chest, Lily moaned softly and wrapped her arms around his neck. Somehow, she'd known he was a man who knew how to please a woman with just a kiss, and he didn't disappoint. Hungrily, tenderly, he kissed her as if he couldn't get enough of her, and just that easily, he made her ache.

''I've been wanting to do this all evening,'' he rasped against her mouth, kissing her sweetly, hotly.

''Me, too,'' she whispered, and gave herself up to another long, drugging kiss.

Lost to all reason and loving it, she could have spent hours just kissing him, but Tony abruptly came to his senses. Groaning, he set her from him. ''I hate to do this, but I've got to go,'' he said. ''Quentin's waiting and it's getting late.''

Giving her one last kiss, he gently steered her back into her apartment, and pulled the door shut between them. ''Lock it, honey,'' he growled from out in the hall.

Still caught up in the heat of his kiss, Lily almost told him no. She didn't want him to leave! Then her common sense reasserted itself and she silently acknowledged it was for the best. Reaching over, she shot the dead bolt into place.

''Good night,'' he called.

A split second later, Lily heard his footsteps disappear down the stairs at the end of the hall. Leaning back against the door, she hugged herself and fought the need to call him back.

* * *

Standing in the black shadows of the alley across the street, Sly Jackson watched with narrowed eyes as the cop and his brat stepped outside through the private street entrance that led to the upstairs apartments. Upstairs, a light switched on in a small window that appeared to be over a kitchen sink. In the darkness, a slow, sinister smile slid across Sly's angled face. So, now he knew which apartment was *hers.* The old man was still in the restaurant even though it was closed, the cop was gone and there was nobody upstairs but Miss Candid Camera.

This was his chance, he thought, pleased. She was alone, and no one had a clue what kind of danger she was in. All he needed was five seconds and he could take care of her once and for all. By the time the old man or the cop discovered her body, he would be long gone and he'd never again have to worry about Lily Fitzgerald and that damn photograph she'd taken of him.

All but rubbing his hands together in anticipation, he started to step out of the shadows, but he never got the chance. Across the street, Angelo pushed open the door to the restaurant and stepped outside with a broom and dustpan. Slowly, methodically, and not going anywhere fast, he began to clean the sidewalk in front of his restaurant.

''Son of a bitch!'' Sly muttered, and quickly, soundlessly, sank deeper into the dark belly of the alley. Did the old goat ever move at any speed other than crawl? he wondered, glaring at him. It was late, dammit! Why didn't he hurry up and go upstairs to bed? Sly wasn't worried about him hearing anything that might go on in Lily's apartment—old strokes slept like the dead. He had to be tired after working all day. So why didn't he go upstairs before the cop came back and ruined everything!

Frustrated, he could almost hear the clock ticking in his head. It seemed the cop had taken the kid home. How long would he be gone? he wondered…just as the black Toyota sedan that belonged to the cop turned the corner at the end of the street and headed straight for him. His heart slamming against his ribs, he swore and pressed up against the building. He was busted, he thought, panicking. All the damn cop had to do was glance over to his right and he was bound to see him plastered to the front of the darkened building like a fly on the wall.

Trapped, he almost bolted, his shifting eyes searching frantically for an escape. He could run down the alley and disappear into the night. The subway entrance was only two blocks away. Or he could go three blocks to the west, where there was a rabbit warren of old buildings in the process of being remodeled. They were linked by underground tunnels that would make it virtually impossible for the cops to find him.

But before he could decide which way to run, the cop pulled over to the curb in front of Angelo's and stepped out of the car to talk to his uncle. He never even looked Sly's way. Relieved, he didn't know whether to laugh or curse. Damn pig! Was he blind? Or just stupid? Either way, the cop hadn't seen him, and that was all Sly cared about. Now if he just had to work the late shift tonight, everything would go just the way he wanted.

But if one of the city's finest had to report to work, he showed no sign of it. He and the old man stood talking as if they didn't have a care in the world. And with every passing second, Sly found himself growing more and more angry. Did they know he was out there, watching them, waiting for his chance to sneak upstairs and kill Miss Candid Camera? Is that why they were lingering? Were they deliberately trying to infuriate him?

His teeth clenched on an oath, he silently ordered himself to get a grip. But the two men across the street didn't make it easy. Five minutes passed, ten, then twenty, and still, neither man showed any sign of calling it a night. And that's when he knew there was no way in hell he was going to be able to kill Lily tonight.

Damn them! he raged as he carefully eased farther back into the darkness of the alley, then turned to silently make his way to where he'd left his car two blocks away. He hoped they enjoyed themselves, destroying his plans. That was all right—his time was coming. And when it did, he'd make them *and* Miss Shutterbug regret they'd ever been born.

"So Lily went out to dinner with you, did she?" Angelo teased, his green eyes glinting with humor. "I thought she had better taste than that."

Tony tried and failed to scowl. "Don't go there, old man. It wasn't a real date. Quentin went with us."

"So? She's single and you're single and you went out to dinner. Sounds like a date to me."

"I don't have time for a woman in my life—"

"Of course you do," his uncle retorted. "You made time tonight."

"The last couple of days have been rough on her," he said with a shrug. "I thought I could take her mind off her troubles if we went out."

Angelo made no secret of the fact that he didn't quite believe him—his doubts were clearly visible in his eyes—but he let the little white lie go and said instead, "What's going on with her case? You did report that threatening call she got, didn't you? What do you think about this bastard who's harassing her? Does she have a clue who it is?"

Tony shook his head grimly. ''She swears she doesn't have any enemies—she certainly can't think of anyone who hates her enough to want her dead. But somebody's got it in for her, and from the sound of it, he's a loose cannon. Although I tried to down play the danger and not make her any more scared than she already was, still, she has reason to be afraid.''

Angelo agreed. ''I've hired her to do a photographic mural for the restaurant. Hopefully, she'll be safer if she sticks close by until the guy is caught.''

''Good. The last thing she needs right now is to be out on the streets alone.''

''Do you have any idea yet why someone's trying to kill her? She's a sweet girl. What could she have done to make someone so angry he'd want to kill her?''

''I don't know,'' Tony said with a frown as he took the broom from Angelo so his uncle could sit and relax while he finished sweeping the sidewalk. ''Whoever this bastard is, he's been damn clever so far. The only clue he's left behind is the abandoned pizza-delivery car he stole, and that hasn't done us a hell of a lot of good. He wiped it free of fingerprints and no one saw him steal the damn thing. We've got nothing on him, and he knows it. Hell, we don't even know why he's doing this!''

''Were you able to trace where he made that phone call from last night? Maybe someone saw him.''

He shook his head grimly. ''He made the call from a pay phone on Fourteenth Street. At that time of night, there wasn't a soul around, and he didn't leave any prints. I warned Lily that would probably happen, but damn, I hate to be the one to say I told you so.''

''You'll catch the jerk,'' Angelo said confidently. ''If he called her once, he's bound to call again.''

''He was taunting her and us,'' he retorted. ''I'd bet a

million bucks he won't call again, but we've got the line tapped just in case."

"Good," Angelo said in satisfaction. Changing the subject, he said, "So when's your next date? This time, Quentin should stay with me. You can't wine and dine her with your son along."

"I'm not wining and dining—"

"That's obvious," his uncle retorted with a grin, ignoring his warning tone. "I can't believe you took her to Mr. Moon's."

"Quentin was with us—I thought she'd be more comfortable if we went someplace casual."

"But a kid's pizza parlor?" Rolling his eyes, Angelo sighed. "I can see right now that you're going to need some advice or you're going to totally blow this. Not that I'm criticizing you," he added quickly, grinning. "I think it's great you're dating again. You should have been doing more of it all along."

"You're pushing me, Angelo."

"Well, somebody has to. You can't even remember the last date you had."

"Yes, I can," he said. "It was with Janice two nights before we got married. She's the only woman I ever loved, and now she's trying to take my son away from me. I'm not looking for another woman, Angelo. All I want is my son."

There was no doubting his sincerity, and Angelo ached for him. Life hadn't been easy for him over the last two years. But locking himself up in his home whenever he wasn't at work was not the way to deal with the problem. "I understand that, and you're going to get him. But don't judge all women by Janice, Tony. From the first moment I met her, I thought she was all wrong for you. She was cold and self-centered and interested only in her career. From what I've seen of Lily, she's the exact opposite."

"I agree," he said. "I would never describe her as cold...or self-centered, for that matter. I like her! But I don't think anything is more important to her right now than her photography. She waited a long time to follow her dreams, and I get the feeling she's not going to let anyone get in her way. Who does that remind you of?"

Angelo scowled. "Will you stop, already? She's not Janice. She's not driven the way Janice is. Of course she wants to succeed with her photography. There's nothing wrong with that. But if she had a son, I'll bet she wouldn't sacrifice his happiness for her own. She's not wired that way."

Tony had to agree. "She's great with Quentin, and he likes her. Just don't get any ideas about the two of us getting together, because it's not going to happen. Okay? Maybe if she'd come along before I met Janice, something could have come of it, but not now. We've both got too much going on in our lives to even think about getting involved with anyone right now. The timing's all wrong."

He half expected Angelo to tell him what he could do with that argument, but he only shrugged. "You would know that better than I. It's your life. I just want you to be happy."

"I'll be happy when I have custody of my son. Nothing else matters but that."

Angelo couldn't argue with that. He knew how much Tony loved his son Quentin and wanted him with him. Right now, nothing else was more important than that. That didn't, however, change Angelo's opinion of Lily. She was just what Tony needed.

* * *

Don't judge all women by Janice.

Long after he'd told Angelo good-night and gone upstairs to bed, his uncle's words echoed in his head. And all he could think of was Lily. She smiled at him in his dreams, teased him, touched him, kissed him until he groaned with the pleasure of it. Somewhere in his head, a voice reminded him that this was just a dream...a very hot, vivid, seductive dream...but it didn't matter. He wanted her. In his sleep, he reached for her, and suddenly the dream shifted, and instead of kissing him as if she couldn't get enough of him, Lily was walking toward him...in a wedding dress. And he couldn't wait to say *I do.*

"What the...!" Abruptly coming awake, Tony bolted up in bed, his heart pounding. He was losing his mind. And it was all Angelo's fault, he thought with a scowl as he punched his pillow into a more comfortable position. If his uncle hadn't kept singing Lily's praises and teasing him about their date, he might have been able to fall asleep without dreaming of her.

Had he really dreamed about marrying her?

No, he told himself firmly. Even if he had, it didn't mean anything. He wasn't getting married again. He wasn't even going to fall in love again. He'd had his heart ripped out once, and he wasn't about to give another woman a chance to do it to him a second time. If he was attracted to Lily, if he couldn't stop thinking about her, it was only because he was physically attracted to her. It was just chemistry. The kiss they'd shared had proved that. His emotions weren't even involved.

So why do you keep thinking about how she felt in your arms?

Swearing, he tried to push the memory away, but he

might as well have told himself not to breathe. The second he laid back down and closed his eyes, he could feel her in his arms, taste her on his tongue. And then there was her perfume. It wasn't anything heavy or cloying, just a subtle, seductive scent that lingered in his mind, teasing his senses, constantly reminding him of her. With no effort whatsoever, he could imagine himself touching her, caressing her, spending what was left of the night slowly driving her out of her mind with pleasure.

Instead, he was the one who was going out of his mind. He didn't sleep at all.

Thankfully, he didn't have to report to work the following morning—it was his day off at the police department—but he was scheduled to work for his uncle the entire day. Groaning just at the thought, he drank what seemed like a gallon of coffee, then took a cold shower to wake himself up and clear his head. Unfortunately, nothing helped much. Resigned, he headed downstairs and hoped Angelo didn't notice that his eyes were bloodshot and he looked as if he'd pulled an all-nighter. Knowing Angelo, he'd figure out that thoughts of Lily had kept him awake and he'd never hear the end of it.

He needn't have worried. Angelo had a meeting with his accountant, then a major problem with one of his suppliers. He was on the phone for what seemed like hours, and by the time he emerged from his office, the morning was half gone. Already behind schedule and the day had hardly started, he didn't have much time to talk.

Relieved, Tony helped in the kitchen and was busy making meatballs for his uncle's famous Italian wedding soup, when Lily walked in with her camera slung around her neck. Dressed in jeans and a T-shirt, with her hair pulled back in a ponytail that swung with every step she took, she looked cute and perky and far more rested than he. And he couldn't take his eyes off her.

Irritated, he frowned. "What are you doing here? I thought you'd be working." Then he had another thought. "You haven't gotten any more threatening phone calls, have you?"

"Oh, no. I'm fine," she assured him. "Didn't Angelo tell you he'd hired me to do a mural for him? I need to take some candid pictures of the staff and customers, then take some measurements of where Angelo wants the mural to go. I'll probably been in and out all day."

Great, Tony thought with a groan that he quickly swallowed. Now he didn't just have to dream about her, he had to work around her all day. Frustrated, he tried to convince himself it wouldn't be that bad. She had her own work to do, and once the lunch crowd arrived, he'd be too busy to even notice her.

And ducks ate lasagna, he thought in disgust two hours later. She didn't come near him, but every time he looked up from what he was doing, there she was, right in his line of vision. And then there was that damn haunting scent of hers. It wafted through the restaurant, drifting under his nose when he least expected it, reminding his senses that she was near. As if he could forget it!

To make matters worse, he had to wait on her at lunch. If she'd just been in a bad mood, he wouldn't have had a problem with it. He could have been all business, taken her order, then brought her her food without a single personal word exchanged between the them. But how was he supposed to keep his distance and just do his job when she was so damn friendly? She only had to smile at him to make him want her.

He had to be losing his mind.

The day only went downhill from there. When Quentin

came in from school, he saw Lily step into the kitchen with her camera to photograph Angelo as he started doing some of the prep work for dinner, and he immediately headed straight for her. "Whoa, boy," Tony said, stepping in his path. "Where do you think you're going?"

"To talk to Lily," he said, surprised.

"Lily's working. She doesn't have time to talk right now."

"But I have to interview her for a project for school," he insisted. "Mrs. Carl, my English teacher, wants us to talk to someone with an unusual job for career week. Nobody else knows a photographer, Dad. Lily's cool!"

No one knew that better than Tony. She was cool, all right, but it had nothing to do with her job. It was her smile and the light in her eye when she saw through his flirting and called him on it. Her skin was as soft as an angel's, and when she was scared, she'd clung to him as if she would never let him go. How could he resist a woman like that?

He didn't have an answer for that, but he had to find a way to keep his distance, and Quentin did, too. "I know she's cool, but she also has to work. Don't get in her way."

"But she told me I could ask for help whenever I needed it. If she couldn't help me right then, she would later. I'm going to go talk to her." And before Tony could stop him, Quentin took a quick step around him and made a beeline for the kitchen.

Swearing under his breath, Tony had no choice but to follow him. Hurrying across the dining room after him, he pushed through the swinging door of the kitchen just as Quentin asked Lily if she could help him with his homework. "I'm sorry he's bothering you," he told her, shooting his son a disapproving scowl. "I told him you were working, but he insisted he needed you to help him with some homework.''

Far from bothered, she only laughed. ''He's not bothering me. I was just about to take a break. Anyway, I told him I'd be happy to help him whenever he needed help if I was home. I've got some chocolate cake upstairs. Why don't we go up to my apartment and have a snack, then work on your homework?'' she told Quentin. ''It'll be quieter there and you'll be able to concentrate better.''

''Can I, Dad?'' he asked eagerly. ''Then you won't have to help me when you finish your shift. Maybe we can go to the park later or something.''

''Brat,'' Tony said, ruffling his hair. Bringing his gaze back to Lily, he said, ''Ever since I told him I needed to find a way to change my schedule so we could spend more time together, he's been using that to his advantage. Are you sure you don't mind? I can help him with his math later, but he needs to interview you for an English project, if that's okay.''

''I never turn down a chance for free publicity,'' she said with a grin. ''Of course I'll help him.''

''Send him back downstairs if he starts to bother you,'' he replied. ''Angelo always needs someone to bus tables.''

''Dad!''

''I don't think you'll have any trouble with him,'' he told Lily wryly. ''He hates busing tables.''

''I can't say I blame him,'' she retorted. ''I don't know about you, Quentin, but that chocolate cake's starting to sound better and better. I think we should get out of here while the getting's good.''

She didn't have to tell him twice. Grabbing his backpack, he headed for the kitchen door that opened onto the apartment stairwell. ''Bye, Dad. See you later.''

When the door swung shut behind them, Tony knew he should have been relieved—at least he no longer had to worry about seeing Lily every time he turned around. But as he returned to work, he found himself looking for her, anyway. That's when he knew he was in trouble.

Chapter 9

At five-thirty the band Angelo had hired to play in the evenings started to play a medley of Dean Martin songs, and by six, nearly every table in the restaurant was taken. Pleased, Tony reminded himself that he would have to thank Lily for keeping Quentin distracted for so long. Quentin had always been good about grabbing a seat at one of the tables and working on his homework whenever Tony had to help out Angelo in the restaurant, but that all changed when Janice announced she was moving to Florida and taking Quentin with her. Since then, Quentin had had a difficult time sitting still for very long, and Tony couldn't blame him. His mother was turning his world upside down for a damn job. That had to hurt.

Every time he thought about what she was doing to the boy, Tony became angry. How could she be so uncaring? She was his mother, for heaven's sake. Didn't it bother her that she was ripping his son away from his father? She knew how close they were. Tony didn't expect her to care about what that would do to him, but what about Quentin? How could she do this to her only child? Didn't she realize this would make him hate her?

Caught up in his musings as he waited on a family of six dining out to celebrate the mother's fortieth birthday, Tony didn't notice the woman who'd just stepped through the front door until she was suddenly striding right toward him. He took one look at the outrage burning in her eyes and knew exactly why she was there. She'd been served with the papers announcing he was fighting her for custody of Quentin.

Lightning quick, he moved to intercept her before she could cause a scene. "We can talk in Angelo's office," he said coolly, and took her arm to steer her away from the rest of the guests.

"You're damn right we're going to talk!" she hissed as she hurried to keep up with his long stride. "How dare you!"

"Excuse me?" Suddenly as furious as she, Tony followed her through the swinging door of the kitchen and into Angelo's office, slamming the door behind him. When she whirled to confront him, her blue eyes blazing, he sputtered, "How dare I? How dare *I?* Maybe you need to take a good look at yourself, sweetheart! I'm trying to save that boy from a childhood of loneliness and unhappiness. What are you trying to do? It sure as hell isn't what's right for him!"

"He's a child," she snapped. "He'll be happy if I'm happy."

"Oh, really? Like he's happy you married Larry? In case you haven't noticed, he can't stand the man! And with good reason. He doesn't like children—including yours!"

"They just need time to adjust."

"It's been two years, Janice. When do you think they're going to adjust? How many more years do they need? Three years? Five? Or maybe Larry will like him when he's eighteen and moves out of the house?"

"It's not that bad," she huffed. "Anyway, my husband is none of your business."

"He is when he makes my son miserable," he retorted. "I've been warning you for the last two years that you needed to talk to him, but you thought it would work itself out. It didn't, and now you want to take Quentin to Florida, where you'll have no one to leave him with but Larry when you're working? You can forget it," he said flatly. "It's not going to happen."

"The hell it isn't! Nothing's getting in the way of my moving to Florida or accepting this job, Tony. Nothing! So you can drop your pitiful little custody suit. You're just wasting your time and money."

Disgusted with her, Tony didn't know why her smug attitude surprised him. She'd been self-centered for as long as he'd known her. "It's all about you, isn't it, Janice? If you'd thought about your son instead of yourself, I wouldn't have had to file a lawsuit."

"You're just being spiteful," she said coldly. "You're still furious with me for divorcing you. This is just your way of paying me back."

Amazed, Tony couldn't believe she really thought he was that vindictive. This wasn't about either one of them, dammit. It was about Quentin. He just wanted what was best for him, and living a thousand miles away from his father with a man who made no secret of the fact that he didn't like him could irreparably harm his psyche. Why couldn't Janice see that?

Because she didn't want to, he thought in disgust. All she cared about was herself—everything always came back to that. He could talk until he was blue in the face, give her a hundred reasons why it was especially important for a child of divorce to be with people who loved him, but he'd be wasting his breath. He'd been married to the lady—he'd learned a long time ago that there was no point in arguing with her when she'd made up her mind about something.

"I'm not dropping the custody fight," he said flatly.

"You'll lose."

"I'd lose even more if I did nothing," he replied. "I have to protect my son."

Livid, she glared at him accusingly. "You act like I'm some kind of monster. I love Quentin, too. I would never do anything to hurt him."

"Oh, really?" he drawled, arching a dark eyebrow at her. "What do you think you did when you told him you were taking him away from his father and moving to Florida? Did he feel the love then, Janice? Did he feel the love when you told him that he'd be stuck spending his afternoons and evenings with Larry most of the time because you'd be working? You did tell him that part, didn't you, Janice?" he growled, knowing damn well she hadn't. "You told him that he had to be quiet so he wouldn't disturb Larry while he was writing one of those boring books he writes, didn't you? Tell the truth. You lied! You made it sound like he'd be going to Walt Disney World every day, and he still doesn't want to go. And you don't care!"

Hot color surged into her cheeks, and if looks could kill, he'd have dropped dead on the spot. She didn't, however, continue to berate him as he'd expected. Instead, she said coldly, "There's no use talking to you. You're totally unreasonable."

Outraged, he sputtered, "I'm unreasonable? You're the one turning your son's life upside down for a job!"

"This conversation is over, Tony. Where is he? I'm taking him home."

Frustrated, angry as hell, he growled, "He's upstairs working on his homework. I'll get him."

Stepping around her, he walked out of Angelo's office and headed upstairs, only to discover too late that she'd followed him. Swearing softly, he could have kicked himself for not anticipating this. He could see it now—she'd follow him right to Lily's door and jump to all sorts of conclusions about his relationship with her when she realized a woman friend of his was helping Quentin with his homework. And she wouldn't be shy about voicing her opinion. It wasn't going to be pretty.

He told himself he didn't owe her any explanations. They were divorced and his private life was none of her business. When Quentin was with him, he could leave his son in the care of anyone he felt was suitable. And Lily certainly fit that description—in the short time she'd known Quentin, she'd shown him more concern and caring than his own mother had in years.

Braced for the inevitable, he reached the upstairs landing and strode over to Lily's front door. Behind him, Janice stopped in confusion. "Where are you going? That's not your apartment."

"No, it's not," he said, and knocked on the door. "Lily?" he called through the door. "It's me. Quentin's mother is here to pick him up."

The door was pulled open almost immediately...by Quentin. His eyes bright with excitement, he cried, "Mom, Dad...look at this! Lily let me take some pictures with her camera, then showed me how to develop the film and print the pictures. It was so cool! Look!"

When he held the picture out to Janice, she hardly looked at it. "That's nice," she said shortly. "Where's your backpack? It's time to go home. Tell Miss...?"

"Fitzgerald," Tony replied. "Lily, this is my ex-wife, Janice." Noticing the way Quentin had wilted at his mother's indifference, he pulled him close for a hug and took the picture he still held. "Here, let me see that. You took this? And developed it and printed it? You've got to be kidding! This is great. We'll go tomorrow and get a frame for it. You can hang it in your bedroom."

"I'm picking Quentin up from school the rest of the week," Janice retorted. "I no longer need you to watch him for me. I'll make other arrangements. C'mon, Quentin."

Jerking up his backpack herself, she stormed out with Quentin following forlornly behind her. Looking over his shoulder, Quentin said glumly, "Bye, Lily. Bye, Dad."

"I'll call you tomorrow after school, son," Tony called after him. "If you need any help with your homework, you make sure you call me, okay?"

He nodded mutely, then disappeared down the stairs with his mother, leaving behind a silence that hummed with tension. His mouth compressed in an angry flat line, Tony said, "I'm sorry you got dragged into that. You shouldn't have had to witness that."

Shrugging off Janice's bad manners, Lily smiled slightly. "Don't worry about it. She was obviously having a bad hair day."

"Oh, it's more than that," he retorted. "She just found out that I'm suing her for full custody of Quentin, and she's furious."

"Oh! Well, that explains it. I thought she had a bee in her bonnet about something. Not that it's anything to joke about,'' she added quickly. ''I'm sure custody battles aren't easy for anyone.''

''I always wanted Quentin,'' he confided huskily, ''but I knew the odds of me getting full custody when we divorced were slim to none. Quentin was only six at the time, and Janice was a lawyer.'' Grimacing at the thought, he said, ''She could afford a court fight—on a cop's salary, I couldn't. And I didn't want to put Quentin through any more than he'd already been through with the divorce.''

''So what changed? She's still a lawyer, isn't she?''

He nodded. ''But Quentin's older, and Janice has accepted a new job in Florida. If I don't find a way to stop her, she's going to take my son a thousand miles away from me. Janice has no family there, no friends, no one except Larry, her husband, and he doesn't like Quentin. Who do you think Quentin's going to stay with after school when Janice is working late? Larry. And he can be a real jerk. I just can't let her do that to Quentin.''

''Of course not,'' she said sympathetically. ''He's such a good kid. For both your sakes, I hope you win.''

''Thanks. Janice isn't making it easy—you saw how she acted.'' Shaking his head over his ex-wife's behavior, he said, ''I was supposed to keep Quentin after school for the next few weeks, but now that's shot. I don't know why I'm surprised. She always did find a way to get back at anyone who stood in her way.''

He looked so miserable that Lily almost stepped forward to give him a hug. But she was still reeling from the kisses they'd shared last night. He'd made her forget her father and Neil and all the years she'd let them control her life, and for no other reason than that, she didn't dare touch him.

Still, she couldn't just let him walk away when he was

so worried about Quentin. ‘‘Why don’t you come in for a while?’’ she said. ‘‘You look exhausted. You’ve worked all day, haven’t you?’’

He grinned wryly. ‘‘Angelo needed the help and I need the money.’’

‘‘That’s why you started working for Angelo,’’ she said as the light dawned. ‘‘You needed the extra money for your legal fees.’’

‘‘I don’t care if it takes everything I’ve got,’’ he retorted. ‘‘I can’t let her take Quentin away from me without fighting for him with everything I’ve got.’’

Touched, Lily had to hug him then. Stepping forward into his arms, she gave him a fierce hug. ‘‘You’re doing the right thing, Tony. Regardless of what happens, Quentin knows you love him and you did everything you could.’’

‘‘I know,’’ he said gruffly, burying his face against her neck. ‘‘But I can’t lose him.’’

Her heart beating in time with his, loving the feel of his breath against her neck, Lily could have stood just as she was for the rest of the night and never cared if it was right or wrong. He needed her and nothing else mattered. ‘‘You’ve got to be exhausted,’’ she said. ‘‘Have you eaten? I’ve got some clam chowder in the refrigerator I can heat up. Take a break and have dinner with me. Angelo doesn’t expect you to work yourself into the ground.’’

Groaning, he hugged her tighter. ‘‘Don’t tempt me.’’

Pressed tight against him, she laughed. ‘‘Is that what I’m doing?’’

‘‘You know damn well it is,’’ he said. ‘‘I’ve got to get back to work.’’

He told himself to release her, but he couldn’t. Not yet. When she was in his arms, she made it so damn easy to forget Janice and her threats to take Quentin away from him.

"Tony?"

Holding her so close, he could feel her start to shake with laughter and had to laugh. "I'm going. Give me a second."

One second led to another, then another, and it was nearly a minute later before he could bring himself to let her go. Drawing back, his arms still loosely locked around her, he smiled down into her eyes. "How about a rain check? My shift ends at nine—I could drop by then."

"That'll be perfect," she said. "I still have some work to do in the darkroom, so just make sure you knock really loud so I'll hear you. The door will be locked, of course. I don't want to take any chances after what happened the other night."

Tony frowned, concerned. "Has something happened you haven't told me about?"

"No, but he's still out there, Tony," she said grimly. "That call wasn't just a prank. I really believe this man, whoever he is, wants me dead."

He didn't want to agree with her, but he'd seen too much meanness in the world to be naive. "There are a lot of crazies out there, and nine times out of ten, the threats they make are just hot air. But there's always that one who crosses the line. I'm not trying to scare you, but—"

"*You* didn't. The minute I heard his voice on the phone, I knew he meant every word he said. And there's not a damn thing I can do about it except wait for him to make a move. Since I don't know who he is or why he would possibly want me dead, I don't know what direction he's going to come from next."

Wishing he could stay and talk and reassure her, Tony pulled her into a fierce hug. "Just stay close to home if you can. Angelo is always downstairs and I am, too, if I'm not on patrol. If you need help, one of us can be here in five seconds flat. All you have to do is scream."

Aching to sink into him, Lily reluctantly pulled back to grin up at him wryly. "Trust me, if there's a problem, I'll scream loud enough to wake the dead. The entire neighborhood will hear me. So go back to work. I'm perfectly safe."

She wasn't, of course—not from a man who was determined to go to any lengths to kill her—and they both knew it. But Tony, thankfully, didn't point out the obvious, and somehow if the words weren't said, she somehow felt safer.

"I'll see you later," he told her.

Closing her front door and locking it, Lily listened as his footsteps died away. He was coming back later, she thought as a slow smile curled the edges of her mouth. Deep inside, a tiny voice questioned her sanity. What was she doing? This time, Quentin wouldn't be here to act as chaperon. Did she really want to go there?

She should have said no. It would have been the smart thing to do. She had no defenses where he was concerned. When he'd come to her rescue after that awful threatening phone call the other night, then spent hours talking to her on the phone just so she'd feel safe, everything had changed. No one had ever done anything like that for her before. And all the time, his own life was in crisis, and he'd never said a word.

This was her time to help him. He could talk about his ex if he wanted, unwind, and maybe for a little while forget that he could lose Quentin. Not that he'd ever really be able to forget that he could lose his son, she thought, sadness squeezing her heart. How did he stand it? she wondered. How did he even bear the thought of Quentin living so far away from him? He was such a good kid, and he and Tony were so close.

If Tony lost the custody battle and Quentin was forced to make the move to Florida with his mother, it would devastate them both. Surely the woman had to know that—anyone with eyes could see that Tony and Quentin were crazy about each other. How could she be so unsympathetic? She might hate her ex-husband's guts, but Quentin was her son, for heaven's sake. How could she not see—or care—what this was doing to him?

Mystified by that, Lily could only shake her head. Poor Tony. It had to be hell for him, knowing he had to depend on the legal system to keep his son in the same city with him when his ex-wife had the advantage of being part of that same legal system. Considering the circumstances, he had to be worried sick.

He was lucky he had two jobs, she thought as she headed for the kitchen. He didn't have much time to think. Of course, coming home to an empty apartment after a run-in with his ex wouldn't be easy for him. Maybe she'd make some cookies…and stay up half the night talking to him, she thought with a smile. It wouldn't solve his problems with the witchy Janice, but hopefully, she could make him forget her for a while.

Smiling at the thought, she quickly began assembling the ingredients for cookies and completely lost track of time. Two hours later, she'd just taken the last batch from the oven and started cleaning up her mess when there was a loud knock at the door. Startled, Lily felt her heart jump into her throat. Just that easily, she was sick with fear.

"Lily? Are you still in the darkroom? It's Tony."

Relief left her weak at the knees. *Idiot!* she chided herself. She'd been so caught up in her cookie making that she'd completely forgotten that she'd told Tony to knock as loud as he could so she'd hear him in the darkroom.

"I'm coming!" she called shakily, hurrying to the front door to throw open the dead bolt. "Sorry about that. I was in the kitchen."

"Hey, I smell cookies," he said with a grin as he stepped through the door. "Chocolate chip! All right! How did you know that was my—what's wrong? You're pale as a ghost."

"It's nothing. Really," she insisted, forcing a smile. "Your knock just scared me. I was doing the dishes and I forgot I'd told you to knock extra loud..."

"And you thought it was your caller," he finished for her.

She nodded miserably. "I hate this! I'm not normally a scaredy-cat, but now I jump like a scared rabbit every time I hear a noise. It's ridiculous!"

"Don't be so hard on yourself," he chided. "So what if you're a little jumpy? You'd have to have ice water in your veins not to be. Somebody's trying to kill you." When she winced, he swore softly. "Sorry about that. You're trying to forget it and here I am blasting you with it. Shall we start over?"

Her lips twitched. "Please."

"Chocolate chip cookies!" he exclaimed again, this time in pretended surprise. "Wow! For me? Where's the milk?"

Giggling, Lily pulled a half gallon of milk from the refrigerator. "Right here."

She poured them each a glass of milk, took a seat at the kitchen table, and grinned when he took a seat across from her and grabbed a handful of cookies. "Don't be shy, Tony. Have a cookie."

His green eyes dancing with wicked laughter, he popped one into his mouth. Almost immediately, he groaned. "Damn! These are incredible. This isn't a mix."

He sounded so shocked that Lily had to laugh. "Bite your tongue. I *can* cook, you know."

"No, I didn't know. The only woman I know who knows the difference between baking powder and baking soda is my aunt Tootsie."

"Then you obviously aren't hanging around the right women," she said. "Don't let me get in your way. Have another cookie."

He had five, in fact, and soon had Lily in stitches as he told her about the time he tried to make cookies and discovered for himself just what the difference was between baking powder and baking soda.

"Stop!" she laughed. "You're making that up! I never heard of cookies blowing up in the oven."

"That just goes to show what you know. You just didn't put the right ingredients together."

"Obviously," she said. "That's because *I* know how to cook."

"Hey, you won't get any argument out of me," he said with a grin as he reached for another cookie. "These are fantastic."

She grinned. "Thank you. I guess this is when I should confess that I burned the first batch. Every oven's different, and I hadn't used this one before."

"Aha! The truth comes out!"

Her eyes twinkling, she smiled. "You have to crack a few eggs to make an omelette. Why do I have the feeling that you've cracked more than your share of eggs in your time?"

"Oh, more than a few," he agreed. "Like that time when I was fourteen and I decided to egg my English teacher's new car."

"You didn't!"

"She threw my six-weeks exam in the trash because I didn't put my name on the right line," he said indignantly.

"Ouch. So what happened? Did you do it?"

"Some other students beat me to it. Apparently, I wasn't the only one she gave a zero to."

"So that was it? You just put the eggs back in the refrigerator and forgot it? After all that planning? What kind of juvenile delinquent is that?"

"What's the fun of throwing good eggs after bad?" he retorted, grinning.

Tony watched her laugh and was completely captivated. He'd never met another woman like her. She looked into his eyes, smiled, and the rest of the world just faded away. He could have talked to her for hours and never thought to glance at his watch.

Emotions he didn't want to name tugging at his heart, he should have come up with some kind of excuse and made a hasty retreat, but he couldn't bring himself to leave. They talked about everything from their favorite movies to sports to their families, and suddenly it was midnight.

"This is all your fault," he told her with a teasing grin as she walked with him to her front door. "You're supposed to throw me out of here at a reasonable hour."

"Me?" she choked out. "How do you come up with that? You're a guest in my home!"

"So? We're friends, aren't we? And you can tell a friend anything, can't you? Especially when they don't have the sense to look at the clock? What's the matter with you, girl?''

''Obviously I lost my head. Go home, Tony. It's late.''

''It's about time you noticed. Of course, I can understand why you would be distracted,'' he added, his green eyes twinkling with wicked teasing. ''You're smitten, aren't you? Go ahead, you can admit it. I saw the way you were looking at me. You couldn't take your eyes off me all evening.''

If he hadn't been so outrageous, Lily would have probably been horribly embarrassed. Because it was true! She was smitten, but she had no intention of admitting it, at least not in a way he would believe. ''You're right,'' she retorted. ''You caught me red-handed. I'm guilty as charged. But I couldn't help myself. You just swept me off my feet and I lost my head.'' Placing her hand over her heart, she gave him a wide-eyed innocent look that was completely ruined by the smile that kept curling her lips. ''It doesn't matter what I tell my heart,'' she confided. ''Every time I see you, it goes…*thump, thump. Thump, thump.* I just can't control it.''

No one had ever given him a taste of his own teasing as well as she did. Delighted, Tony burst out laughing and snatched her into a bear hug. ''Damn, I like you! Where'd you get such a smart mouth?''

''I don't know,'' she chuckled. ''You just seem to bring out the worst in me.''

His arms snug around her, holding her close, Tony knew he should have released her, but she felt too good in his arms. The minute he touched her, he knew he wasn't going to be able to let her go. Not yet.

His smile fading, he rasped, ''Do you have any idea how much I like holding you like this? When we went to dinner the other night, all I could think about was reaching for you and kissing you. That's why I sent Quentin downstairs to talk to Angelo. I just couldn't leave without kissing you good-night.''

''I'm glad you came back,'' she whispered, sliding her arms around his neck. ''I wanted to kiss you, too.''

His gaze dropped to the sweet, sensuous curve of her mouth and he felt his body temperature rise ten degrees. ''You're driving me crazy,'' he said hoarsely. ''You know that, don't you?''

A slow smile flirted with the edges of her mouth. ''So why don't you do something about it?''

She couldn't believe her own daring, but she wanted him to kiss her so badly, she ached. And he felt the same way—she could see it in his eyes. His gaze never leaving hers, he slowly leaned down and brushed her mouth with his, barely rubbing her lips. He was so gentle, Lily could have cried with the wonder of it.

Teasing her, seducing her, he did it again, then again, the touch of his mouth featherlight. Her body already starting to hum, she melted into him, her eyes closing on a sigh of pleasure as his mouth finally, completely, settled over hers.

Her blood heated, her mind blurred, and every bone in her body dissolved. In a saner moment, she could have come up with a dozen reasons why she had no business being within touching distance—let alone kissing distance!—of Tony or any other man, but she couldn't think of a single one now. And she didn't care. With a murmur that was his name, she crowded closer and loved the feel of him against her. More, she thought dreamily. She wanted more.

What could it hurt?

Lost in the taste and scent and heat of her, Tony told himself he had to stop this madness now, while he still could. But he couldn't remember the last woman who'd knocked him out of his shoes so completely, so easily. Did she have any idea what she did to him when she slid her arms around his neck and pulled him close against her? He just wanted to sweep her up in his arms, carry her off to bed and spend what was left of the night making love to her.

But even at the thought, alarm bells clanged in his head. Swallowing a groan, he knew he couldn't afford to take the risk. Not with her. She was the kind of woman a man didn't walk away from easily, the kind a man gave his heart to if he ever made the mistake of making love to her. He couldn't let himself do that. Not now. Not when the only thing that mattered to him was winning custody of his son.

''I have to go,'' he rasped, pulling back abruptly and gently setting her from him. ''Thanks for the cookies.''

He kissed her again, then a split second later, he was gone, quietly shutting the door behind him. Dazed, her heart pounding a thousand beats a second, Lily instinctively reached for the dead bolt and turned it, but she hardly noticed when it clicked into place. All she could think about was Tony...and how much she wanted him.

She dreamed of him all night long and woke up feeling as if she were floating on air. Outside, thick, low-lying clouds were dripping with moisture, but Lily had never seen a more perfect day. Wishing she'd thought to ask Tony last night if he would like to meet her for breakfast this morning, she almost called him, only to think better of it. Just because he'd kissed her like there was no tomorrow didn't mean that he wanted to spend all his free time with her, she reminded herself. It wasn't as if they were dating...well, not exactly, anyway. And even if having dinner with him and Quentin could be classified as a date, they'd made no future plans. If they happened to meet by chance, though…

Grinning at the thought, she quickly changed into jeans and a lime-green T-shirt and pulled on tennis shoes. When she checked her image in the mirror, she couldn't stop smiling. When was the last time she'd been this happy? She couldn't remember. She told herself it had nothing to do with Tony, then looked herself right in the eye in her dresser mirror and had to laugh. Liar! Okay, so maybe her current mood did have more than a little to do with him. There wasn't anything wrong with that. He made her laugh. And when he kissed her… Her heart pounding, she smiled at the memory.

That's when she first smelled the smoke.

Surprised, she frowned. Something was definitely burning. Was Angelo having some kind of problem in the restaurant kitchen? Maybe she should call downstairs and make sure everything was okay.

She started to reach for the phone on the nightstand next to her bed and gasped in horror. Smoke was pouring out of the air-conditioning vent over her bed.

"What the—"

Alarmed, she rushed into the living room, only to discover that the room was already thick with smoke. With her next breath, it filled her lungs, choking her. Coughing, her lungs burning and her eyes streaming with hot tears, she turned blindly toward the front door. She had to get out. Now!

Sobbing, she ran into a chair and nearly fell. This couldn't be happening! she thought as she caught herself and stumbled toward the door. Was the building on fire? Where were Tony and Angelo? She had to find them, then call 911.

Her mind jumbled, her thoughts hardly coherent, she finally found the door and cried in relief. Thank God! Thank God! Was Tony still in his apartment? Did he even know there was a fire? Please, please, let him be safe, she prayed, and quickly threw the dead bolt.

Later, she never remembered reaching for the doorknob. She turned it and tugged, but the door didn't budge. "N-no!" she choked out. "Dammit, why is it stuck? It has to open!"

She might as well have asked the Statue of Liberty to step down from its granite base and walk. Crying, struggling for breath, she tugged and pulled and cursed, and the door never budged.

That's when it hit her. She was going to die.

"Help!" she cried hoarsely, banging on the door. "Somebody help me!"

Her only answer was silence.

Terrified, she whirled and stumbled toward the window, never even noticing when she slammed into the coffee table, then a wing chair. Sobbing, every breath she took burning like fire in her lungs, she finally reached the living room's double windows, but the air in her lungs suddenly just seemed to give out. She couldn't think, couldn't breathe. Her vision blurred, but still she tried to open the window. A split second later, everything went black.

How could he have forgotten his wallet? Tony thought as he braked to a stop in front of his apartment and turned off the ignition of his patrol car. Maybe if he got his head on straight and thought about what he was doing instead of constantly daydreaming about kissing Lily, he might be able to get through the day without making a complete fool of himself. But then again, who could blame him? he thought with a grin. She was incredible.

Rushing up the stairs, he played with the idea of stopping by her place for a few minutes. Just to say good morning, he told himself with a grin. And maybe kiss her again.

Then he saw the smoke pouring out from under Lily's front door.

"Lily!" His hoarse cry echoing through the upstairs hallway, he ran the rest of the way to her apartment and tried the door. It was unlocked, but it wouldn't open. Confused, he stepped back and examined it, and only then saw someone had screwed the door shut with three screws.

Horrified, he bit out a curse and wanted to believe that Lily wasn't locked inside. But why else would the bastard who did this have screwed her door shut? He was trying to kill her and doing a damn good job of it.

"No!" he roared, and threw his weight against the door, slamming his shoulder into it. Through the pain in his shoulder, he felt the door give slightly, and that was all the encouragement he needed. He threw himself against it again and again, until the screws finally gave and the door flew open. Before he could drag in a bracing breath, smoke engulfed him.

"Lily? Where are you, honey? Dammit, answer me, sweetheart! I know you're here."

His eyes burning, he dragged his handkerchief out of his pocket and pressed it over his nose and mouth, then pushed through the smoke to Lily's bedroom. There was no sign of her anywhere.

He liked to think that he kept his head in any crisis—his job demanded it—but at that moment, he knew true panic. Running out of her room, he looked wildly around, trying to see through the thick smoke, but the apartment appeared to be deserted. Then he saw her lying on the floor by the living-room window. His heart stopped dead in his chest.

Later, he never remembered calling for his uncle, but he must have. Suddenly, Angelo was there, helping him get Lily outside as a fire truck pulled up and an ambulance wailed in the distance. Before Tony could do much more than lie her on the sidewalk out front, the ambulance pulled up beside them and the EMTs jumped out to take over. They worked over her frantically, but even as they loaded her into the ambulance long minutes later and roared off to the hospital, Lily never once opened her eyes.

Chapter 10

Her dreams haunted by a man who hid behind a wall of thick smoke, Lily shifted restless in bed, whimpering. Somewhere in the back of her mind, a voice gently told her to open her eyes—there was nothing to be afraid of—but fear gripped her by the heart and she couldn't. She had to run; he was after her! Even though she couldn't see him, she knew he was there, just beyond the smoke. She could feel him, feel the hatred that emanated from him in icy waves. Any second now, he was going to grab her and kill her, and no one would ever know why.

A sob rising in her throat, she wanted to scream, "*No!,*" but her throat felt as if someone had stuck a knife in it, and she couldn't do anything but moan. Help! she cried silently. Someone help me!

"It's okay, Lily. You're safe, sweetheart. Please don't cry. No one's going to hurt you. I promise."

In the darkness of her dream, she heard Tony call to her from what seemed like a long way away. How could she be safe, she wanted to cry, when she was lost and he couldn't find her? Didn't he know there was someone else there who was waiting for the chance to choke the life out of her when no one else was around? Couldn't he feel the other man's fury in the fog that made it difficult to breathe? He was in danger, too. She had to warn him!

"Tony? You have to run!" she murmured hoarsely, tossing restlessly on the bed. "He'll kill you, too."

From out of the darkness, his hand closed over hers, squeezing reassuringly. "No one's going to kill either one of us," he said huskily. "Open your eyes, sweetheart. There's a guard at the door who's going to make sure no one gets in who doesn't belong here. We're both fine."

Surprised by his closeness, she jerked awake, forcing open her heavy eyelids to find him standing next to her hospital bed, holding her hand and smiling down at her reassuringly. Confused, she frowned. "What happened? How..." Her memory suddenly came rushing back like a tidal wave and she gasped in horror. "Oh, my God, there was a fire!"

"There were some rags in the attic of your apartment that caught on fire," he said. "They were just smoldering when the fire department discovered them after you were taken to the hospital."

Her hand still in his, she stared up at him searchingly. "Rags? What do you mean...there were rags in the attic? How did they get there?"

His expression grim, he said, "Unfortunately, we don't have the answer to that yet. The fire department is investigating."

"How did they catch fire? Was there some kind of electrical short?"

"Not that the anyone could tell."

"What about Angelo?" she croaked. "He's okay, isn't he? Please tell me no one died—"

"He's fine," he assured her. "He's been worried to death about you, but the fire was contained in your attic. Angelo was downstairs in the restaurant when I found you. He didn't even know there was a fire."

"Thank God!" Sighing in relief, she relaxed back against her pillow, only to bolt straight up in bed, her eyes wide with terror. "My door was jammed!" she cried, suddenly remembering. "I couldn't get out!" Tears spilling over her lashes, she reached for him. "Oh, God, Tony, I thought I was going to die!"

Tony folded her close, his heart aching for her. Given the chance, he would have done anything to erase the horror from her eyes. He hadn't been on the other side of that door with her, but he'd been in the hallway, trying to get in, imagining her trying to get out, and it had been hell. If he lived to be a hundred, he'd never forget the moment when he realized the bastard had screwed her door shut. What if he hadn't forgotten his wallet? he thought. He would have never had to come back for it, and no one would have realized she was in trouble until it was too late. Trapped in her apartment, she would have lain there and died of smoke inhalation.

Just the thought of that shook him to the core.

Something had happened between them over the course of the last few nights. When he'd held her and kissed her, she'd knocked him out of his shoes, and nearly twenty-four hours later, he was still reeling from it. She was no longer just a woman to flirt with and tease, no longer just a friend, though he wasn't ready to ask himself yet where or how she fit into his life. He just knew one thing—he needed time. Time to get to know her better. Time to kiss her again and make love to her and learn everything there was to know about her. Then if she walked away or he did, fine. But he couldn't lose her to death…and certainly not to the monster who was trying his best to murder her.

Fury burned in his gut just at the thought of the bastard who'd done this to her. The day would come, Tony promised himself, when he'd make him wish he'd never been born. In the meantime, Lily had to know that the fire this morning had been no accident. He hated to tell her when she was still so weak, but he really had no choice. She was in danger.

His hand tightening gently around her fingers, he said huskily, "There's something you need to know, sweetheart. The reason you couldn't get the door open was because it was screwed shut. The fire was deliberately set."

She was already as white as the sheets of her hospital bed. With his words, what little color there was left in her face drained away. "What?"

"We don't know the specifics," he admitted. "I left early for work, and Angelo was in his office by a quarter to eight, doing some paperwork. The bastard must have found a way into the building after that."

Her eyes as big as saucers in her pale face, she shrank back into her pillow as if he was the monster who wanted her dead. "No!"

His fingers tightened around hers. "I had to break in the door to get to you, sweetheart. You'd already passed out trying to get out through the living-room window."

Her blood roaring in her ears, Lily felt as if she was going to throw up. Her tormentor couldn't have gotten so close to her without anyone seeing him. Tony had to be mistaken.

But who else would screw her door shut, then start a fire?

Starting to shake, she hugged herself, but it didn't do any good. She was cold all the way to her bones. "It has to be *him,* doesn't it?" she said hollowly. "He's found another way to get to me. And this time, he almost succeeded."

He nodded grimly. "Whoever he is, he's damn clever. He didn't leave any prints, and all the materials he used to start the fire were common things that could be bought at any home-improvement store. Nothing, unfortunately, can be traced."

"How did he get into the upstairs hallway? The stairwell doors are always locked."

"Apparently, he broke in through a fire escape in the roof. No one saw or heard anything. Do you remember what time you woke up this morning?"

"It was fairly early," she said, frowning. "Seven-thirty or eight. I took a shower, then dried my hair. I remember it was misty, but the sun was breaking out."

"Did you hear anything unusual? Or happen to look out the window and see anyone hanging around outside that didn't belong there?"

Her lungs hurting, her throat sore from the smoke that she'd inhaled, she could only shake her head miserably. "No, nothing. I didn't know anything was wrong until I saw the smoke and tried to open the door to the hall. When it was stuck, I ran to the window, but the smoke was getting to me then. I must have passed out."

Just thinking about what could have happened if Tony hadn't found her terrified her. "He's getting closer, Tony," she said quietly. "You know that, don't you? Next time, you might not be around to rescue me."

"There isn't going to be a next time," he growled.

"We're going to catch this guy—you have to believe that."

Lily wanted to believe it, but how could she? She knew Tony would do everything he could to protect her, but how much could he really do? A maniac had nearly killed her in her own apartment, and no one had seen a thing. And Tony, one of D.C.'s finest, lived right across the hall from her! How could he or the police department protect her from someone who was so damn bold? Obviously, the monster would try anything.

"How can you catch him when you don't have a clue who he is? Who hates me that much? It's not Neil—"

"Or your ex-boss or your father," he added for her. "We checked them all out, and they were all clean."

"You talked to my father?"

He nodded. "We had to eliminate all possible suspects."

"What did he say?"

"That he wasn't the kind of man that would kill anyone, let alone his own daughter."

Kenneth Fitzgerald had said a few other choice things, the majority of which were cold and unfeeling, but Tony had no intention of repeating them to Lily. Her father had been cleared as a suspect, mainly due to the fact that he'd cooperated fully, lived halfway across the country, and had no suspicious contacts or phone calls that could connect him to the attacks. That didn't mean, however, that Tony had to like him. The concern the older man had expressed for Lily had been stiff and grudging, and though Tony didn't doubt that he loved his daughter, the man's pride wouldn't let him show it.

Idiot! Tony thought silently. Didn't the old man realize he could lose her in a heartbeat? How could he not be speaking to her, especially now that he knew the circumstances? Somehow, though, Kenneth Fitzgerald had found a way to justify his actions and seemed to feel quite proud of himself. Let him enjoy his pettiness, Tony thought grimly. He'd already hurt Lily once; Tony wasn't going to help him do it again by repeating what he'd said about her.

Not that it mattered. He could tell she knew that her father realized she was in danger—and he still hadn't called to check on her. Tears glistened in her eyes, but she didn't give in to them. Blinking them back, she raised her chin and said stiffly, "I told you he wouldn't do anything like this. He's washed his hands of me, and so has Neil. That just leaves my old boss, Meredith, and she's the last person I know who would do something like this. Anyway, that threatening phone call I got was from a man. So that takes us back to square one. Whoever this guy is, he hates my guts, and I don't have a clue why. Neither, apparently, do the police. So where do we go from here? How do you catch someone who leaves no clues, no motive? We don't even know what he looks like."

"He's going to make a mistake," he assured her. "It's just a matter of time. When he does, we'll be there to catch him."

"Before or after I'm dead?"

Tony winced. "I can understand why you're frightened, sweetheart, but I promise I'm not going to let anything happen to you. I've already made arrangements for a uniformed officer to be outside your room round the clock—"

"You're leaving?"

"I have to for now," he said. "But there's nothing for you to be afraid of. Your guard's not going to leave your side—or let anyone near you who doesn't have a right to come in this room. He's already met your doctors and the nurses who'll be taking care of you, and I'll be back before there's a shift change. You're safer than you would be in your own home. Okay?''

For a moment, he didn't think she was going to let him go, and that tore at his heartstrings as nothing else could. Then she nodded reluctantly. ''I'd feel better if I just knew who to be afraid of. You said yourself that whoever's trying to kill me is damn clever. He could disguise himself as an orderly or a nurse and no one would blink twice.''

''I've already spoken to your doctor about that,'' he assured her. ''Only a limited number of staff is allowed in here and, like I said, your guard's met them all. Trust me, sweetheart. You're safe. Not even a Hummer could get in this room with Jimmy Bishop at the door. Let me introduce you to him.''

Giving her hand a reassuring squeeze, he stepped out into the hall and returned a few seconds later with a uniformed police officer who looked as big as a house. Six foot five if he was an inch, he must have easily weighed two hundred and fifty pounds. There wasn't, however, an ounce of fat on him. All muscle, he towered over her bed and would, no doubt, be as intimidating as hell when he was in a temper.

But then he smiled and held out a massive hand to her, and he looked like a big teddy bear. ''It's nice to meet you, Lily,'' he said in a voice that rumbled. ''I'm Jimmy Bishop. I'm going to be here all day, protecting you, so don't worry about anyone hurting you. It's not going to happen.''

Lily didn't doubt him for a second. Taking his hand,

which completely engulfed hers, she smiled. ‘‘Thank you, Jimmy. I feel a lot better knowing you’re right outside the door.’’

‘‘If you need me for anything, just holler,’’ he told her. ‘‘I’ll come running.’’

Returning to his post, he slipped outside into the hallway and quietly shut the door behind him. With a single step, Tony reached her bedside and took her hand again. ‘‘Better?’’ he asked.

She nodded. ‘‘I’m sorry to be such a baby.’’

‘‘Don’t,’’ he cut in. ‘‘You have every right to be scared. Just remember…you’re not alone. I have to go to work, but I’ll be back. So you rest and just take it easy, and I’ll see you later. Okay?’’

She forced a smile that didn’t quite reach her eyes. ‘‘Okay,’’ she said huskily, but when he stepped back, she couldn’t bring herself to let him go. With a will of their own, her fingers curled tighter around his.

He should have squeezed her fingers reassuringly, then gone to work, as he needed to. But leaving her was turning out to be a hell of a lot harder than he’d thought it would be. He told himself it was because he couldn’t shake the image of her lying unconscious on her living room floor when he’d found her, but it was more than that. It was Lily herself, the softness of her skin and mouth, the scent of her, the feel of her against him…

Swallowing a groan, he ordered himself to quit torturing himself and just leave. ‘‘I’ve got to go,’’ he told her again, but instead of turning toward the door, he leaned down and gave in to the temptation to kiss her.

It was a mistake, of course. The second his lips touched hers, everything he’d felt last night came rushing back, and all he wanted was more. Tearing himself away, he rasped, "I'll see you later." Before he could change his mind, he hurried out of her room without a backward glance.

Carrying a large fall floral arrangement, Sly Jackson exited the elevator on the hospital's third floor and nodded politely at the orderly who passed him in the hall. When the other man only returned his nod and kept on walking, Sly almost laughed aloud. Yes! He'd stolen a cap advertising the florist out of a truck parked in front of the flower shop where he'd bought the flowers, and the chance he'd taken was well worth it. Clothes made the man, and anyone who happened to see him strolling the hospital halls wouldn't question his right to be there—after all, he was delivering flowers.

It was the perfect disguise, he thought in satisfaction. In all likelihood, no one would even notice what he looked like—the first thing everyone looked at was the flowers. If everything worked out the way he'd planned, he could waltz right into Miss Candid Camera's room, kill her, and no one would even remember that he'd been there.

Bitch. He still didn't know how she'd managed to escape with her life this morning. He'd planned it right down to the last detail. He'd watched the cop leave for work and had waited for the old man to go down and open up his restaurant, all before the irritating Lily showed any signs of stirring, let alone leaving her apartment. Seeing his chance, he'd slipped around behind her building and climbed the fire escape to the roof.

Trapping her in her own apartment had been the easiest thing he'd ever done. All he'd had to do was quietly screw the door shut with the screwdriver and deck screws he'd hidden in his pocket. Then it was time to set the rags smoldering that would kill her.

Only they hadn't killed her.

Livid, he still couldn't believe it. He'd gone to work and had one of the best days he'd had in years. The economy had rallied, and investors were ready to jump back into the stock market. Sales had been brisk and he hadn't been able to stop smiling. Then on the local evening news, he'd seen the tape of a reporter standing on an all-too-familiar street in Georgetown, telling the world the miraculous story of Lily Fitzgerald, a local photographer, and how she'd just barely escaped dying from smoke inhalation from a fire in the attic of her apartment.

The cop had rescued her! Furious, Sly kept his pace slow and easy as he headed down the hall toward Lily's room. He'd get Officer Giovanni, he promised himself. But first, he intended to take care of Miss Candid Camera once and for all. She may have managed to evade death so far, but her luck had just run out.

This time, he'd planned the hit instead of going off half-cocked. He'd called the hospital earlier and gotten her room number from patient information, then waited for the next shift change. Right about now, the nursing staff would be at the nurses' station, updating their notes, checking meds, punching out and in as the shift changed. No one would be in the patients' rooms. All he had to do was act as if he belonged there and it would all be over in a matter of moments.

His heart pounding, he saw the nurses' station just ahead on his left. He strolled past without bothering to glance over at the busy station, and no one paid the least bit of attention to him. Pleased, he followed the signs that pointed out the room numbers and turned the next corner.

Already picturing the horror in Lily's eyes when she discovered that her murderer had tracked her down and this time she wasn't getting away, he didn't notice the man standing outside a room at the far end of the hall until he was three doors away. Then he saw the police uniform the man was wearing.

"Son of a bitch!"

Swearing under his breath, Sly quickly stepped into the nearest room, only to find it occupied by an old woman who was laid up in bed with a broken leg in a cast that was hung from a contraption at the end of the bed. Wide awake, she saw him almost immediately and frowned. "You must be in the wrong room."

"No, ma'am, I'm not," he growled, and set the vase of flowers at her bedside. "These are from your son."

"But I don't have a son!"

She might as well have saved her breath. Striding out, Sly turned down the hall, away from where the policeman stood, and never looked back. His face expressionless, he appeared perfectly in control of his emotions, but inside he was seething. Damn her! She wasn't going to get away with this. He didn't care how many cops she had protecting her, he'd find a way to get to her, and when he did, she was dead!

Wide awake in the darkness, Lily listened to the steady, squeaky tread of a nurse as she walked down the hallway. In the last hour, she'd made six trips down the hall and back again. Lily knew because she'd counted every trip. She didn't even try to go to sleep. There wasn't any point—she was too scared.

True to his word, Tony had come back, as he'd promised, but only to introduce her to Vince, her guard for the rest of the night. Disappointed, she tried to make Tony understand that she couldn't stay there—she felt too vulnerable, even with a guard—but he couldn't take her home until the doctor released her. Stuck, there was nothing she could do but wait.

The doctor had left a sedative for her if she needed it, but she wouldn't even consider taking the medication. Just the thought of being drugged when her tormentor walked in to kill her horrified her—she wouldn't stand a chance. So she sat up in her bed and listened to the sounds of the hospital at night. And every time someone even came close to her room, she froze, half expecting to hear a gunshot in the hall as the killer took care of her guard.

Thankfully, there were no gunshots, or for that matter, any unusual sounds, period. The night passed peacefully, but she still wouldn't allow herself to sleep. When there was a shift change again at seven in the morning, she was exhausted, but still wide awake. Activity picked up in the hall outside her door, and the new day began. She should have been able to relax then—there were more people around and chances were that the maniac who wanted her dead wouldn't be able to make a move against her without someone in the hospital seeing him. Still, she couldn't sleep. Her heart pounding and her eyes on the door, she just sat there in bed, waiting.

It was barely eight in the morning when her doctor, Aaron Thomas, walked in, looking fresh and alert and a heck of a lot more rested than she. He took one look at her and started to frown. "I was going to say good morning, but it's obviously not for you. Did you sleep at all?"

She didn't even consider lying to him. What was the point? He'd already guessed. "I have a lot on my mind," she said with a shrug.

"You were afraid," he said flatly as he stepped over to her bed to listen to her lungs. "It's perfectly normal, Lily. A maniac tried to kill you. You wouldn't be normal if you weren't scared." Checking her eyes, pulse and blood pressure, he unwrapped the blood pressure cuff and frowned down at her. "So other than being exhausted, how do you feel? Is your throat feeling better? What about your head? Any headaches or any other aches and pains?"

"My throat's still a little sore," she admitted in a raspy voice, "but it's better than it was last night. Other than that, I'm fine."

"And what about your lungs? Are you having any trouble breathing?"

"Not now. I was coughing some last night, but I haven't had any problems since about midnight."

Studying her with shrewd eyes, he smiled and patted her hand. "Then I don't see any reason why you can't go home later today."

Startled, horrified, she cried, "Home? I can't go home!"

"But—"

"No! You don't understand. I live alone and the man who tried to kill me knows where I live. He'll try again, and next time, he might succeed!"

"Maybe you could go stay with a relative for a while," Dr. Thomas suggested. "Or a friend…"

"And put them in danger, too? I couldn't. Anyway, I don't have any family in the area, and I wouldn't feel comfortable imposing on my friends."

"You can stay with me," Tony said quietly from the doorway. "I have a spare bedroom, so there's plenty of room." Stepping farther into the room, he held out his hand to the doctor. "It's nice to see you again, Dr. Thomas. When can I take her home?"

"Later this afternoon," he replied with a smile. "I'll notify her nurse and get the ball rolling."

He was gone before Lily could stop him, leaving her sputtering in frustration. "Dammit, Tony, this is never going to work," she told him with a frown. "Whoever set that fire yesterday knows where I live. Obviously, he's been watching the place, since he timed the fire yesterday when you and Angelo were both out of your apartments. What good will it do to stay at your place when he's going to know I'm there? Instead of setting my apartment on fire, he'll burn down yours!"

"Not necessarily," he replied. "First of all, you won't be alone—"

"Of course I will. You have to work."

"I'm on vacation. I have a week off from the force, starting today."

"But what about Angelo? You still have to work at the restaurant, don't you? You need the money for your legal fees. I can't interfere with that."

"You won't be," he assured her. "You're still working on the mural for Angelo, aren't you? While I'm working, you can take pictures of the customers or study for your classes or just take some time off and relax on the patio or visit with Angelo in the kitchen. Whatever you decide to do, I promise you won't be alone."

Hesitating, she wanted to say yes more than she had ever wanted anything in her life, even a career in photography. And that shook her to the core. When had spending time with him become so important to her? When had *he* become so important to her?

Shaken, she didn't have an answer to either question. Considering that, she should have thanked him for his offer and made immediate plans to leave town before she found herself involved with him in a way she would have sworn just weeks ago that she didn't want. But it was too late for that. She refused to question why, but she couldn't leave. Not now. Not when he was all she could think about.

She could hardly tell him that, however. Instead, she said huskily, ''You have your own problems. You don't need another. I don't want to take advantage.''

''I appreciate that, but how could you be taking advantage? I'm going to be at the restaurant, anyway. You might as well be there, too. And I do have an extra bedroom. You're welcome to use it. This way, you can have twenty-four-hour police protection for the next week. I know a week's not very long, but I want you to feel safe. I don't know any other way to do it until this bastard is caught.''

Just that easily, he touched her heart. Her eyes searching his, she said, ''Are you sure? I don't want to impose.''

''I'm sure,'' he laughed. ''Enough already. Now that that's settled, let's have breakfast. As soon as we get the green light from the powers that be later this afternoon, we're out of here. Okay?''

When he smiled at her with a twinkle in his eyes, she couldn't refuse him anything. ''Okay,'' she said softly.

Ten hours later, Tony unlocked the door to his apartment, flipped on the lights in the living room and welcomed her inside. ''You can sleep in Quentin's room,'' he told her, showing her to a small bedroom that was decorated with sports wallpaper and pictures of Quentin's favorite athletes. ''I'm sorry the bed's so small—''

''It'll be fine,'' she assured him. ''After not sleeping last night, I'll probably crash the second my head hits the pillow.''

''Good. You need the sleep.'' Nodding toward the door halfway down the small hall, he said, ''The bathroom's the first door on the right. There are towels and shampoo in the closet, and if you get hungry, feel free to raid the refrigerator. You didn't have dinner. If you don't see anything you like—''

Smiling—she'd never seen him so nervous and she found that incredibly endearing—she stepped forward and stopped him with a kiss on the cheek. ''Thank you—for everything. I'm not really hungry, and I'm too tired to take a bath tonight, so I think I'll just go to bed.''

When she stepped back, she should have stepped into the bedroom and shut the door behind her. But then her eyes met his, and suddenly her heart was skipping every other beat and she just wanted to step into his arms. ''Tony…''

''It's been a long day,'' he said huskily. ''Go to bed, sweetheart. And I don't want you to worry about anything. You're perfectly safe. I'll be right down the hall, and I'm a light sleeper. If you so much as whisper for help, I'll hear you. Okay?''

''Okay,'' she said, and gave him a quick hug. A second later, she stepped into the bedroom and quietly shut the door.

Considering the pounding state of her heart, she would have sworn that she'd never be able to sleep. But the minute she stretched out in Quentin's twin bed, exhaustion hit her. A heartbeat later, she was asleep.

At three o'clock in the morning, she woke with a start, her heart slamming against her ribs like a jackhammer. Had she heard something? She couldn't be sure. Holding her breath for long seconds at a time, she listened, but the apartment was perfectly quiet.

Call Tony, a voice in her head whispered. *He told you to call him if you were scared. You're scared. Call him!*

She should have, but the longer she listened, the more

she was convinced she had nothing to be afraid of. Lying there for what seemed like an eternity, she finally accepted the fact that she wasn't going to be able to go back to sleep any time soon. Sighing quietly in the darkness, she rose to her feet and padded barefoot into the living room.

Tony had left the drapes open, but the apartment was totally dark, so she didn't have to worry about anyone seeing her. From outside, the pale glint of moonlight drew her to the windows and a view of the street. Not surprisingly, there wasn't a soul out at that time of the morning.

Hugging herself, she stared out at the dark shadows of the night created by the moonlight and shivered. The man who wanted her dead was out there somewhere in the dark, possibly watching, waiting, planning. He would strike again—she knew that as well as she knew her own name—though there was no way to predict when. She'd given up asking herself why. Madness needed no reason.

"Lily? Are you all right?"

Caught up in her musings, she nearly jumped out of her skin when Tony spoke in the darkness. Whirling, her hand flying to her throat, she gasped, "You startled me! I didn't hear you!"

His teeth flashed in the darkness. "Sorry about that. Are you okay? Why aren't you in bed? What's wrong?"

"Nothing. Really," she insisted. "I woke up and got to thinking about everything that's happened and I couldn't go back to sleep. Oh, please don't turn the light on," she said quickly when he stepped over to the lamp by the couch. "The drapes are open. Someone could be out there."

On silent feet, he joined her at the window. "Did you see something?"

Staring out at the night again, she searched the shadows across the street. ''No,'' she said quietly. ''But if someone's out there watching, I don't want him to know I'm awake.''

Tony couldn't even imagine what it was like for her, knowing there was a monster out there who was stalking her, patiently waiting for a chance to kill her, and she didn't even who he was or why he hated her so much. For all she knew, he could be a teller at her bank, a fellow student in one of her classes, someone who just lived down the street. No wonder she was terrified.

Slipping an arm around her shoulders, he pulled her gently against him until they stood hip to hip. ''You're safe, Lily. No one's going to hurt you as long as I'm around.''

Her gaze, like his, still trained on the dark, empty street below his apartment, she lay her head on his shoulder. ''I know,'' she said. ''I keep telling myself that, but it doesn't matter. I'm always on guard, waiting for the other shoe to drop. It's just so tiring.''

She was worn out and Tony couldn't believe she was still standing, considering how little sleep she'd had in the last thirty-six hours. He could feel the exhaustion in her. She didn't even have enough energy to stand on her own.

''You need to be in bed,'' he growled, and surprised them both when he swung her up in his arms.

''Tony! What are you doing?''

Cradling her as if she weighed no more than a feather, he asked himself the same thing. What the devil was he doing? They were alone together in his apartment in the middle of the night and he wanted her so badly, he physically ached. The only problem was, she was a guest in his home, dammit, and there because she needed his protection. He had no business touching her.

His eyes locking with hers in the darkness, he sternly ordered himself to set her down. He might as well have ordered himself to fly to the moon. How could he release her when she felt so right in his arms?

"I'm carrying you to bed," he said. "If that's okay with you."

When she hesitated, he thought she was going to say no. Then she looped her arms around his neck and looked him right in the eye. "That depends," she said quietly.

Surprised, he arched a dark eyebrow at her. "On what?"

"Whether you're taking me to my bed or yours."

Already heading toward the short hallway that led to the bedrooms, he stopped in his tracks. "You're exhausted. I should take you to yours."

All she had to do was agree with him and she knew he would carry her back to her bed, tuck her in, then he'd return alone to his own bed. And that was the last thing she wanted. Later, she knew she would have to deal with that, but for now, she didn't want to think about anything except the feelings he stirred in her with nothing more than his nearness.

"No," she said softly. "I don't want to go to sleep. I don't want to go to my room. I want to be with you." And just to make sure there was no misunderstanding, she lifted her mouth to his and kissed him hungrily.

Any worries that he might not want her as much as she did him died a swift death. With a groan, he kissed her back and strode quickly into his bedroom. Still kissing her, he brought her straight down to the bed with him and wrapped her close in his arms.

He kissed her again and again, and with every slow,

seductive kiss, with every tender touch of his hands as he caressed her as if he couldn't get enough of her, he made her forget…everything. He made her forget the smell of smoke in her lungs, the horror of realizing she was trapped in her own apartment and about to die, the terror of seeing a car bearing down on her as if she was a deer trapped in its headlights. And within a matter of minutes, he made her forget her own name.

Her breath tore through her lungs, the thunder of her heartbeat echoed in her ears. She wanted to tell him everything she was feeling, but words escaped her. All she could do was feel and it felt wonderful. *He* felt wonderful. With slow hands, he pulled her nightgown over her head, then shed his own clothes, and then they were skin to skin. Moaning, she moved against him, aching for more.

She didn't have to say a word—he knew. Every time she moved, every time he touched her, the fire that burned between them grew hotter. Outside, the night was cool, but inside the bedroom, the air was steaming. Tony never noticed. There was only Lily and the way she made him burn with every touch, every sigh, every pounding of her heart. When she took him into her, he felt as if he was coming home. She caught his rhythm, and just that easily, they were moving in time to a melody only they could hear. Then she trailed her fingers down his chest and stroked him in a way he'd never expected. Just that easily, he lost what was left of his control. Her name a groan that was ripped from the very heart of him, he buried himself in her and felt her come apart in his arms. With nothing more than that, she took him over the edge.

Chapter 11

The thunder of her heartbeat loud in her ears and her face buried in Tony's neck, Lily felt his arms tighten around her, cradling her close, and tried to figure out what had just happened. She wasn't falling in love with him, she told herself firmly. Love had nothing to do with what they'd just shared. After all, how long had she known him? A couple of weeks? A month, at the most? People didn't fall in love that quickly. They had to have time to get to know each other, to learn their likes and dislikes and what they had in common. And even then, what seemed like love wasn't always. Look at her and Neil.

She pushed thoughts of that time in her life away, but pushing away her doubts wasn't nearly as easy. True love took months to develop and grow. Anything that happened faster than that was just physical.

How many times had she told herself that in the past?

she wondered. So why was she having such a difficult time believing it? She didn't love Tony. She couldn't.

But even as conflicting emotions pulled at her heartstrings, she had to admit that there was something different about Tony. There was something different about the way he made her feel. She'd thought she knew what need and desire were, but no one had ever stirred the emotions in her that Tony had. And every time she saw him, touched him, kissed him, those emotions grew stronger and stronger.

Still, she told herself she could handle it. She had a career to think of, dreams she'd waited a lifetime to follow. Nothing was getting in the way of that. Not Tony, not these crazy, mixed-up feelings he ignited in her so easily, not love. Especially not love! All of her life, love had held her back and kept her from being the woman she'd always wanted to be. Ultimately, it had nearly cost her her dreams. Other people could fantasize about love and their soul mates—she wanted nothing to do with either one.

Satisfied that she finally had sorted out her priorities, she told herself that whatever emotions she did feel for Tony didn't have to ruin the time she had with him. They could enjoy each other without putting a label on things. Today—tonight—was all that mattered. Pleased, she released the breath she hadn't even realized she'd been holding and snuggled more comfortably in his arms. Within minutes, she was asleep.

Holding her close, Tony felt the exact moment she fell asleep. Her muscles relaxed, she sighed in contentment, and her breathing turned slow and deep against his neck. Sated, he should have closed his own eyes and gone to sleep, too, but his thoughts wouldn't let him.

He'd only loved one woman in his life, and that was

Janice. Even after they'd divorced, he would have found a way to forgive her for her betrayal of their marriage vows because he'd still loved her. She hadn't been interested in forgiveness, however—she'd already moved on with Larry. Devastated, he'd sworn then that he'd never put his heart on the line and let himself care for another woman.

Keeping that promise to himself hadn't been difficult. He had work and his son and that didn't leave much time for dating. He appreciated a beautiful woman just like the next man, but the rare times that he had dated, no woman had tempted him to do anything other than flirt. Until now.

He wanted to believe what he felt for Lily was just lust, but he couldn't be sure, and that had him worried. How could this be happening? he wondered, irritated with himself. He had a major court fight ahead of him for the custody of Quentin, and he couldn't afford to be distracted by a woman—any woman. He wouldn't lose his son.

Considering that, he should have been able to put his attraction for Lily in perspective. It was chemistry, lust, voodoo. Call it what you will, it certainly wasn't something that should have dominated his every waking—and sleeping—moment. But somehow it did, and honesty forced him to admit that not even Janice had tied him in knots the way Lily had. And as much as he hated to admit it, he knew in his heart that it wasn't just lust. He couldn't forget the fear he'd seen in her eyes when she'd first realized that the maniac who nearly ran her down in the park really was trying to kill her. He'd never felt so protective of a woman in his life. And she was still in danger.

Just thinking about the bastard who was terrorizing her

infuriated him. The guy's days as a free man were limited, Tony promised himself. He couldn't play this game forever—no one was that good. He'd get cocky, overplay his hand and make a mistake. And when he did, Tony planned to be on him so fast, he'd never know what hit him.

In the meantime, he couldn't worry about the future. There was only now...and Lily. Feeling her against him, drawing in the scent of her, he realized nothing else mattered. Tightening his arms around her, he held her close for the rest of the night.

The sun was high in the morning sky when Lily woke with a start. Disoriented, she glanced around the bedroom and saw nothing familiar except her nightgown, which lay across the foot of the bed. Then she remembered Tony...and last night...and started to smile.

Later, she couldn't say how long she lay there, daydreaming about last night, when she noticed how quiet the apartment was. Startled, she stiffened, listening to the silence that echoed in her ears. That's when she realized she was alone.

No! she thought, alarmed, her heart suddenly pounding wildly in her chest. Tony had to be there somewhere. He'd promised to protect her. He wouldn't just leave without waking her up to tell her where he was going.

Maybe he didn't leave voluntarily, a voice whispered in her head. *Maybe he was lured away, then knocked out from behind. The monster who's trying to kill you could be coming up the stairs right now and no one knows you're alone.*

''Oh, God!'' she whispered, horrified. ''I've got to get out of here!''

The taste of fear bitter on her tongue, she jumped up

and grabbed her nightgown and jerked it on. Her shoes! she thought wildly, glancing around frantically. Where were her shoes?

"Hey, sleepyhead, I brought you breakfast—" Stopping short in the bedroom doorway, a laden tray in his hands, Tony took one look at her ashen face and immediately set the tray on a nearby chest. "What is it?" he asked, alarmed. "What's wrong?"

Concern etching his forehead in deep lines, he eliminated the distance between them in two long strides. Mortified, Lily wanted to sink right through the floor. "I'm sorry," she said. "When I woke up and saw you weren't here, the apartment was so quiet, I thought I was alone."

"And you were afraid." Swearing softly, he pulled her into his arms. "I'm sorry, sweetheart. I was just in the kitchen. I thought I'd surprise you with breakfast in bed. It never entered my head that you might wake up and be scared."

"I'm just being paranoid," she choked out, wiping at the foolish tears that welled in her eyes and spilled over her lashes. "I'm sorry. I hate to be a crybaby. It's just that every time I think I'm doing okay, something like this happens and I turn into a basket case."

"Sweetheart, I'm amazed you're able to hold it together as well as you do. Of course you're scared. Who wouldn't be?"

"I hate it," she sniffed, pulling back to force a grimace of a smile. "You're probably wondering if you're going to have to peel me off the ceiling one of these days. I'm really not that bad."

"You were just trying to get out of here before you had to eat my cooking," he teased. "C'mon, you might as well confess. I'm a cop, remember? I've got ways of making you talk."

For the first time since he'd walked into the room, she smiled naturally. "Your cooking's the last thing I'm worried about. You couldn't have been around Angelo all these years and not learned something."

"Good point," he said with a grin. "So now that you don't have to worry about me poisoning you, why don't we eat? I don't know about you, but I'm starving."

Her smile faded. "Would you be terribly offended if we ate downstairs in the restaurant? I know I'm being paranoid, and it was so sweet of you to go to so much trouble, but we're just so isolated up here."

"And you'd feel more comfortable if there were more people around," he said, understanding perfectly. Pulling her close for a hug, he said, "Don't worry about it. I understand. Obviously the bastard who's after you has no trouble getting in the building in broad daylight, and you don't want to take any chances. I don't, either. So we'll just take everything downstairs and have breakfast with Angelo."

"You don't mind?"

"Of course not. I want you to feel safe." Giving her a quick kiss, he pushed her toward the bathroom. "Go get dressed. The food's getting cold."

Relieved, she turned back into his arms and raised up on tiptoe to give him a slow, hungry kiss. When she finally pulled back, ending the kiss, her eyes were shining. "Thank you."

Grinning crookedly, he rasped, "Sweetheart, you can thank me anytime you like. I should warn you, though, that if you keep that up, we're never going to make it downstairs for breakfast."

Laughing, she turned and hurried into the bathroom.

That day and the previous night set the pattern of their time together. Every morning, they went downstairs for breakfast with Angelo, then, while Tony worked, Lily took candid shots with her camera and began to plan the layout of the mural Angelo had commissioned. At night, she and Tony would go to her apartment. Angelo had sent in a cleaning crew to take care of the smoke damage, and the scent of smoke was nearly gone. For several hours each night, she worked in the darkroom, developing and printing the pictures she'd taken during the day. As fascinated by the process as Quentin had been, Tony was right by her side in the darkroom, asking questions and enjoying it as much as she. He identified many of the diners in the pictures for her, helped her with the design, and even tried his hand at taking a roll of pictures and developing them himself.

Considering the fact that the monster who wanted her dead was still out there somewhere, waiting for another chance to get close enough to her to kill her, she should have been a nervous wreck, jumping at every unexpected sound. Instead, she couldn't remember the last time she'd had so much fun. The Giovanni men had a way of taking her in and making her feel as if she was a part of the family, and she loved it. She felt right at home in the restaurant, and Angelo was wonderful. He teased and joked with her, and even had her helping him in the kitchen.

And then there was Tony. He was the most incredible man—there was no other way to describe him. Somehow, he made her feel safe and protected, even though the restaurant was a public place and anyone wishing her harm could have just walked in off the street. He was in and out of the kitchen a lot, waiting on customers, watching the door. Just the touch of his eyes reassured her that he was always nearby, quietly watching over her. And if her tormentor cased the joint, looking for her, she wasn't aware of it. There were no threats directed at her; no strangers approached her. She'd never felt so safe.

It was the nights, however, that turned her world upside down. Every night, when they retreated to his apartment, he made love to her as if she was the most precious thing in the world to him, and every morning, she woke up in his arms. And though she tried to deny it, she could no longer lie to herself—with every passing day, she was falling more and more in love with him. In the dark of the night, when she was sated from his lovemaking and so content in his arms that she couldn't imagine being anywhere else, she silently sent up a silent prayer that her time with him would never end.

Four days later, the dinner crowd had just started to thin when Tony got a call from the precinct. He wasn't surprised. The department was shorthanded, and all week he'd been expecting to be called back early from his vacation. Assuming his boss, Frank Hodges, was on the other end of the line, he teasingly said, "You've got the wrong number, Frank. There's no Tony Giovanni here. The only one I know by that name isn't supposed to report back to work until Monday."

"This is Charlie, Tony. I just wanted to let you know we made an arrest in the Fiztgerald case."

Shocked, he nearly dropped the phone. "What? When?"

"A half hour ago," he replied. "He was hanging around the alley across the street from the restaurant, acting suspicious. Ted Hawk saw him when he was making a pass in front of the restaurant, and followed him to the back of the alley. He had a gun."

Tony swore. "Son of a bitch! Did he confess?"

"He's singing like a bird right now," he said with a

chuckle. Quickly giving him the highlights, he added, ''I thought you'd want to know as soon as possible.''

''I owe you,'' Tony said gruffly. ''Thanks, Charlie.''

When he hung up, he turned to find Lily standing in the office doorway, her eyes wide. ''Angelo said you got a call from the precinct?''

Nodding, he grinned, and before she could even guess his intentions, he pulled her into his arms for a fierce hug. Laughing in confusion, she pulled back slightly so she could see his eyes. ''What was that for?''

''A suspect has been arrested.''

If he hadn't already been holding her, Lily was sure her knees would have buckled. ''What? When?''

''That was Detective Charlie Drake on the phone,'' he replied. ''He's one of the officers on the case. He knew I was keeping a close eye on you this week and wanted to let me know that they made an arrest about a half hour ago. The man was spotted in the alley across the street. He had a gun.''

She blanched. ''Oh, God!''

''It's all right, sweetheart,'' he assured her. ''He was arrested. You'll never have to worry about him again. He confessed.''

''Who is he? Why was he doing this?''

''He used the name Joe Smith, but he's got a long list of aliases. He has a history of stalking. According to Charlie, he claims he saw you in the park one day and became infatuated with you. He didn't have the guts to speak to you, and in his mind, that was your fault. Apparently, you walked by him on a number of occasions without speaking to him, and he wants you to suffer for that.''

''He sounds crazy.'' Horrified by a sudden thought, she gasped, ''They're not going to let him out of jail, are they? Tell me they won't let him out on some technicality, Tony. I think that would just push me over the edge.''

Pulling her back into his arms, he hugged her tight. ''He's behind bars and he's not getting out, sweetheart. You can relax. The nightmare's over.''

Held close to his heart, the warmth of his arms around her, she knew he wouldn't lie to her. That's when his words finally sank in. The nightmare really was over. Overwhelmed with relief, she started to cry.

''It's okay,'' he murmured, kissing her. ''It's okay. You can cry if you want to. Hell, after what you've been through, you deserve a good cry. Go ahead—let it out.''

She'd dreamed of it dozens of times—the moment when she discovered that the monster who'd turned her life into hell was finally in police custody. She'd pictured herself laughing and crying and dancing in relief. The one emotion she hadn't expected to feel was sadness. She didn't want her time with Tony to be over. Burying her face against his neck, she drew in the clean, masculine scent of him and never wanted to move.

When the phone rang again, they both jumped. Swearing, Tony reached for it and growled, ''Angelo's. Tony speaking.''

''Tony, this is Janice. I need to talk to you if you have a minute.''

Alarm bells rang in Tony's head. Anytime Janice cared one way or the other if he was busy, something was wrong. ''What's wrong, Janice? Quentin's all right, isn't he?''

''He's fine,'' she replied stiffly. ''I'm sorry I didn't let you see him all week—I was mad.''

He almost told her that sorry was a poor apology for denying their son the opportunity to be with his father just to get back at him, but he bit the words back just in time. He didn't want to start another argument with her—he didn't even want to talk to her. The minute Lily heard him mention Janice's name, she started to pull out of his arms, and he hated that. Any feelings he had for Janice had died a long time ago, and suddenly it was very important that he tell Lily that, but he couldn't, dammit, not when Janice was on the other end of the phone, listening. As much as he resented her and everything she'd done to take his son away from him, he couldn't humiliate her that way.

"I need to go, Janice," he growled. "Your apology's accepted. If that's all—"

"Wait!" she cried before he could hang up. "I wanted to know if you'd like to have Quentin tomorrow. He has a school holiday, and I thought you might like to spend the day with him since he told me you're on vacation."

There'd been a time when Tony would have naively fallen for such a line, but he'd learned a long time ago to read between the lines when it came to his ex-wife. Because she never did him a favor...unless it benefited her, too. "Larry's still in Florida, isn't he? You need someone to baby-sit Quentin, don't you?"

Irritated that he'd seen through her ploy, she snapped, "Yes, but I would hardly call it baby-sitting. He's your son."

"And it's high time you remembered that," he retorted. "Of course I'll keep him."

Her ruffled feathers somewhat soothed, she said, "Good. You can pick him up at Bryan Taylor's house in the morning. You remember Bryan—he and Quentin have been friends since kindergarten. They're having a sleepover at his house tonight since they don't have school tomorrow."

"I have the address in my address book," he replied. "I'll pick him up in the morning at ten."

Satisfied she'd gotten what she wanted, she hung up. Then Tony turned his attention back to Lily, who'd moved to the door of Angelo's office to give him some measure of privacy during his call. "I'm sorry about that," he said. "Quentin doesn't have school tomorrow, and she wanted me to take him for the day. Are you all right?"

Lily nodded, the forced smile that curved her mouth not quite reaching her eyes. "Isn't it weird the way everything just works out right when you need it to? My case gets solved, I can go home tonight, and tomorrow, Quentin has his room back. What are the odds?"

"I don't want you to go home tonight," he growled. "I know it's just across the hall, but stay one more night."

She couldn't refuse him. "What time do you get off?" she asked.

"In twenty minutes."

Her heart skipping a beat in anticipation, she smiled. "So I guess I'll see you then." She leaned up on tiptoe and pressed a kiss to his cheek. He reached for her, but he was too late. Sailing toward the door in the kitchen that gave access to the apartment stairwell, she glanced over her shoulder to give him a flirty wink, then disappeared into the stairwell. Ten minutes later, when she was immersed up to her shoulders in her favorite bubble bath in his apartment, she was still smiling. Maybe she'd just lie right here until he came home.

It was a nice thought, but she knew she wouldn't. She just wasn't that decadent. So she soaked in the steaming water for a few minutes, then began to shampoo her hair. Too late, she realized she'd have to hurry, after all, if she was going to have time to blow it dry before Tony's shift ended. *Idiot,* she chided herself, and quickly began to rinse.

"Lily? Where are you? I'm home."

In the process of applying conditioner to her hair, she glanced up, startled. "Tony? I'm taking a bath," she called through the partially open bathroom door. "Give me a minute and I'll be right out."

Her heart starting to pound, she quickly rinsed her hair with the hand sprayer on the old-fashioned claw-foot tub, then reached for her bath gel. Five minutes later, she'd just wrapped a towel around her wet hair and another one around her body when he softly knocked on the bathroom door. "Mind if I come in and shave? I feel a little rough."

When he peeked around the door and grinned at her, his green eyes dancing with mischief, he was impossible to resist. Grinning, she stepped back, allowing him room to join her in the small bathroom. "Of course. I was just going to dry my hair."

"I could help you with that," he said huskily. "Or you could just let it dry naturally." Stepping close, he pulled the towel from her head and watched as her damp hair tumbled about her bare shoulders. Just that quickly, the light in his eyes turned dark and sensuous. "Do you have any idea how beautiful you are?"

She'd never thought of herself as beautiful—her chin was too stubborn and her nose could only be described as pert, at best—but when he looked at her that way, he made her feel like Cinderella at the ball. "You make me feel beautiful," she said softly. "Whenever I'm around you, I just feel like smiling all the time."

"I feel the same way," he admitted in a voice as rough as sandpaper. "I don't know what it is about you. Just looking at you does something to me. I think it's your skin.''

Surprised, Lily laughed. ''My skin?''

He grinned. ''Yeah. Like this spot right here. It's so soft, I can't resist it.'' Leaning down, he dropped a gentle kiss to the spot where her neck met her shoulder. ''Mmm. See? And then there's your neck...and shoulder...and here...''

He kissed the top of her breasts, just above where the towel was wrapped around her, and just that easily, turned her bones to water. She moaned softly and leaned into him. ''Hold me,'' she whispered. ''I need you to hold me.''

''My pleasure,'' he rasped, and drew her into his arms.

Her pulse raced and her head swam. Kissing the side of his neck, just as he had kissed hers, she wondered how it could have taken so long for her to realize she loved him. He made her laugh and smile and ache with need in a way that stole her breath. With him, she felt as though she'd become the person she'd always wanted to be, and she loved it. She loved him. And even though she didn't know if they could ever have a future together—considering the way his ex was trying to take his son away from him, she wouldn't blame him if he never trusted a woman again—she couldn't worry about that now. Tomorrow, she'd return to her apartment and her life, but for tonight, she was going to enjoy her time with him. The future would take care of itself.

Reaching for the buttons of his shirt, she unbuttoned them and slowly kissed her way down his chest. When he groaned, she smiled. ''You've got a few interesting spots of your own, Mr. Giovanni. I would love to explore them.''

''I'm all yours, sweetheart,'' he retorted with a grin as

he held his arms wide. "Go ahead—have your way with me. I promise I won't offer a single word of complaint."

Just that easily, he teasingly threw down a challenge, and without a blink of an eye, she accepted it. Smiling, she parted his shirt and slid it off his shoulders with agonizing slowness. Before it hit the floor, her fingers were trailing over his bare torso, heating his skin with just a touch. Then, everywhere she touched, she kissed.

His teeth clenched on a groan, Tony had to fight the need to snatch her tight in his arms and kiss her until they were both wild with need. But he couldn't, not yet. She was showing him a side of herself he'd never seen before, and he loved it. So he kept his hands out to the side and waited to see what she'd do next.

He didn't have to worry—she didn't disappoint him. Reaching for his hands, she brought them to where the towel she still wore wrapped around her had been secured by simply tucking it between her breasts. Closing his fingers around the end of the towel, she molded her fingers to his and tugged, helping him pull the towel loose. Before it could hit the ground, she pulled his head down to hers for a long, slow kiss that curled his toes.

His blood heating to flash point in the time it took to blink, he never even had a chance at control. Deepening the kiss, he kissed her until they were both hot and breathless and she was clinging to him as if she'd never let him go. And still, it wasn't enough. On fire for her, his hands stroking, rubbing, caressing, he slowly walked her backward toward the bedroom, dropping kisses on her mouth and face and neck all the while. And for every kiss she gave him, for every touch, every teasing playing of her fingers, he did the same, until they were dancing a sensuous dance of give-and-take and driving each other out of their minds.

Later, Tony never remembered the moment when they reached the bed—or when he removed the rest of his clothes. Suddenly, they were on the bed, skin to skin, and nothing had ever felt so good. His mind blurred, and all he could do was feel…Lily under him, surrounding him, moving with him in perfect time to a rhythm only they could hear. And when she came undone in his arms, he groaned and lost himself in her. The world could have exploded, and he never would have noticed. There was only Lily, and the feelings she stirred in him.

She wanted to tell him she loved him. The words hovered on her tongue the next morning as they got dressed, but she couldn't bring herself to speak them. He'd given no indication that his feelings for her were anything more than lust and liking, and she just couldn't bring herself to put her heart on the line. Not yet. So she kept her feelings to herself and acted as if nothing had changed in her world. Only, she knew that everything had.

"So what are you doing today?" Tony asked as he finished dressing. "Now that you don't have to worry about some bastard trying to kill you every time you stick your head out the door, you can do whatever you want. It looks like it's going to be a gorgeous day, and the leaves are changing in the park."

"Actually, I thought I'd stick around here and work on Angelo's mural," she said as she twisted her hair up on her head and secured it with a clip. "It's really starting to come together and I'd like to get it finished."

The phone rang then, and Tony said, "That's probably Angelo. He was going to make his famous strawberry tart for you for breakfast this morning. It's probably ready."

Grinning, he snatched up the phone. "We'll be down

in just a second,'' he said by way of a greeting, only to frown when he recognized his boss's voice on the other end of the line. ''Sorry about that, Frank—I thought you were my uncle. What's up?''

''I don't know if you heard,'' Frank growled, ''but there's a nasty stomach virus going around, and it's wiping us out. I've already got six men out, and two others are feeling lousy. I know this is your vacation, and I hate to do it, but I've got to ask you to come in today. We're so shorthanded, we've already got people working double shifts and it's still not enough.''

If anyone else had asked him to give up the rest of his vacation, he might not have done it. But Frank wasn't the type to panic or exaggerate the circumstances. If he said the department was in a crisis, then it was. ''I'll be in as soon as I change into my uniform,'' he promised.

''Thanks, man,'' he sighed in relief. ''You don't know how I appreciate this.''

It wasn't until he hung up that Tony remembered he was supposed to have Quentin for the day. Swearing, he told Lily, ''I forgot I'm supposed to have Quentin today. He's waiting for me to pick him up at a friend's house, and now I've got to go into work. I'll have to call Janice—''

''I can pick him up for you,'' she volunteered, ''and bring him back here. He can help me with the mural.''

''You don't mind?''

''Not at all. We have a great time together, and I can use the help. If that's all right with you...and you don't think your ex-wife will mind if I pick him up.''

He hadn't thought of that, but she was right. Sometimes there was no way to predict how Janice was going to react to something, and right now he didn't want any more problems with her than he already had. ''You never know with Janice,'' he admitted. ''It probably would be better if I picked him and brought him back here before I went to work. Then there won't be any problems.''

''You won't be late?''

''My sergeant will understand. Anyway, this is the best I can do.'' Pulling her close, he gave her a quick kiss. ''I wish I could stay for breakfast, but I've got to change into my uniform and get out of here. Will I see you for dinner?''

''I think that can be arranged,'' she said with a smile. ''Maybe Quentin and I will cook something special.''

''Quentin's idea of special is beef burritos,'' he said with a chuckle. ''Don't forget your Tums.''

The police station was usually bustling with activity, but the stomach virus that had made its way through the force had also, apparently, taken its toll on the criminal population. Compared to the usual hustle and bustle that took place during shift changes, the place was like a tomb. No wonder Frank had called him in, he thought in amazement. It looked as if half the force hadn't showed up for work.

''Hey, Tony! Thank God you're here. I was just about to call you.''

Tony grinned at Charlie Drake. ''Just the man I wanted to see. I wanted to thank you for calling me about Joe Smith. Lily was so relieved he was finally off the streets, she cried.''

''The confession was bogus, Tony. We just found out this morning.''

He didn't have to ask him what confession. There was only one that mattered. ''This is a joke, isn't it? Quit fooling around, Charlie. The perp confessed.''

''It was a setup,'' he said flatly. ''Somebody paid him

five thousand dollars to hang around in the alley until he got caught, then he was supposed to sing like a canary so you and your lady friend would drop your guard.''

Furious, Tony swore. ''Are you sure? Why'd he recant his confession, then?''

''He swears that was part of the deal.''

''Maybe he's just messing with your mind and trying to get out of the confession.''

''We thought of that, but the money was deposited in his bank account this morning.''

''So he had someone do it for him so he can get out.''

''This scumbag's never had that much money in his life,'' he retorted. ''And we ran the surveillance tapes at the bank.''

A sick feeling of dread spilled into Tony's stomach. ''Let me guess. Whoever made the deposit was wearing a red wig and a pizza-delivery hat.''

Charlie nodded grimly. ''We just verified it with the bank. I looked at the film myself. It's impossible to tell what the bastard looks like.''

Horrified, Tony felt sick to his stomach. ''Lily thinks she's safe,'' he said hoarsely. ''She doesn't have a clue the bastard's still on the streets. I've got to call her!''

Grabbing his cell phone, he quickly punched in Lily's number, but after what seemed like an eternity, all he got was her answering machine. He hung and immediately called Angelo. ''Where's Lily?'' he asked the second his uncle answered.

Surprised at his sharp tone, Angelo drawled, ''Well, good morning to you, too. I guess I don't have to ask what side of the bed you got up on this morning. Obviously, it was the wrong one.''

Struggling to hold on to his patience, he growled, ''She's in danger, Angelo. She thought the man who was trying to kill her had been arrested, but it was a setup. She said she was going to work on the mural this morning with Quentin. She's there, isn't she? I need to talk to her.''

His tone grim, Angelo swore. ''She and Quentin left fifteen minutes ago. They were going to get darkroom supplies.''

Chapter 12

"I can't wait to see Angelo's face when we unveil the mural," Lily told Quentin as they walked out of the camera-supply shop carrying boxes of developer and photographic paper. "He's going to be so surprised."

"So will Dad," Quentin said as he helped her load the supplies in the cargo section of her SUV, then climbed in the back seat and buckled up. "Wait until he sees the pictures I took. Maybe I'll get a camera for Christmas."

Chuckling at his enthusiasm, Lily slammed the rear door on her truck and walked around to the driver's side, grinning at the thought of Quentin hounding Tony until he bought him a camera, then snapping candid photos of him every time he turned around. She couldn't wait to see them.

Already picturing them as she pulled open the driver's door, she never saw the man who suddenly appeared out of nowhere behind her. He grabbed her from behind, startling her, and shoved a gun in her side before she could do anything but cry out in surprise. ‘‘What—’’

‘‘Get in the car!’’ her abductor growled, jabbing her with the gun again, only this time harder. ‘‘In the passenger seat…now! And don’t say a word.’’

Terrified, Lily didn’t argue with him. She awkwardly climbed over the console—with the help of a rough, hard hand in her back—and completely forgot that Quentin was in the back seat until he said hesitantly, ‘‘Lily? Are you all right?’’

‘‘Shut up, kid!’’ their kidnapper snarled, shooting him a sharp, narrow-eyed look that drained the color out of Quentin’s cheeks. ‘‘Just shut up!’’

‘‘Leave him alone!’’ Lily snapped, her outrage overcoming her fear. ‘‘He’s just a kid.’’

Lightning quick, he backhanded her. ‘‘When I want your opinion, bitch, I’ll ask for it.’’

Stunned, her cheek burning and tears filling her eyes, Lily quickly glanced in the mirror of her visor to make sure Quentin was all right, but he was obviously scared to death. Hugging himself, there were tears in his eyes and he was shaking like a leaf. *Don’t!* she wanted to tell him. *Don’t let him terrorize you. We’re going to get out of this.*

But even as his eyes met hers in the mirror and she tried to send him a reassuring look, she was as afraid as he was. She couldn’t, however, afford to let their abductor see that. For all she knew, he was the kind of man who thrived on fear, and she’d be damned if she’d give him that kind of satisfaction.

Turning on him with fierce eyes, she prayed he couldn’t hear her heart slamming against her ribs. ‘‘Who are you? What do you want from us? I don't have any money—''

''I don't want your damn money!'' he growled as he threw the SUV into gear and jerked the vehicle out into the traffic. Driving with one hand, he pointed the gun right at her heart. ''I want you dead.''

His words were eerily familiar. Horrified, Lily stared at him searchingly. Who was he? She would have sworn that she'd never seen him before—surely she would have remembered his thin, sharp features and beady eyes—then it hit her. ''I remember you,'' she said hoarsely. ''I was taking pictures in front of Angelo's Italian Restaurant, and you stopped and talked to me about photography. You wanted to know what kind of camera to buy your girlfriend.''

''I wanted to see how close I could get to you,'' he sneered, ''to see if you recognized me. For a photographer, you don't have much of an eye.''

Confused, she didn't understand why he acted as if he knew her. If they'd met some other time before he spoke to her on the street that day, she didn't remember it. What did he want from her? And why did he want her dead? Was he just trying to scare her so she'd do what he wanted? That had to be it, she decided. It was just a coincidence that his words were so similar to those of the man who'd been trying to kill her for weeks now.

But even as she tried to convince herself her imagination was just playing tricks on her, she had a sick feeling that there was no such thing as coincidences. And somehow, she knew deep in her gut that this was her tormentor, her nemesis, her would-be killer. He was the same one who'd tried to run her down in the park, the man who'd trapped her in her apartment and set the attic on fire. And he had a gun.

Oh, God, she thought, swallowing a sob. How had he gotten out of jail?

"You're supposed to be in jail," she said hoarsely. "Tony said you confessed."

He laughed sharply. "Someone did confess, but it wasn't me. It's amazing what people will do for money, isn't it? All I had to do was find an addict on the street and he was willing to say anything I wanted him to. I imagine your friend Tony and the rest of the pigs he works with are finding that out just about now." Pleased with himself, he said smugly, "Idiots. They don't have a clue who I am and I plan to keep it that way. That's why I'm getting rid of you."

"But why?" she cried. "Who are you? Why would you want to kill me? I don't even know you. What could I have possibly done to you to make you hate me so much?"

"You took my picture!" he snapped. "Right after I killed a hooker in the park. No one else but you can place me at the scene. So make your will, sweetheart. You're dead just as soon as I can arrange it—and so is the kid. I can't afford any more witnesses."

Confused, Lily frowned. "I took your picture? When? I've never even seen you before."

That was the wrong thing to say. In the blink of an eye, he was enraged. "Bitch!" he screamed at her, back-handing her again. "Don't lie to me! I saw the damn picture hanging in a gallery right around the corner from your apartment!"

Stunned, Lily pressed a hand to her stinging cheek. He was the runner in the mist, she thought, horrified. He hadn't been jogging in the park on a rainy day, as she'd thought. He was running from a murder!

"But I didn't even look at your face!" she cried. "I was concentrating on the light and taking the picture at just the right time. I didn't *see* you. I just saw the overall image. I couldn't have picked you out of a lineup if my life depended on it."

"Yeah? Well, it looks like the joke's on you," he taunted. "Because now you can identify me and so can the boy. Say your prayers. You're both going to die."

Terror nearly choking her, Lily wanted to scream at him, to cry and plead and beg and completely give in to her fear, but she couldn't. Quentin was just as scared as she was, and he was depending on her to somehow rescue him from this mess. She couldn't just sit there and let this maniac drive them to their deaths. She had to keep her head, had to think! There had to be a way.

Racking her brains, she shifted slightly in her seat and felt something hard poke her hip bone. Her cell phone! she thought, relieved. She'd shoved it into the right pocket of her jeans when she'd gone into the camera store. Now she just had to find a way to use it to signal for help.

Her heart in her throat, she glanced over at their abductor to discover that he was too busy weaving in and out of traffic to take his eyes off the road. This was her chance. With agonizing slowness, she silently pulled the phone out of her pocket and slid her hand between her seat and the passenger door so that she could soundlessly hold the phone out behind her to Quentin.

For a minute, she didn't think he understood what she needed him to do. *Take it!* she silently urged. *Find a way to call for help!*

When his fingers suddenly closed over hers, clinging for a moment, she wanted to cry. Poor kid, he was scared out of his wits, and all she wanted to do was crawl in the back seat with him, give him a fierce hug and assure him that everything was going to be fine. But that was out of the question at the moment. All she could do was squeeze his hand again and pray that he knew she needed him to call his father or Angelo or 911, anyone who could save them.

When he took the phone and released her hand, she realized that she had to create some kind of distraction so that their abductor wouldn't hear him punching the buttons on the phone. "Why don't you just pull over and let us out," she said loudly to him. "You're not going to get away with this, so why don't you cut your losses and make a run for it. We'll give you time to catch a plane and fly out of the country before we call for help. We don't even know your name—the police won't know where to look for you."

"Yeah, right," he laughed, his tone ugly. "Like I'm going to believe you. I wouldn't even be out of sight before you'd be on the phone calling for help."

"No, we wouldn't! I give you my word."

"Shut up!" he snapped. "Do you really think your word means anything to me? You're dead, lady! And so is the kid. It's just a matter of time. Accept it!"

Halfway across town in her office, Janice frowned when her cell phone rang, and she almost didn't answer it. She'd told her secretary to hold all calls, but she'd forgotten to turn off her cell. She'd just let the answering service get it, she decided. She had too much to do to chat on the phone with every Tom, Dick and Harry that called. Whoever needed to speak to her could wait for her to call them back later.

But what if one of her clients had an emergency…?

Not even looking up from her computer screen, she reached for her cell phone. "Janice Coffman," she said coolly. "Who's calling, please?"

"Why are you getting on the beltway if you're going to kill us? What's wrong with the park? Isn't that where you killed the other lady?"

Surprised, she frowned. What the devil! That was Quentin—or at least it sounded like him, but he seemed to be speaking from a long ways away. Shaking her head, she reminded herself to speak to him about calling her at the office. She didn't know what kind of joke he was playing, but he knew he wasn't supposed to disturb her when she was working.

"I told you to shut up, kid, and I meant it. When I want your opinion, I'll ask for it."

Straining to hear the cold, angry words, Janice stiffened. She didn't know who the man was who spoke to her son like that, but she knew it wasn't Tony. He'd never spoken to Quentin that way in his life. What was going on? she wondered. Whatever it was, she didn't like the sound of it. And she damn sure wasn't going to tolerate anyone talking to Quentin that way.

Opening her mouth to tell Quentin just that, she couldn't have said later why she hesitated. Something—a sixth sense, her angels—warned her to be quiet and listen. Her heart suddenly racing, she pressed the phone closer to her ear and held her breath, listening.

"At least let the boy go," a woman pleaded. "He'll cause you nothing but trouble and his father's a cop. You don't want Tony coming after you. He'll search heaven and hell for anyone who harms his son. You don't need that kind of complication. Let him go."

"No!" the man shouted. "Both of you shut up or I'll kill you right here! Do you hear me? I don't want to hear another word! Do you think I give a flip about the boy's father? He can't hurt me—he doesn't have a clue who I am. And I don't plan to leave any evidence with your bodies. Not that he's going to find you," he added smugly. "You're going to be spending eternity at the bottom of a deep, dark, abandoned well."

"Where?" the woman asked hoarsely. "We have a right to know where."

"Yeah, I guess you do," he replied with a mocking chuckle. "How does Arlington sound? Arlington, Virginia," he added, "not the national cemetery. There's an old well on my grandmother's place. It'll be perfect for the two of you."

"And do we get to know the name of our killer before we die? We're entitled to that, if nothing else."

Holding her breath, Janice didn't think he was going to answer, but then he laughed. "What the hell. What can it hurt? It's not like you can go to the police and turn me in, is it?" Laughing at that, he said, "The name's Sly Jackson. But you can call me Mr. Death."

Janice didn't wait to hear more. Her heart in her throat, she snatched up the office phone on her desk and quickly punched in Tony's cell-phone number. Tony picked up a second later. Not wanting her voice to carry to the cell phone that Quentin had called her on, she said in a hushed voice, "Tony, Quentin's in trouble. I just got a call from him on my cell phone—"

"Where is he?" he asked sharply. "I've been worried sick about him and Lily."

''A man named Sly Jackson has them. He's taking them to his grandmother's farm somewhere on the outskirts of Arlington, where he's going to kill them and dump their bodies down an abandoned well. You've got to do something, Tony! This bastard's not fooling around. He's going to kill our baby!''

''I'm going to do something, all right,'' he said grimly. ''I'm going to catch the son of a bitch and make him wish he'd never been born. What else did Quentin say?''

''He didn't say anything to me. He must have just dialed my number, then kept it out of sight when I answered. I can hear everything being said.''

''You mean he's still on the line? Are you at the office? I'll be right there!''

The drive to Janice's office would have normally taken twenty-five minutes. Sick with fear for Quentin and Lily, Tony made it in ten minutes flat. Racing into the parking lot of Janice's law firm, he pulled up at the front door just as she rushed outside with her cell phone.

''I took notes of everything they said,'' she told him and handed him a notepad. ''You should have heard Quentin. He was so brave. He kept making comments to the creep who kidnapped them about where they were going, and he even told him he'd be in big trouble if he wrecked Lily's SUV.'' Tears flooded her eyes. ''He wanted us to know what vehicle they were in. You've got to find them, Tony.''

Scared to death for his son, Tony wrapped his arms around Janice and gave her a fierce hug. Regardless of their differences, they both loved their son and they were in this together. ''He's going to be okay,'' he said huskily. ''Just hang tight and pray.''

Taking her cell phone, he held it up to his ear and could barely make out his son's voice as he said, "My dad says there's a lot of speed traps in this part of the beltway. Are you sure you don't want to go through town? The Fourteenth Street bridge is coming up..."

Pride swelling his heart, Tony told Janice, "I've got to go. They're coming up on the Fourteenth Street exit."

Her face as white as snow, Janice gave him another hug, then stepped back. "I know you'll keep him safe. Call me as soon as you know anything. I'll instruct the receptionist to put any calls from you through immediately."

Hurrying to his patrol car, Tony hit his lights and siren, then pulled out of the parking lot with tires squealing. His eyes on the road, he grabbed his radio and called for backup. "The suspect is driving a red 2003 Ford Explorer, D.C. license-plate number AGH–113, and heading south on the beltway near the Fourteenth Street exit. His name is Sly Jackson, and he's believed to be heading for a farm outside of Arlington that belongs to his grandmother. He's holding two kidnapped victims hostage—a nine-year-old boy and a thirty-three-year-old woman. He's considered armed and dangerous.

"He intends to kill them," he told the dispatcher. "Make sure you pass it down the line to everyone to be careful not to do anything that will set this bastard off. My son's in the car with him and so is the woman I love."

It wasn't until Tony heard the words that came out of his mouth that he realized just how true they were. He loved Lily. Stunned, he didn't understand how he could have been so blind. He'd tried to convince himself it was lust, but lust didn't make a man's heart ache, it didn't make him dream of her laugh and the way her hair glinted in the sunlight. It didn't make him think about her at all hours of the day and night and long to be with her, even if that meant doing nothing more than sitting at one of Angelo's patio tables and watching the world go by.

He just wanted to be with her…for the rest of his life.

Stunned, he didn't know how she hadn't gotten past his guard, but it no longer mattered. He loved her more than he'd ever thought possible and just the thought of losing her and Quentin sickened him.

His radio crackled and the unemotional voice of the dispatcher said, "Attention all units in the vicinity of the Fourteenth Street bridge. The red Ford Explorer, D.C. license-plate number AGH–113, has been spotted crossing the Fourteenth Street bridge and heading south. Proceed with caution. Suspect is armed…"

Tony didn't need to hear more. Flattening the accelerator, he raced toward Fourteenth Street, praying all the while that he'd make it in time to save the two people in the world he loved most.

"Please don't do this," Lily pleaded as Sly Jackson reached the outskirts of Arlington and took a quick turn onto a dirt road that led back into a thick stand of trees. "I'm not a threat to you—neither is Quentin. We'll tell the police that you were wearing a disguise. Please—"

Lightning quick, Sly jerked the gun up and pointed it in her face. "Shut up."

He didn't scream it, as he had earlier. In fact, he was cold and calm and totally in control of his emotions, and somehow, that made him even more frightening. Chilled all the way to the bone, Lily didn't dare look in the back to see how Quentin was faring—she didn't want him to see her despair. Had he been able to call for help? She wanted to believe that he had, but she hadn't seen a police car since she and Quentin had been abducted, and she was starting to lose hope. They'd left the main road and were now traveling down a dusty private gravel path that seemed to disappear into the trees. How was Tony ever going to find them back here in the middle of nowhere when he had no idea where to even begin looking for them?

Swallowing a sob, she was forced to accept the inevitable.

They were dead unless they could find a way to save themselves. The question was…how? He had a gun, and she had a child to protect. Would Quentin understand what she was trying to do if she created some kind of distraction? Sly wouldn't give her a chance to talk to him in private, to warn him. She could pretend to be sick and faint…or trip, anything so Sly's attention would be on her, and Quentin would have a chance to escape. Would he leave her alone with Sly and run for help? He had to. Otherwise, they'd both be dead for sure.

Her stomach knotting at the thought, she felt her heart stop as the dirt road they were on came to a dead end at an old house that look as if it hadn't been lived in in decades. The yard was knee-high with weeds, the wooden porch was rotted and leaning, and even as she watched, a bird flew through a hole in the roof. Surrounding it for as far as the eye could see was nothing but trees. There didn't appear to be another house for miles.

It was the old well in the clearing to the right of the house, however, that terrified her. She took one look at it and felt her stomach turn over. He hadn't been lying, she thought, nauseated. He really did intend to dump their bodies down the well.

''All right, boys and girls,'' he said with sadistic cheerfulness. ''We're home. Everybody out. It's time to die.''

His siren and lights off, Janice's cell phone pressed to his ear as he used the cover of Sly Jackson's dust to race down the dirt road after him, Tony swore at the other man's words. Bastard! He wanted to scream at him, to tear him apart, but then the phone went dead and so did Tony's heart. ''No!''

Jackson couldn't have found the phone, he told himself. He would have said something before it went dead. Quentin must have turned it off and put it in his pocket so it wouldn't be discovered. That was the only logical explanation. He was just playing it smart. Damn, he was proud of him! And he'd get the chance to tell him that, he vowed. And Lily…God, he couldn't wait to hold her and tell her that he loved her.

But first, he had to take care of Sly Jackson.

Through the dust, he could just barely see the brake lights of Lily's SUV light up as the vehicle was brought to a screeching halt. Reaching for his radio, he growled softly, ''This is it. They're getting out of the Explorer right now. This is where he's going to kill them.''

He didn't have to say more. The line of patrol cars behind him followed his lead and pulled over and cut their engines, then quickly, soundlessly, the other policemen fanned out into the woods with their guns drawn. Taking the lead, Tony had never been more afraid in his life. If he was too late…

* * *

Later, Lily couldn't have said when or how she knew they were no longer alone. Brandishing the gun at them, Sly forced her and Quentin to walk the short distance to the well, and over the thunder of her heartbeat, she couldn't help but notice how eerily silent the surrounding woods were. Even the birds were quiet. Was Tony out there somewhere, waiting for just the right moment to save them? Frowning, she quickly searched the surrounding woods, but nothing moved. Still, she knew Tony was out there. She could feel him.

Quentin felt it, too. He didn't say anything, but as he walked beside her, she saw his eyes darting to the woods. When he glanced back up at her, she could see in a single glance that he wasn't nearly as afraid as he had been. He knew, as well as she did, that Tony was there.

They couldn't, however, underestimate Sly Jackson. He meant to kill them and he wasn't going to let anyone get in his way. Even if Tony fired at him at the same time he shot at them, there was a good chance that one of them would be killed. They couldn't wait to be rescued—they had to save themselves.

"Turn around," Sly called out coldly. "Even I won't shoot someone in the back. I have my standards, you know."

"I'm going to trip, Quentin," she whispered hurriedly. "When I do, I want you to run straight for the woods. Don't look back. Understand?"

Wide-eyed, he said softly, "Dad's here—"

"I know. Do as I say." Not giving him a chance to argue, she started to turn. A heartbeat later, she pretended to stumble. "Run!"

Caught off guard, Sly Jackson screamed, "No!" Lightning quick, he jerked his gun up, aimed and fired.

The bullet slammed into her shoulder like a runaway train. Screaming at the pain that ripped through her, Lily fell backward and hit her head hard on a rock. Before she could do anything but whimper, bullets were suddenly flying overhead.

Where was Quentin? she wondered, panicking. Had he made it to the trees? If something happened to him, Tony would never forgive her. Tears flooding her eyes, she tried to crawl behind the well, but she felt as if she was moving in slow motion. Blood seeped from the wound in her shoulder in a steady stream. Dazed, she collapsed face first in the dirt and could do nothing but lie there and wait to die.

Livid, Tony saw Lily fall a split second before he shot Sly Jackson in the wrist. Dropping to his knees, his gun falling out of his reach, he grabbed his wrist as blood dripped from his fingers. Tony couldn't have cared less. All he saw was Lily lying face first on the ground. Her blood was already turning the dirt underneath her body red.

"Lily!" Later, he didn't remember shouting her name. Running toward her as the rest of his fellow officers rushed to take Sly Jackson into custody, Tony stopped in his tracks as his son threw himself into his arms. Sending up a silent prayer of thanks, he hugged him fiercely. "It's okay," he said huskily. "Everything's okay, Quentin. You're safe. He'll never hurt you again."

"I knew you would come, Dad. I knew it. Lily did, too. Is she okay?"

"She has to be, son." Quickly striding the rest of the way to Lily's side, Tony set Quentin back on his feet, then dropped to his knees beside Lily as Sam Taylor, one of the other officers who'd responded to his call for help, carefully rolled her to her back. The second Tony saw her ashen face and blood-drenched shirt, fear tightened like a noose around his heart.

"An ambulance is already on the way," Sam told him as he pressed a hand to a pressure point to stop the flow of blood oozing from the bullet wound. "She was lucky, Tony. It could have been a hell of a lot worse."

Tony hardly heard him. Kneeling at Lily's side, he took her hand and tenderly cradled it in his. "Wake up, sweetheart," he said huskily. "You're going to be fine. Do you hear me? There's an ambulance on the way, so just hang on, honey. Okay? Lily? Sweetheart? Say something."

Pale as a ghost, she didn't respond by so much as a flicker of an eyelash, and that scared the hell out of him. "She should be conscious, Sam," he said worriedly, glancing up at the other man. "Something's wrong. She must have hit her head when she fell. Where's the damn ambulance?"

In the distance, the high whine of ambulances carried easily to them in the silence of the woods. Five minutes later, two ambulances pulled up, but it wasn't soon enough for Tony. He was losing her, he thought, and that terrified him. Helpless, he stood with Quentin at his side as the EMTs worked on Lily, quickly bandaging her shoulder, then checking her vital signs as she was carefully loaded onto a stretcher and into the ambulance.

Thirty feet away, the EMTs from the second ambulance bandaged Sly Jackson's wrist while two other officers stood guard, ready to shoot him again if he was stupid enough to make a break for it. He wasn't. Leaving his co-workers to take care of the paperwork and booking Jackson after he was treated at the hospital, Tony told

Sam, "I'm going to the hospital with Lily. I'll report back to the precinct when she's out of danger."

"I'll cover for you," his friend said. "Go."

He didn't have to tell him twice. With Quentin buckled up in the back seat of his patrol car, Tony switched on his light bar and raced after Lily's ambulance, praying all the while.

While Quentin called his mother from the hospital emergency room to let her know he was all right, Tony put in a call to Lily's father. He knew Lily probably wouldn't be happy with him when she discovered what he'd done, but he'd just have to take that chance. He'd just come damn close to losing his own son, and as far as he was concerned, Kenneth Fitzgerald had a right to know just how close he had come to losing his daughter and that she still wasn't out of danger. If he chose to turn his back on her because he was still angry with her for not making the choices in her life that he thought she should, then that was his loss. At least he could look at his own son and know he'd made the right decision.

"Hello," a cool male voice said on the third ring.

"Mr. Fitzgerald? This is Tony Giovanni, a friend of Lily's. We spoke several weeks ago."

"You're the police officer with the District of Columbia. Is she all right?" he asked sharply. "Why isn't she calling me, herself?"

"She's in surgery, sir. She was shot in the shoulder, but she's going to be fine. I thought you should know."

For a moment, Kenneth Fitzgerald didn't say a word, and Tony was afraid he was going to just hang up. Then he said, "What happened?"

"Apparently, she unwittingly took a picture of a man

who had just killed a prostitute in the park.'' He gave him the story Quentin had told him, explaining how Sly Jackson had seen his picture hanging in the gallery and decided that Lily had to die because she was the only one who could place him at the scene of the murder. ''She's safe, sir. We have the shooter in custody, and trust me, he won't be released any time soon. If I have anything to do with it, he'll spend the rest of his life in prison.''

''Good.'' Silence fell, then he added huskily, ''Will you tell Lily when she comes out of surgery that we spoke, and I hope she's feeling better? When she's up to it, I'd like to come and see her.''

For a man who up until then had appeared not to lack for confidence, he sounded surprisingly unsure of himself. ''I'll tell her, sir,'' he promised, and quietly hung up.

At his side, Quentin leaned against him. He hadn't been two steps away from him since he'd run into his arms at the edge of the woods after Lily was shot. ''Is Lily really going to be okay, Dad? What's taking so long? She's not going to die, is she?''

''No, son,'' he said, hugging him close. ''The doctor said they just need to repair the damage to her shoulder.''

''But she didn't wake up.''

''The paramedic said she came to in the ambulance,'' he said. ''She hit her head really hard when she fell, but she's going to be fine.'' Tightening his arm around him, he ruffled his hair. ''Did I tell how proud I am of you for what you did today? If you hadn't called your mom and left the phone on so she could hear what was going on, I never would have known where you and Lily were.''

"It was Lily's idea," Quentin told him, grinning. "She slipped the phone to me when *he* wasn't looking, then she talked real loud so he couldn't hear me dialing Mom's number. I would have called you, but you always said don't call you at work because you might be in court and not have your phone, so I called Mom."

"It's okay," Tony said, ruffling his hair again. "I'm glad she was there for you. Just for the record, though, you can call me anytime there's an emergency, son. I don't care where I am or what I'm doing, you call me when you're in trouble. I'll always come running."

"I know," Quentin said, reaching up to return the favor and ruffle his hair. "I knew when I called Mom, she would find a way to get in touch with you and you would find us. He was really going to kill us, wasn't he, Dad?"

"Yes, he was." Wanting to get his son's mind off of it, he corralled Quentin around the neck. "C'mon, I'll buy you something from the snack machine. How about some hot Chee•tos?"

"Yeah!"

When Janice stepped into the waiting room, she stopped short at the sight of Quentin sitting next to Tony, his head propped against his father's shoulder as he popped chips into his mouth. Tears stung her eyes, shocking her. She never cried! Or at least, she never had until today. But then again, she'd never come so close to losing her son.

God, he loved Tony. Just watching the two of them together, she could feel the love between them from across the room. How, she wondered, had she ever thought she could split them up? Quentin loved her, but not the way he loved his father. They were like two peas in a pod—they had the same walk, the same mannerisms, the same grin. If she insisted on taking Quentin away from Tony, she realized now that her son would never forgive her.

There was a time when she would have shrugged that off and convinced herself that he was a child—he would adjust. But she'd almost lost him today, and everything had changed. She wanted him to be happy. Nothing else mattered.

"Hey, guys," she said huskily, stepping farther into the waiting room. "You don't know how glad I am to see both of you. How's Lily?"

"The doctor's cutting the bullet out of her shoulder, Mom," Quentin said, jumping up to hug her as Tony rose to his feet. "Dad says she's going to be okay, though."

Stepping over to Tony, she hugged him, then had to laugh when she saw the surprise in his eyes. "Don't look at me like that. I haven't lost my mind. I'm just so glad you're both safe and Lily is, too. She and Quentin were lucky to have each other today."

"So were we," he said roughly. "We could have lost him, Janice. If you'd seen how close—"

She stopped him with a touch of her hand. "Don't." Tears welling in her eyes, she forced a smile. "Let's don't go there. He's safe and happy, and we have to make sure he stays that way." Hesitating, she added, "I'm not going to move to Florida, Tony."

"What?"

"I realized today how much I love my son…and how much he loves you," she said simply. "The two of you need to be together, and that can't happen if I'm living a thousand miles away. Some things are more important than a job. So I'm staying.''

Whatever Tony had been expecting, it wasn't that. Stunned, he blinked. ''Are you serious? You're really going to stay in D.C.?''

''He'll be happier with you close by,'' she said huskily. And after a moment she added, ''perhaps even living in the same home.''

His eyes shining with happiness, Quentin could hardly stand still. ''For real, Mom? You mean, living with Dad?''

''Yes, honey. I mean living with Dad,'' she said with a smile. ''If that's what you really want.''

''Oh, it is!'' Suddenly realizing that he might be hurting her feelings, he added, ''It isn't that I don't love you, Mom.''

''I know,'' she said with a chuckle. ''You love both of us. You'll just be happier with your dad. I don't have a problem with that.'' She ruffled his hair affectionately. ''Besides, it's not like I won't ever see you.''

Elated, Quentin let out a shriek and threw himself into Tony's arms. Laughing, Tony hugged him close and didn't care that there were tears in his eyes when they met Janice's. ''Thank you. You know I never wanted to fight with you.''

''All I could think about was how much I wanted him with me. This really opened my eyes. It really isn't all about me, is it?''

Tony grinned. ''Nope.''

Cocking her head, she narrowed her eyes at him and couldn't quite suppress the smile that tugged at her lips. ''You don't have to be so quick to agree, you know.'' Sobering, she said, ''I thought I'd take Quentin home with me for tonight. You have enough on your plate worrying about Lily. We'll talk more tomorrow."

He hadn't expected such consideration from her. "I appreciate this, Janice. Thank you."

"I hope she's okay," she said sincerely. "Call me when she's out of surgery. We'd both like to know that she made it through the operation without any problems."

With a kiss and a hug, Quentin and Janice were gone, leaving Tony alone in the waiting room, watching the clock. An hour passed, then another. By the time the surgeon came out to say that Lily was in recovery and doing well, it was going on eleven, and all Tony wanted to do was tell her how much he loved her. But she was still groggy when she was finally wheeled into her own room, and with a groan, Tony was forced to accept the fact that the timing wasn't right. Sinking into the chair by her bedside, he stayed there all night.

Lily came awake slowly and couldn't understand why her shoulder was throbbing as if she'd been burned with a hot poker. She frowned and reached for her shoulder, only to have her fingers encounter a thick bandage. Surprised, her eyes flew open, and only then did she realize she was in the hospital.

She glanced around, confused, trying to remember what had happened, then her eyes landed on Tony, who was asleep in the chair next to her bed. Only then did her memory come flooding back. "Oh, God!"

Tony jerked up before he was even fully awake. "What? Are you okay? What's wrong?"

"Where's Quentin? Is he okay? He was able to get away, wasn't he? If something happened to him…"

"He's fine, honey," he said gruffly, rising to his feet to move closer to her bedside and take her hand. "He's with Janice. Thanks to you, he doesn't have a scratch on him."

"I was so afraid," she choked out, blinking back tears. "I knew that son of a bitch was going to kills us, and I didn't know if Quentin understood what I needed him to do. But he was wonderful. The second I handed him the phone, he immediately started asking questions and dropping clues so you'd know where to find us."

"You were pretty damn wonderful yourself," he said huskily, leaning down to kiss her. "I saw how you diverted attention from Quentin so he could get away. I thought I'd lost you, sweetheart. When I saw you fall, all I could think was that I loved you and I never got a chance to tell you."

Stunned, she looked up at him with tears once again misting her eyes. "Oh, Tony, are you sure?"

Laughing, he kissed her again, this time with all the love in his heart. "Yeah, I'm sure," he rasped, grinning crookedly. "You've been tying me in knots from the moment I met you. Didn't you know?"

"I was too busy fighting my own feelings," she admitted huskily. "After the way my father and Neil reacted to my photography, I didn't think I'd ever find a man who would understand how much it meant to me. I can't give it up, Tony."

"Of course you can't," he replied. "You're too damn good at it. I would never ask that of you. And if your father had it to do over again, I don't think he would, either. I called him."

"What? When?"

"When you were in surgery," he admitted. "I know

it wasn't my place, but he's your father, honey, and he needed to know what happened to you. What if you'd died on the operating table? Think how he would have felt."

"What did he say?"

"He wanted me to tell you that we spoke and that he hoped you were feeling better. He'd like to come and see you."

Whatever Lily had expected, it wasn't that. Tears clogged her throat and flooded her eyes. "I'm sorry I'm so emotional," she said thickly, wiping at the tears that streamed down her cheeks. "Maybe it's the anesthetic."

"Maybe it's you," he said with a smile as he brushed the hair back from her face. "You love your father. Why shouldn't you cry? He practically disowned you. You had a right to be hurt."

"He's just so stubborn," she replied. "But I'm glad you called him." Pulling him down to her with her free hand, she kissed him sweetly. "Thank you," she murmured. "Did I mention that I love you?"

Nose to nose, his green eyes twinkled into hers. "As a matter of fact, you did. Now that we have that established, there's one more thing we need to discuss. How do you feel about living with a couple of bachelors?"

Whatever she'd been expecting, it wasn't that. Confused, she cocked an eyebrow at him. "Do you have a split personality I'm not aware of?"

Chuckling, he said, "As a matter of fact, I do…sort of. His name's Quentin."

"I'd love to live with both of you," she said honestly, "but the custody fight—"

"Is settled," he cut in with a grin. "Janice has changed her mind about moving to Florida. Almost losing him was a real wake-up call for her. She realized how much she loved him and how she wanted him to be happy. She's agreed to let him come live with me.''

''Oh, Tony, that's wonderful! You must be thrilled.''

''Only one thing will make me happier,'' he admitted. ''How do you feel about being a stepmother?''

Lily didn't pretend to misunderstand what he was asking. Her heart in her eyes, she lifted her chin slightly, bringing her mouth into whisper-soft contact with his. ''Is that a proposal?''

Leaning a heartbeat closer, his lips brushed hers, setting her body humming. ''Would your answer be yes if it was?''

Seduced, more in love than she'd ever been in her life, she didn't even hesitate. ''Oh, yes!''

He grinned...and still didn't kiss her the way she longed to be kissed. ''Did I tell you that's one of the things I love about you? You know what you want.''

''Yes, I do,'' she purred, smiling. ''And I want you.''

''I'm yours,'' he growled, and gave her the kiss they were both longing for. And without saying another word, they both knew it was for always.

* * * * *

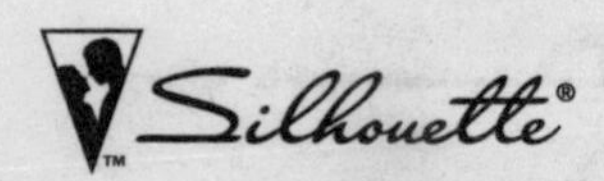

INTIMATE MOMENTS®

COMING NEXT MONTH

#1309 IN THE DARK—Heather Graham

Alexandra McCord's life was unraveling. The body she'd discovered had disappeared—and now she was trapped on an island with a hurricane roaring in and someone threatening her life. To make matters worse, the only man she could rely on was the ex-husband she'd never forgotten, David Denhem, who might be her savior—or a killer.

#1310 SHOTGUN HONEYMOON—Terese Ramin

No one had to force Janina Galvez to marry Native American cop Russ Levoie. She'd loved him since his rookie days, but their lives had gone in separate directions. Now his proposal—and protection—seemed like the answer to her prayers. But would he be able to save her from the threat from her past, or would danger overwhelm them both?

#1311 TRIPLE DARE—Candace Irvin

Family Secrets: The Next Generation

Wealthy recluse Darian Sabura had resigned himself to a solitary existence—until he heard violinist Abigail Pembroke's music. Then Abby witnessed a murder, and suddenly it was up to Darian to keep her alive. But would she feel protected—or panicked—when she learned he was empathetic and could literally sense every private thought?

#1312 HEIR TO DANGER—Valerie Parv

Code of the Outback

The Australian outback was about as far as Princess Shara Najran of Q'aresh could go to escape her evil ex-fiancé. With her life at stake, she sought sanctuary in the arms of rugged ranger Tom McCullough. But when her past loomed, threatening Tom's life, would Shara run again to protect the man she loved—or stay and fight for their future?

#1313 BULLETPROOF HEARTS—Brenda Harlen

When D.A. Natalie Vaughn stumbled onto a murder scene, Lieutenant Dylan Creighton knew the sexy prosecutor had just placed herself on a crime kingpin's hit list. And when they were forced to work together to bring him down, their powerful attraction for each other became too irresistible to deny.

#1314 GUARDING LAURA—Susan Vaughan

When it came to guarding Laura Rossiter, government operative Cole Stratton preferred jungle combat to a forced reunion with his old flame. But having someone else protect her from a madman determined to see her dead wasn't an option. Would Cole's nerves of steel see him through the toughest battle of his life—winning Laura's heart?

SIMCNM0704